A Dangerous Dance

BOOK 1 OF A DANGEROUS LIFE SERIES

Y M ZACHERY

WILD DREAMS PUBLISHING

1

Sweat ran down Melody's back as she danced to the music. She twirled and spun, spun and twirled as she choreographed her admission tape for Juilliard.

There was nowhere she loved more than being in the dance studio at the Denver University for the Arts. Melody could still remember the rush she'd gotten when she opened the mail four years ago to find out that she had been accepted to the University, the happiness she had felt lasted weeks. Denver University was the stepping stone to her future and she knew the feeling she'd felt that day would be nothing compared to the feeling she would get if she received her place at Juilliard.

Melody wouldn't except anything less than an acceptance, she *needed* to get a spot in the prestige's school as that was the only way she was going to achieve what she wanted in life. Ever since Melody was little and had attended her first dance lesson when she was five, she knew that dancing was all she wanted to do in life.

It didn't matter what was happening around her dancing brought a calmness to her life that alleviated all of her stress. It was her saving grace throughout high school and the pressures of her teenage years and it was during high school that she realised she wanted to dancing on stage for the Royal Ballet and in musicals across the world.

It didn't matter to her which she got first as long as she was dancing. Dancing was her life and she wanted to make it her career.

Now that dream was closer than ever before.

When the music came to a stop Melody sat down to stretch out her legs and as she did her mind wandered back a few weeks to the day where her dreams became that little bit more achievable. Throughout the four years that she had studied at DUA, learning all the techniques she would need to fulfil a career in dancing, Melody had remained at the head of her classes and would graduate with honours next summer.

This should have taken some of the pressure off of her, but she knew that now was not the time to rest on her laurels, she still had one more year to get through.

While it had been hard work and left little time for a social life, the benefits that Melody was about to reap were worth the trouble.   A smile spread across her face as she remembered the conversation with her professor three weeks ago. Juilliard were offering a summer program that would allow potential future students a chance to train with the best dancers and instructors across the world, it was basically a stepping stone to help with admissions. It was a three-month program that ran for the first term every year. Only the top twenty students across America were chosen for a placement.

Melody had been one of those twenty offered a spot.

Thankfully Melody's professor had helped her fill out the application of acceptance, and financial aid package three weeks ago, now they were waiting on the confirmation which should arrive any day now. The confirmation of acceptance and financial aid would be the answer that either helped her achieve her dreams or broke them for good.

Melody was brought out of her musing when the door to the studio opened. Turning around to see who had entered, she smiled when she saw Quinn. Quinn was another student who studied the lighting and sound side of performances. He was a quite young man and was always around when he was needed. Quinn was usually at the campus late and often stopped in to check if Melody was alright when she was here alone.

"Hey Quinn, how are things?" She asked as she continued to sit on the floor and stretch out her legs.

Quinn gave her a shy smile, she had no idea why he wasn't more outgoing, he was nowhere near average looking, in fact he was quite the opposite.

With his dark mahogany hair that curled just on his shoulders, deep blue eyes and a buff body, he was typically what most girls drooled over. However, his quiet and reserved nature tended to keep people away.

"The usual," he answered leaning against the door and placing his hands in his pockets. Melody was just going to ask him another question when he suddenly looked out the door and straighten.

"Well I had best be going, I just wanted to check in and make sure that you were alright."

Melody gave him a smile. "I am thank you."

"No problem. I'll see you tomorrow." With that he walked back out the door letting it close behind him. Melody gave a nervous laugh as she thought about his strange behaviour.

Putting Quinn out of her mind Melody went back to stretching, her mind once more running through everything she needed to get done for her admission tape and she started to worry about whether she had done enough.

"Hey, I have been looking all over for you." Isla remarked as she came through the door.

"Been here the whole time." Melody offered. "What's Up?"

"Professor Klein needs to see you in her office."

"No worries. I will just change and head there now. Thanks for letting me know."

Isla nodded, "once you've finished why don't you come and meet us at the usual hangout."

"Will do." Melody waved Isla off as she shut the door and headed away. Standing up Melody grabbed her bag from the back of the room before heading to the lockers for a shower. Thirty minutes later Melody was knocking on the door of her professor's office. It didn't take long before "come in," radiated through the door.

Pushing the door open Melody walked into the office of her mentor and professor. She had spent many days in here stressing over assignments and getting much needed advice for how to improve her tencniques.

"I have some news for you regarding your application."

Melody's heart rate picked up, she took a deep breath to try and calm her nerves. She loved how her professor always got straight to the point.

This was it.

This was the news she had been waiting for.

This was the news that would change Melody's life forever.

Melody sat across from her professor as she pulled out an envelope from a stack of papers on her desk.

"So is it good news?" Melody asked, unable to hold back her anxiety. The suspense was killing her.

Her professor didn't offer her any answers however, she simply smiled at her as she handed Melody the envelope.

"Why don't we find out together." She added.

"Haven't you read it yet?" Melody was perplexed. The letters were often addressed to the university and therefore were opened before the student even saw it.

"I wanted to give you the pleasure." Professor Klein offered with a kind smile.

Melody could only nod. This was it. Crunch time.

Taking a deep breath, Melody pulled out the paperwork that the envelope contained. Instantly, her eyes were drawn to her own handwriting, which was scrawled across the application form, but that wasn't the only thing her eyes were drawn to. Across the handwriting was a big green approved stamp.

Once again, her heart started to beat rapidly. Half of the battle had been won. Her application had been approved.

She had been accepted into the program, Melody couldn't believe it. For a few seconds her eyes stayed on the approved sign. All of her hard work over the years made everything she had lost worth it. All of the late night parties that she'd missed, all of the friends she'd had lost, and all of the potential dates she'd given up were a thing of the past. Her future lay in front of her.

There was only one thing left that could potentially pose a problem. Melody's excitement started to wean a little as she sat the papers down on the desk and started to flip through them. She could feel the professor's eyes on her waiting for an explanation, but before she got too excited she needed to find out if her financial aid had been approved. That would be the final factor that would determine if her dreams were going to come true.

The course cost twenty thousand dollars and without some kind of financial aid or scholarship there was no way Melody would be able to afford it. She couldn't ask her parents for the money as they were already paying enough to send her here. What little money she did make from part time jobs and her summer job was spent on bills and saving for the four years of Juilliard.

Finally, Melody hit the finance section and she wanted to laugh and cry at the same time. She had been approved for a dance scholarship, but it was only going to pay half of the full cost. If Melody wanted to attend the program she needed to come up with the other ten thousand dollars. Tears started to run down her face she had been so close.

Melody looked over the table when the professor's hand touched hers. "What seems to be the problem?"

Melody handed the professor the papers so she could see for herself.

"I only got half of the funding. I got approved to go, but I can't afford to go." As the words left her mouth her heart broke a little more, she had been so close.

Melody knew that this would have been the ticket she needed to put her one step above the other applicants when she applied to Juilliard, now she was going to have to make sure that her audition tape was above reproach. Melody wasn't sure she would be able to go home for the holiday's now. As she sat at the professors table watching her dreams get further away from her, Melody tried to come up with ways that she could get the money.

At one stage robbing a bank even crossed her mind, but all joking aside Melody knew that it would take a miracle for her to raise that kind of cash.

"Well that is a bit of a pickle isn't it?" Professor Klein stated from across her desk.

Melody could only give a half-hearted smile. "I guess it was too good to be true." Melody replied. "I guess that's it then. I will just have to work that much harder to get in." She finished.

Melody knew she should leave the professor's office, there was no more to be said. She was just about to get up and go when the professor spoke again.

"Look, don't go counting your chickens yet. You still have three months of summer break left ahead of you before the payment is due. You have been given a chance here, and you only have to come up with half of the money, not all of it. So, before you go giving up on the idea all together, spend the summer trying to come up with a way to get the funds, and if you still don't have it on the first week back, we will figure something out."

Tears were falling down Melody's face again.

Getting up she walked around the table and hugged Professor Klein. This woman had been her rock for the last three years and here she went again, not letting Melody give up.

"Thank you." She said simply. Melody knew that there was no way she would get the money in time, but she would not let her professor's faith go un noticed.

"I will not let you give up on this once in a lifetime chance, you hear me?"

Giving her one more squeeze, the professor added, "now go on with you. You only have a few more days before the end of the year and summer break is here. I suggest you spend that time coming up with a plan for how you are going to get the money."

Melody nodded as she made her way back over to her side of the desk. She collected the paperwork and her bag and with newfound hope Melody started making her way out of the office. She had so much to consider.

Melody had to ring her mom at home and get her onto making sure there were extra shifts for her at the diner this summer and she had to try and figure out what else she could do to earn some extra cash.

As she reached for the door, Melody turned to face Professor Klein. "Thank you."

The professor looked up from her desk and with a serious expression, one Melody had never seen before, she replied. "You are very welcome. I am very proud of the person you are becoming and I truly believe there is no-one who deserves this opportunity more than you. Now go and work at getting your dream."

Nodding once more, with fresh tears in her eyes Melody headed off to do just that.

This summer was already looking up, while she had no idea how she was going to do it, Melody was prepared to embrace her future with both hands.

Nothing was going to stop her now.

2

"What can I get you folks to eat?"

Melody had been back in her hometown of Pagosa Springs for a week and every moment spare moment she had she worked at her family's diner. It wasn't hard work, she spent most of the time waitressing and on a good day she would make at least fifty-dollars in tips.

The problem was most days were not good days.

Melody groaned inwardly. *At the rate I am going I won't even make half of what I need.* She was brought back to the present when the couple in front of her placed their order.

"We would both like to try the old-fashioned bacon cheeseburger please."

"Will you be wanting any drinks with that?"

Melody watched as they perused the drink menu. She knew that the customers in front of her were going to go with an old-fashioned milkshake, but she still had to wait. It was what their family diner was famous for.

Her parent's had created a diner that was well known for bringing you meals that took you back to the days when you were young. Besides she knew that the burgers and shakes sold here were some of the best in the country, even if she was a little bias.

"We would love an old-fashioned vanilla malt shake please."

Melody gave them a warm smile, "your order won't be long. Please let me know if you need anything in the meantime."

Once her customers nodded their understanding, Melody took the order back to the kitchen.

"Here ya go Pops, have another one for ya." Melody said as she slid the paper slip into the hanger with the other orders.

"Thanks, Darlin. How's things going out there?"

Melody laughed at how Texan her father still sounded. He'd met her mother over thirty years ago in New Orleans. They were both there for Spring Break and as the tale goes her father fell so madly in love with her mother he followed her back to Colorado, where he spent the next six months wooing her.

However, while he was falling in love with her mother he was also falling in love with the state she lived in. So after their wedding they moved down to Pagosa Springs as it was close to her father's favourite skiing and hunting area, and that folks was the end of the tale.

"Its okay, a bit slow today."

"Well enjoy the quite while ya can. Y'all know that as soon as those hunting parties get here there will be no rest for the wicked."

"I know Pops." Didn't she what.

Melody had learnt long ago that once hunting season kicked off in a few weeks the place would be constantly packed. Melody also knew that she wasn't going to be making enough tips to help her reach her goal.

The problem she faced was that there were no other jobs around here that would offer her any more money than she got working here.

Well none that were legal anyway.

"Dee, a new customer just came in." Both Melody and her father smiled at each other when her mother stuck her head in through the order window to let Melody know about the new customer. There were three other waitresses in the diner today, yet her mother knew that she needed the tips so when she could she would let Melody know about the customers before the other waitress.

Melody had asked her not to play favourites so many times over the years, but her mother was her mother, and no matter how much nagging Melody did her mother would simply say, "you are my daughter and you will always come first."

"You might as well take this when ya go darlin.'" Her father stated as he handed her a basket of fries and a 'Loaded Burger.' Grabbing the meal from her father Melody made her way out of the kitchen, placed the meal on table four and then headed to the new table.

As she neared booth seven she noticed there were two people sitting there, she could see the male from the front. She knew his face from somewhere but couldn't place it, the girl that was with him had long jet-black hair and faced away from her, but Melody would know her anywhere.

Picking up the pace, she practically ran to the table.

"When the hell did you get back?" She exactly exclaimed as she stopped at the table.

Gabby, her best friend since she was two, beamed back at her.

"Just got in today. I came straight here to see you." Gabby jumped up from her chair and embraced Melody in a huge bear hug. It had been almost six months since they had physically seen each other. They talked on messenger and Facebook every day, but it wasn't the same. After school Gabby moved to Arizona where she went to school. She was working on becoming a psychologist. Before than the two of them had been inseparable.

"Mom I am going to take my break." Melody shouted to her mother as she sat down in the booth with Gabby and her friend.

"I thought you might." She replied. It didn't take long for the girls to get back into their old habits.

"Dee this is Tobin." Gabby introduced the guy who was with her. Now that she had heard the name Melody realised where she knew him from. He was Gabby's roommate down in Arizona.

"Nice to meet you." Melody replied offering him her hand. "What brings you this way?"

Tobin gave her a smile before he answered. "I was on my way to New Mexico to visit family, so I offered to bring Gabby home with me. I will collect her at the end of the summer on my way back through."

"What happened to your car?" She asked Gabby.

Gabby laughed. "Nothing, it's at home. When Tobin offered me a ride I thought it was a great idea as it saves the miles on my car. Besides, when I am home I usually use one of the spares at Mom and Dad's anyway."

Melody nodded that made sense. The talking stopped for a few seconds when one of the other waitresses came by to take their order. Melody placed one as well as she decided she might as well eat while she was on her break.

"I thought you had planned to go to California for a few weeks?" Melody asked Gabby once the waitress was gone.

"I was going to but when you pulled out and told me you were coming home I decided that I would rather spend time here with you than in California without you."

"Well I for one am glad you are here. It is going to make this summer so much more fun." The catching up and laughs continued right through lunch, until her break was over.

Getting up Melody gave Gabby one more hug before she turned to Tobin, "it was nice to finally meet you."

"And you." Tobin replied.

Turing back to Gabby, Melody added before she left. "You have to come over tonight. We have so much more catching up to do and I have some news to tell you." Melody didn't want to tell Gabby about her shot at Juilliard and her money issues in front of a stranger. Besides she needed time to prepare what she would tell her friend.

"You got it." Gabby replied and with one final hug and with that Melody headed back to finish her shift.

For the rest of the afternoon Melody felt a little happier knowing her friend was here. If there was anyone who could help her figure out this mess it was Gabby.

* * *

It was five o'clock by the time Melody arrived home from work. Walking up the stairs inside the garage to her granny flat that her parents built her when she went off to college, Melody was once again grateful to have her own space. She loved her parents but since being at collage Melody was used to having her independence and since she saw her folks at work all day it was nice to have some personal time.

It would also give her and Gabby some privacy.

Once inside she placed all of her stuff on the counter then headed into her bathroom to have a shower. She wanted to get rid off the smell of bacon and fries before Gabby arrived. That was the only downfall to working in the diner all the time, you started to smell like the food. Thankfully the food was nice smelling.

Fifteen minutes later, Melody was stepping out of the shower when there was a knock at the door. Looking at her watch she realised that Gabby was early. Wrapping a towel around herself Melody went to let her friend in.

"You're early." She stated as she opened the door.

"The pizza is going cold." Gabby retorted.

Melody laughed and opened the door wider to let her friend in. "I'll be back in a minute." Then headed to her bedroom to get dressed.

"Don't be long, or I will eat all the pizza." Gabby shouted back, as Melody heard her fridge open.

She knew Gabby would be looking for the drinks to go with the Pizza. There was always a stash of Jack Danials and cola in the fridge when she was home. Even though Melody was a dancer, and it was well known that most dancers had a strict diet, it was not so for Melody.

When she was at Collage she ate healthy and exercised a lot, but the way her body worked it was not necessary to be that extreme all of the time. Melody was gifted with a body that, even when she did splurge a little, it didn't take her long to get fit again. A night of pizza and alcohol with her friend was not going to make a huge difference. She would just work it off when she got back to school.

Putting on her comfy track pants and sweatshirt Melody made her way out to the lounge where Gabby was currently surfing Netflix for something to watch and eating pizza. Sitting down beside her Melody grabbed a piece of pizza, took a bite and closed her eyes to savour the flavour.

Gabby's laughter had Melody opening her eyes.

"The noise you just made sounds like something I make during sex." She mocked.

Melody poked out her tongue and finished her bite. She was not going to play into her friend's teasing.

Placing the pizza back on the box she wiped her hands, took a long drink of Jack and then turned to her friend.

"So how is everyone?" she asked Gabby. Melody didn't need to elaborate as her friend new she was asking about her family. Gabby laughed it was the same routine every time they got together, they would get the mundane chitchat out of the way before they moved on to more important stuff. Usually when Melody asked Gabby about her family it meant she had big news.

"How big is the news this time?" Gabby asked before she took another bite of her pizza.

"Big, but first I do want to hear about your family."

Smiling Gabby put her pizza down before answering. "Mom and Dad are good as always. Both are busy at the hospital. Peter and his wife still live in Kansas and are expecting their first baby at the end of this year. Oscar is on tour in Afghanistan again, and the cousins, well they are the cousins. You know them always up to no good. Oh, speaking of cousins did you know Rome is working as a detective in Denver?"

Melody loved hearing about the lives of Gabby's family. She had grown up with them all, but there was only one of the names that Gabby had mentioned that made her heart skip a beat.

Melody could still remember the moment she fell in love with him. It had been in high school.

He was in his final year and they were a year under him. Melody had been having trouble with a guy harassing her at school, although she didn't see it until it was too late. Everyone always commented on how beautiful she was, but Melody never saw it. She had long blonde hair, bright blue eyes and a body that most girls would kill for, well at least that was what Gabby often told her.

The problem was that it often led to a lot of boys wanting her. Most of the time it was harmless flirtation, until it wasn't. Melody still remembered the day as though it were yesterday, and to this day only her and Roman knew about it. Gabby had to go and see a teacher about some work, which left Melody alone in the cafeteria. Not that she minded, opening her book she had started to study for an exam. That had been when Trent, the quarterback, decided to come over and ask her to go with him to the formal for the tenth time.

Melody had no interest in going anywhere with Trent, normally he took the news well and would joke that he would make her change her mind. But on this particular day he wouldn't leave it alone. It got to the point that Melody decided to get up and go and find Gabby. She had just rounded the end of the block between the cafeteria and the east hall when Trent grabbed her and forced her into an alcove. There he pushed her up against the wall and once again asked her to go with him. When she said no he pushed himself up against her and started rubbing his hand up under her skirt while saying, "just think of what you will be missing."

Melody could still remember the fear she'd felt. She had been terrified. Everything inside of her was telling her to scream and yet no sound would come out. He outweighed her by a ton and panic started to race through her blood. Tears started to fall down her face as he tightened his palm around her thigh, "please let me go," she remembered begging him. Instead of letting her go though he laughed, that was when someone grabbed him and pulled him off of her.

Melody sagged to the ground her body wracked with shivers. She had no idea what had happened to Trent, all she remembered was falling to the ground and then the next thing she was looking into the deep blue eyes of Roman Fox, best friend to Gabby's cousins.

He had saved her.

He didn't say anything he simply wrapped Melody in his arms and held her until she could stand. Still to this day he'd never mentioned the incident again. They both knew that he had saved her that day and it was that day that her crush of four years grew into full blown love.

Some may say that it was puppy love but even as the years went on every time she saw him her heart missed a beat, Melody knew there was no-one else for her. If only he felt the same way. She hoped one day he would either notice her or her heart would find someone else to love.

For now though, he was it.

"…but I don't know much more than that, as the cousins say, he is often busy with a case, so they don't hear from him much." Gabby's voice brought Melody back to the present. Thankfully her friend hadn't noticed her lack of interest.

"So now it is your turn, tell me your big news."

Melody pulled her legs up underneath her then placed her arm on the back of the couch bending it up so that she could rest her head in her hand. Taking a deep breath she got ready to share her news with her friend. Maybe she could come up with some way for Melody to get the money.

"Well it started about a month ago when I got news that I had been accepted into a program at Juilliard." Melody waited for the news to sink in. Aside from her parents and Professor Klein, Gabby was the only other person who knew how big this was for Melody.

"And…." Gabby asked excitedly.

Melody told her all about how the opportunity had come up and then she told her about the money.

"You have to go." Was all Gabby said.

"And how do you propose I do that?" Placing her feet back on the ground Melody busied herself with closing the lids of the empty pizza boxes. "I am doing as many shifts at the diner as I can and I still won't even have half the money I need by the end of the summer."

The mention of not having enough money to follow her dream was once again bringing her down. Getting up from the sofa, she took their empty cans to the kitchen and replaced them with full ones. Gabby had turned on the couch to face her.

"You are going to that workshop; I will sell my car if I have too." That brought a smile to Melody's face. Trust Gabby to know how to lighten the mood.

"You are not selling your car." Melody stated as she sat back down on the seat.

"Okay, but you have to figure out how to get more…"

Melody looked at her friend as she cut her sentence short, that usually meant she had an idea. Sometimes the ideas were not always good and yet other times they were.

"What are you brewing up now?" Melody asked.

"Okay before you say no, hear me out."

Melody looked at her friend with scepticism. This could not be good but at this point Melody had a feeling that she would give anything a try.

"Okay shoot."

Gabby gave her a surprised look before she rushed on to tell Melody her plan. It was as though she expected Melody to change her mind. "Okay, well you know how the cousins own the bar just outside of town….."

"You mean strip club."

"It is not a strip club, it is a bar, where girls just happen to take their clothes off for the patrons who stop in." Gabby defended.

"So, a strip club." Melody added sarcastically; not sure she was liking where her friend was going.

Gabby gave her an annoyed look before stating, "if you don't wish me to continue just say so."

Melody simply waved her hand in recognition for her friend to continue.

"Okay as I was saying, I have been working there…"

"Gabby what are you thinking?"

"God would you stop butting in and let me finish." She

waited a moment to see if Melody would say anymore, but when she didn't Gabby continued. "As I said I have been working there, not as a stripper you dope, but as a bartender."

Melody relaxed a little. "How does this help me?"

"Well in three days of work I make triple what you make in tips." With that statement Gabby sat back and folded her arms across her chest. Melody almost chocked on the drink she had just taken. With that kind of money, she could save up in no time. Melody didn't have to think about it for long. Bar tending was no harder than waitressing and she did say she would do anything to make this opportunity happen.

"Do you think your cousins will let me work there?" She asked a little bit excited now.

She knew she should think about it more but she didn't have the time or the luxury to wait around for another opportunity.

"Of course they will. I am their favourite cousin and that also makes you their favourite. I will be seeing them tomorrow so I will ask, hopefully you can start Friday."

"You're the best." Melody lunched forward and threw her arms around her best friend. Once the news was out of the way they spent the next hour reminiscing about all the fun they used to have and the trouble they had caused through high school, well the trouble Gabby had caused.

Melody glanced down at her watch and noticed that it was after midnight. She didn't want the night to end but she also knew that she had to get up for work early tomorrow. Stretching out her legs she stood, "well I guess I had better call it a night, you can crash here if you like."

Gabby smiled, "you bet your arse I will. Don't wake me in the morning though or I will have to kill you, best friend or not."

Melody laughed, "you know where the spare room is."

Gabby waved her off as she picked up her phone and surfed for a bit. Melody knew her friend would be up for a few more hours, she was a night owl that was why working at a bar suited her so well.

Walking into the bathroom Melody pulled her phone out of her pocket, placed it on the counter and then continued to get undressed and into the shower. Even though she'd had one before Gabby arrived Melody felt the need to have another. As the warm water sliced over her body she let some of the tension that had been riddling her body leave. She didn't know what she would have done if Gabby hadn't offered to help her get a better paying job, now she just hoped she had enough time to save.

As Melody continued to shower and go over in her mind what she had to do to make her dream a reality she heard her phone ding. She wondered briefly who would be texting her at this hour and then shrugged it off. It was probably Gabby texting her to tell her to leave a towel out or something. Putting the phone out of her mind Melody finished her shower.

Twenty minutes later she was turning off the water, grabbing the towel that was hanging over the glass door and stepping out of the shower. Wrapping the towel around her she walked over to the vanity, cleared the mirror of fog and brushed her teeth before grabbing her phone. With her phone in her hand she padded out of the bathroom and entered her room. As she went to shut the door, she heard Gabby yell from the lounge room, "hope you left some hot water for me?"

Melody smiled, "do you feel lucky?" the only reply she got was laugher.

Shutting her door Melody padded over to her bed, chucked her phone down and went to get something to wear.

Once dressed she scooted into bed, picked up her phone

and opened the message to see what Gabby had to say.   T h e first thing Melody noticed was that the message was from an unknown number. Melody should have clued on that the message should have been ignored, but it had been at least three weeks since the last incident and she had become comfortable once more.

She should have known better.

The moment she opened the message Melody's blood ran cold and fear enveloped her. This could not be happening, how had he gotten a hold of her new number. Melody's eyes scanned the message over and over again, the words before her swimming in the tears that were now falling. She couldn't go through this again, not now, not when her life was heading in the right direction. If only she knew who was behind the messages then she could make them stop. But she didn't know and that only made it more terrifying.

Turing her phone off she placed it on the nightstand before turning off her light and trying to go to sleep. She had to put the incident of her head and get on with her life. But in the darkness of her bedroom, the shadows adding to the forbidding feeling, the message rang out to her like a whisper in the night telling her that her stalker was back.

Closing her eyes, the words were replaced with a dark stranger creeping back into her nightmares repeating the words from the text,

So, you thought you could get away did you? Changing your number and leaving town will not stop me. How dare you leave me. You are mine Dancer, no matter where you go I will find you. There is no point trying to run from our love, it is destined to be. The more you try and run the more pain I will cause you. You need to understand and accept that you will be mine forever, one way or another. I will find you pretty Dancer.

3

Roman walked through the department, past his desk and on to the Captain's office, his anger and frustration building with each step he took. The moment he walked through the glass doors and Wilkin's had told him that the captain wanted to see him, he knew what was coming. Roman knew that going to the University had been a bad idea.

One of the suspects – the stalker in Roman's opinion – had been there and Roman had been unable to control himself. The suspect, who Roman currently marched through the precinct in cuffs, smirked at him. That smirk only added to his anger as did his comment when he handed him off to another officer.

Roman would have loved to have interrogated the punk further but his Captain was not known for his patience.

The scene from earlier today was still played in his mind.

***

Roman was at the university to see if he could find any more leads on the latest missing girl but all he found was more dead ends.

Erica was the fifth victim to go missing in the last nine months. The detectives on the case knew they were dealing with a serial killer but had yet to find any concert evidence that would link any one person. The only reason they knew it was a serial killer was because every case started the same way.

A girl, usually one that came from a background of means, would be stalked for a few weeks before they were finally kidnapped. A ransom would be sent to the families, promising the safe return of their daughter once it had been paid, however after payment the body of their daughter was delivered to their door, in peices.

At first they had taught it was a one of thing, but with each dead girl detectives had an idea of what type of person they were dealing with. The killer was meticulous and left now evidence behind. From the moment he took the victim to the moment they showed up on their parents doorstep the killer was in control. Detectives knew he got off from the power he was holding as it seemed as though the faster the family paid the ransom the faster the girls ended up dead. But no matter how much law enforcement pleaded with each family to hold off paying the ransom, it never worked. The families payed and then the bastards would kill the girl, once again leaving the police with no option but to wait for the next victim in hopes that the bastard messed up.

After the first two murders Roman and his team were called in, they were the local homicide detectives in Denver. At first Roman had treated this case as he did any other, but with each murder that happened and the lack of evidence they found it acme harder for him to sit on his hands and wait for something to happen. He knew that if they didn't eventually catch this guy they would need to call in the FBI.

That was the last thing Roman wanted to do.

It was why he found himself back at the campus for the third day in a row, there was something he was missing and it was driving him mad. After leaving the Dean's office where he had talked to the victim's friends agin, Roman headed out of the main building. His plan was to head over to the building where the dancers performed, he was hoping to catch a break, maybe someone would finally remember seeing something that night. His foot had barley hit the bottom step when his name had been called.

"Detective." Roman stopped to see a tall young man coming down the stairs towards him. Roman took him in trying to figure out if he'd talked to this young man before but he was someone he hadn't spoken to before.

Roman had a hunch on who was behind the kidnappings. He just didn't have enough evidence to prove it.

Sometimes he hated the system. He was getting so sick of seeing dirt bags go free due to a lack of evidence, even though everyone knew they were guilty.

Roman leaned against the railing of the stairs and waited for the young man to reach him. "Yes." He answered when the young man stopped in front of him.

"I was just wondering if you had any more information on the missing girl?"

Roman raised his eyebrow. "And you are?"

The young man cleared his throat before continuing, "my name is Quinn Uncer sir. I am asking because I've made it my mission to make sure no more women go missing. Any little detail you can give me will help me provide the police with any details of things that seem strange around here."

Roman knew that the young man was wanting to know the same answers that everyone at the campus was wanting to know, but the case was an open investigation. He also knew that at some point the unsub may try and place himself into the investigation. While Roman did not consider the man in front of him as a suspect he gave the usual response anyway.

"Thank you, Quinn, as you would be aware while the case is open I cannot share any information that may affect the case."

The young man in front of him simply nodded. Roman looked at him one more time, making sure to get the measure of the man, before turning to leave he was stopped once more. This time for a different reason the person he believed to be the perp walked right up to him, a smug look covering his face.

Neil Solomon was a rich kid who believed he was untouchable. He was your typical good-looking jock, tall, dark hair and was usually followed around by a bunch of Neanderthal goons. The problem with his good looks was that it was coupled with money and this made Neil feel as though he was better than everyone else.

He was also the boyfriend of the latest missing girl.

Normally Roman wouldn't have put any stock in a douche bag like him. He was no different to any other rich jock who had been interviewed by the police. However, his actions after the disappearance of his girlfriend were what made Roman suspicious. Sure he acted like the concerned partner when the police asked him of his whereabouts the night of his girlfriend's disappearance, he even handed over his phone so that the police could check his messages. But as Roman knew, that meant nothing. It was nothing these days for people to have more than one phone and he was almost certain that the stalker would have just that. While none of that made Neil a killer, what did make him suspect however was the numerous complaints filed by ex-girlfriends in regards to his violent nature.

Even his behaviour when questioned about the complaints made Roman suspicious of him. No longer had he been the co-operative, polite rich boy, instead he became evasive and squirrelly. Roman tried pushing the matter, but rich boy called in his parents, who in turn called in their lawyer. From there everyone was told to leave Mr. Solomon alone. Roman had no choice but to follow his captain's orders, however he refused to let the matter rest. Roman made it his mission to gather information on Mr. Solomon under the ruse of following all leads.

Thankfully the friends of Erica Hatchman, the current missing girl, were more than happy to fill him in on the relationship between Neil and Erica. Roman was more than pleased to find out that their relationship was anything but loving. Neil was still his number one suspect.

Now all Roman had to do was remain calm and not do anything stupid, but the first words out of the kids mouth were making it hard.

"Well well well, what brings you here this time *Detective?*" Roman didn't miss the infliction he placed on the word. As though it was something that one found in a toxic waste dump.

"Have you found another innocent person to harass?"

Roman simply smiled. One day he was going to love putting this germ behind bars. The streets of Denver would be much safer for it. Even if he didn't turn out to be the killer. For now, Roman would play the weasel's game.

"Not at all Mr. Solomon. I am simply following more leads so that we can find *your* girlfriend as quickly as possible. As you are aware, the first forty-eight hours are the most important in a missing persons case. I know that you along with her family want nothing more than her safe return. Correct?" Roman put just enough scathing sarcasm into his voice, so as not to directly call Neil a liar, but insinuate it enough so that the slime bag knew Roman was looking into him.

Roman got a slight bit of pleasure out of seeing the young man's back go a little bit more rigid. It didn't take him long to regain his composure though, especially with his band of goons standing behind him.

"Well it's about time we see our money going to work." He

remarked.

Roman wanted nothing more than to roll his eyes but being that he was an officer of the law it would not be at all professional. "Well gentlemen, it's been *nice* talking to you as always, but I need to get the information I have gained back to the police station. Quinn, remember if you have anything to add just call me."

"Ha what the hell would Queer Quinn have to tell you about girls. His preferences run the other way. Isn't that right Quinn?"

Neil walked forward and grabbed Quinn in a head lock while rubbing his hair.

"Get off me." Quinn ordered weakly as he tried to get out of the hold.

Roman knew he should have walked away but one of the things he hated about this world was the power that bullies had. Once he saw Neil's friends start to make their way towards the young man who was outnumbered, he knew he had to do something. Walking forward Roman grabbed Neil by the scruff of his neck and threw him down the stairs where he landed in the dirt on his knees.

Roman knew that the young man was afraid of him, he hadn't expected him to make the move he had. But Roman also knew that Neil would not let himself be humiliated in front of all of his preppie pals.

Roman was counting on just that.

Roman gave a little smile and started slowly walking down the stairs as Neil stood, brushed off his pants and cracked his knuckles. The moment Neil threw the first punch Roman spun him around and pressed him up against the stone wall of the stairs. Without care he reefed Mr. Solomon's arms behind his back, where he handcuffed him and read him his rights. Finally, with his friends looking on Roman walked Neil off towards his squad car and for his own pleasure leaned forward and whispered in his ear, "this is just the beginning."

The only answer he got was the loogie Neil spat at him. Roman laughed and wiped it off, it wasn't the first time he had been spat on and it wouldn't be the last.

"Is that the best you got? The boys in lock up are going to love you. Now watch your head."

Roman pushed the boy ceremoniously into his car, before he himself got in and drove to the precinct with Neil cussing him the whole way. Roman paid him no mind, he was only too happy to have a reason to bring the tool in, he simply turned up the music and whistled along, hoping like hell that he still had a job after today.

* * *

Roman gave a quick knock on the captain's door and waited to be acknowledged. It wasn't long before his partner walked out, patted him on the shoulder and said, "you got this." Before heading back to his desk.

"Enter." Followed those words.

Roman walked in and sat before his captain. Captain Walters sat in his leather chair behind a mahogany desk that was littered with case after case. Working in homicide took its toll, and cases such as the one Roman was working on now were the worst. His captain would often remind them that they had to remain impartial to the case they were working on, if they didn't it would burn them out quicker than anything else they knew.

They had to see the victims as evidence, not people. But the more victims that turned up, the harder for Roman that was becoming. Roman waited for his captain to look up from the computer, it didn't take long.

"Sit." He ordered.

Roman did as was commanded and sat waiting for his captain to discuss the reason he was brought in.

"What were you doing at DUA today?"

Roman's eyes shot up, he had only just gotten back, how was it the captain knew about his visit already. Roman squirmed in his seat. He had been ordered to stay away from Neil after the last time he'd been brought in for questioning. His country club mother and father didn't like how their little boy had been treated; so they had demanded, through their lawyers, that no-one was to approach him without their consent. They were of course happy to help in anyway they could with the case, they told the department, as long as it was on their terms. That meant keeping their precious son and his reputation out of the limelight.

"I went to speak to the missing girl's friends once more."

"Right. So please explain to me how is it then that you got into an altercation with Mr. Solomon?"

Roman looked up in surprise.

"How...?"

He didn't get to finish the question before his Captain spun his computer around and Roman was watching himself on YouTube arrest the young man. From the way the film had been shot it looked like one of those average Police brutality films. They did however leave out the bit where Neil had attacked the young man still standing on the steps. The young man looked frightened alright, but he looked afraid of Roman not Neil. This was just great.

"It's not what...."

"It doesn't matter what it looks like. All that matters is we now have a shit storm about to descend down on our heads and although I don't like having to do this I am going to have to place you on paid suspension."

Roman was outraged.

"This little shit attacks me and another member of the

public and I'm the one being punished. How long am I on *leave* for?" He asked sarcastically.

"For however long it takes for this shit storm to blow over." His captain answered. "Now you know the drill." He added. Roman stood up and placed his gun and badge on the table before he started to make his way out of the office.

"You know I am right about this guy." He stated, stopping half way across the room, turning to look at his boss. Captain Walters looked at Roman and nodded. Roman shook his head and finished making his way out of the room. He had just gotten to the door when his captain stopped him.

"We will catch him, just so you know I plan to lock him up with one of our scary inmates until Mommy and Daddy come get him." Roman smiled and left the room. He knew the captain's hands were tied when it came to cases such as these, but it was still nice to know he had his mens' backs.

Walking to his desk he started to collect his things, his partner joined him leaning against the desk. "So, what happened?"

"I guess I am taking a small break."

"If only we could all be so lucky." He quipped trying to make light of the situation.

Roman smiled at him, "see ya when I get back." He stated slapping his friend on the shoulder as he walked by. "Try not to get dead while I am gone."

His partner snorted. "Try not to get in trouble while I'm not with you."

Roman's laughter could be heard as he continued out of the offices and down the stairs. He had just hit the bottom one when he heard a whistle come from the balcony above.

"Where are you headed? You know in case I need to find you."

"Home."

Roman saluted his friend as he made his way out of the

precinct to his car. Chucking his bag in the back, he decided that he wouldn't bother going to his apartment instead he made his way out of Denver to highway 285. A highway that would start his five-hour journey home to Pagosa Springs.

Roman was not heading home because he wanted to, he was heading home because he needed to. Over the last few weeks he'd felt as though he was slowly losing himself and there was only one place in the world he knew where he could find breath enough to work through what was bothering him. He had to admit he was looking forward to going home, it had been ages since he had seen his friends and family. Maybe his captain was right, maybe he was too close to the case. The break may just allow him to clear his head enough to see things more logically.

He hoped so anyway, because they needed a break in the case and soon. Switching on the radio, Roman settled back for the long drive, imagining all the things he would do when he got there. The first thing he was going to do was stop in at the 'Just a Peek' Bar that his brothers from another mother owned. A smile played on his face as he realised that if traffic allowed he would get there just as things were warming up. Yes, a drink and a catch up with old friends was what he needed, and the eye candy wouldn't hurt either.

4

He couldn't believe it, there was still no sign of where Melody went. For the last year it had not been his decision on which girls he would stalk and kidnap, they had all be part of a bigger picture. He had been fine with that until Melody.

She had not been part of the plan.

The plan had been simple, kidnap dancing girls that people would notice were missing, girls whose families would pay to have back. Not that ever giving them back was part of the plan. It just helped fund the project. The idea was that the loved ones needed to believe they would get their daughters back so that the money for the ransom would be paid.

Yes, that had been the plan. Make the rich pay in more ways than one. In the meantime he could have a little fun as well.

Then he had seen her.

The first time he had seen her dancing in the studios on campus, he had been mesmerised. The only reason he had been there in the first place was to monitor the routine of Erica, his current catch.

It had been easy for him to gain the knowledge he needed, he was expected to be in the halls outside of her room, having inside information on her helped. Everything had been going to plan until one Tuesday afternoon, It all changed. He had been walking past the dance rooms on his way to Erica's room, when the music from within drew him closer. The haunting Melody seemed to call out to something dark inside of him, and when he saw a woman dressed in black, dancing to the music of his soul he knew instantly that he had to have her.

She was not going to be someone that he took because of the plan. She was not going to be someone that he took for a ransom. No, this one was for him, taking her was purely for his own need.

Nothing more. Nothing less.

He had spent the last couple of months carefully constructing how he would implement his plan and now she was gone and worst of all, he had no way of finding her.

That was not the only issue he was facing. Currently he found himself once more in the Police station trying to figure out what, if any leads the police had on the kidnappings. He was certain they had nothing on the killings but the arrival of the detective at the university today worried him. So far he had outsmarted everyone, the police had not been able to find any traceable evidence on his victims. The courses in forensic Science at the university truly did help with that part. Little did the professors know that while they were teaching students how to become great forensic scientists who would eventually help solve crimes, they were also teaching criminals how to beat the system they were trying to enforce.

He had always known he was different and for many years he had tried to deny the impulses he felt. But the moment his first victim of 'the plan' had spoken up in his forensic class, he knew that he could no longer deny them.

The idea that someone could be smarter than the police and the forensic evidence they relied on thrilled him to no end. Once the reports had started coming in about how he had beat the system he knew that he could never stop.

His first victim was also the inspiration on how the victims following her were chosen. Not only was she an academic, she was also rich and a dancer. Although she didn't study dance at the university, she did however dance weekends at a local club to pay for her classes, and so it began.

Each new victim was chosen from the pool of potential scholars/dancers and with each new murder the title of the 'Denver Dancer' Serial Killer was born and with it his confidence and need to kill again grew. The pathetic title they gave him showed the intelligence that he was dealing with and the thrill was no longer in finding the girl, it came after his kill, waiting to see if he would be discovered.

That had been until Melody.

When he saw her, she brought back all the feelings he had first felt when he'd started stalking his first victim. He would watch her read the messages from afar and could practically smell the fear radiating off her. As an added bonus, he learnt that the more he texted her the more dancing she would do. That only added to his need for her and he often found himself hiding in one of the back rooms, pleasuring himself while she danced away her worries.

He promised himself that when the time came, and he finally did kidnap her, he would spend hours making her dance for him. Then when the time came to kill her he was going to fully enjoy watching her life essence leave her.

Now all he had to do was find her.

First though he had to deal with the problem at hand. For weeks he had been trying to figure out how he could get into the police department without drawing suspicion to himself. He couldn't just walk in and start asking how they were going on the case, that would draw more suspicion to him straight away, as it was they were already suspicious of him.

Most serial killers got impatient and let their hand show too soon.

He knew better.

Thankfully Detective Fox gave him the perfect excuse to walk right into the department and find out what they knew. From the moment he had taken over the case he had a feeling that the detective was going to be a pain in his arse. Unlike most of the other detectives, this one seemed to grow more determined with each kill to catch him and that worried him. It was almost like it was personal for him.

He also knew the minute the detective had shown up on the campus today, even though he had been ordered to stay away, that things were getting real. Thankfully that little visit today played into his hands perfectly. Now, not only had he found all he needed to know about what the cops had on the case – which was nothing – he was also happy to find out that Detective Fox had been removed from the case. That was going to make his movements a whole lot freer. He had been in the interview room for well over an hour and was just making his way out of the building and had just rounded the corner when Detective Fox walked off the stairs just in front of him.

The last thing he needed was a face to face with the detective again, no his best move was to stay as inconspicuous as possible. Pulling the hood of his jumper up over his head, he quickly sped up and continued to make his way out of the police station just behind the detective.

He had almost made it when someone from above called out to the detective. Having to think fast he quickly lowered his head, hoping the hood offered some amount of protection. Thankfully the detective was too busy talking to another officer to notice him. He knew he should have gotten out of there as soon as possible but he had to know what information the detective had.

Anything that could help him stay ahead of the game was beneficial. Seeing a bubbler ahead he leant over and pretended to have a drink as he listened.

"Where are you headed? You know in case I need to find you." His partner yelled.

"Home." Detective Fox yelled back before he headed out of the station.

He had only caught the end of the conversation but it was all he had needed.

Of course why hadn't he thought of that. Melody would have gone home for the summer. A sick smile spread across his face as he thought of the pleasure he would get seeing the shock on her face when he finally kidnapped her. Unlike here on the campus, there was not going to be anyone around that knew what was going on. People would not be as vigilant as they were on campus and police would simply think another young girl had gone missing.

This time there was not going to be a ransom.

No Melody was not like the others, she was special.

She had been made just for him.

Placing his hands in his pockets he pulled out his phone. He would have to go back to campus to break into the administration office so he could gain her home address. Then he would make plans to leave.

But first thing was first.

Time was up for Erica. It was time to put the last wheels of her time in motion. Punching in the code to his phone he opened up the message tab and sent off the message he knew would end Erica's life.

It only took a few minutes for the reply to come, but with that reply came the rush that he loved. Now he could end Erica and start the hunt for Melody. Opening his photos he looked at the one he had of Erica strung up, defeated.

Oh, he loved these pictures. He had one for every girl that

had been taken and killed it was what gave him pleasure on the long, cold, lonely nights. Nothing could bring him pleasure like these photos.

He couldn't wait to add Melody's to his collection.

Swiping the picture into the special folder marked fun, he turned off his phone, placed his hands and phone in his pockets and started to make his way down the street to his car, whistling as he went.

It was a glorious day to be alive and he couldn't wait for the day when he was once again reunited with the woman he wanted to possess more than life itself.

"I hope you're ready Melody, because I am coming for you." He whispered into the air.

5

Melody placed her tray on the bar and read the order of drinks off to Jax. "I need them asap," she relayed to him over the music. Jax smiled at her and leaned up against the bar.

"You know if you keep working this hard I am going to have to give you a raise and that's bad for business."

Melody threw her napkin at him, he smiled and handed it back to her. Jax was one of Gabby's three cousins who ran this place, but they weren't just her bosses, they were her family too. Melody had practically grown up with the three boys and Jax, being the youngest, was the closest to her in age. He was also the mischievous one of the bunch. He thrived on trouble and that was why he often wound up working the bar, he also doubled as the bouncer.

Jax was the most protective of her, that was why it only took a guy laying his hands on her once for the others to get the message never to do it again. It had been a miracle that the guy had walked out of the bar when Jax had finished with him, all he had done was touch her ass and ask if she was available to hire for a lap dance. Something that was not that far-fetched in this place.

From that night on all of the patrons were nothing but respectful to her and those that were not from around the area soon learnt that they were only to talk to her in a respectful manner. At first Melody had been unsure about what it would be like to work here. When she had first put on the tight, short-shorts that left nothing to the imagination, and the form fitting shirt that housed a slit that showed off her ample cleavage and a peek of her belly and the ring that lay there, she had almost backed out. But after a rocky first night, Melody had to admit she loved the work. She loved talking with everyone that came in and as a bonus she got to spend more time with her best friend.

"Did you see the guys who just walked in?" Gabby whispered in her ear.

Melody looked at the table her friend indicated to and Melody knew instantly that they were not from around here. They looked more like the surfer types rather than the hunting type.

"What do you think brought them all the way out here?" She asked leaning on her palm.

"I don't know, but I can tell you I want to find out." Gabby laughed.

"Hey don't talk like that around me. You are still as innocent as the day you were born." Jax grumbled as he placed the drinks Melody ordered on her tray.

Giving Gabby a sly smile and a wink she lifted her tray and added, "well I guess I will have to take the table then because while Gabby is innocent and all, I am far from it." Melody chucked Jax a smile that would melt butter, when a cuss word left his lips. Gabby simply laughed. Melody didn't hear what happened next as she was too far into the crowd of people. After placing the drinks on the table and collecting the money and her tip from them, she made her way over to the new table. She had been right, the group of men weren't from around these parts, they were actually making their way from New Mexico over to California. They were in these parts checking out the layout of the ski fields in preparation for winter. Melody spent a few minutes chatting to them, giving them the lay down on the best places to ski. She had to admit, while the Aspen was the favoured place for most to hit during winter, not many knew of their own little piece of paradise, 'Wolf Creek.'

The locals knew of it, the best part was it had just as many runs as the top resorts, but it was half the price. Melody was happy to pass on this information and she even shared the best places to stay while they were here. She spent a good fifteen minutes talking to them, she could see Jax seething at the bar, arms crossed just waiting for one of them to make a move. Deciding she had made him stew long enough she took their final order, then with a, "I'll be right back with your drinks." She made her way back to the bar.

"That was not funny you know." Jax snapped as she handed him their orders.

Melody smiled, "I love it when you go all big brother on me." She teased. That just earned her a darker look.

Melody decided that she was having too much fun messing with Jax, so she kept it going. Picking up the napkin that one of the guys had written his name and number on, Melody ran it around in her fingers.

"I wonder if it would be too soon to call when I get off work? I'm sure my parents will be asleep by then."

Melody laughed when Jax reached over the bar, grabbed the napkin and threw it in the bin. "Let's get one thing straight. You are as innocent as Gabby is and don't tell me any different. Now take these drinks over there and don't make me have to hurt any of those nice boys. It is not good for business."

Melody pouted, "fine, but when did you become so uptight?" she asked picking up her tray.

Jax smiled, "when you and Gabby grew boobs." Melody

shook her head, she was grateful to have people who were protective of her. Melody made sure not to linger at the table of randy young men for too long, she didn't want to test the validity of Jax's threat. She spent the next few hours taking orders and around eight-thirty the joint picked up. It happened every night on the weekend as everyone knew that at nine o'clock the first lady of the night would appear.

That was the thing about this place, during the day the bar was a respectable place where men could bring their wives for lunch and a drink, even families came in to eat. But on a Friday, Saturday and Sunday night, it doubled as strip joint. It's positioning on the main road made it great for bringing in travellers, especially lonely truck drivers. Because of this it was from the hours of nine and two on those days that Melody made the most tips. On average she made at least two hundred dollars a night, yet she still worried that she would not have enough time here to make up the money she needed. She only worked Friday and Saturdays and even if she got two hundred every time, with the tips she made at the diner she would be lucky to crack six grand. Melody looked at her watch and noticed that it was five to nine. She smiled to herself and walked up to the bar.

"I'm taking my break." She informed Jax, who simply smiled and nodded.

She took her break at the same time every night and she was sure Jax knew why, but he never said a thing. Melody made her way through the crowed to the door on the far side that said employees only. Opening the door she entered the hallway that would lead to the back of the stage, the employees lounge, and locker room, Melody smiled as she enjoyed the quiet and made her way to the edge of the stage. She was just in time to see Honey make her way up from the dressing room.

"You ready for a great show?" she asked as Melody

hugged her.

"You know it." She answered returning her hug.

Every night the girls were on Melody would come back here and watch the show from the side of the stage. She was not interested in the stripping part and would usually be back at work before the girls were down to nothing, earning their tips, but she loved watching the beginning of the show. Watching the girls as they danced and parlayed with the pole was enchanting. During her years of dance instruction, Melody had often found herself dancing on poles. While many people associated them with strippers, what they didn't know was that it took skill and strength to use them probably. From the moment Melody had watched these girls dance, she knew they were not just lose women out to show off their bodies. They were professional dancers, women who simply needed a little more money.

Here they were afforded that luxury, with the knowledge that they would be well protected and their identities were also kept a secret, they could earn the money they needed to get them where they needed to go in life. The beauty of dancing here was that each girl wore a mask and a wig, so only a select few actually knew who they were.

Melody was one of those people, and during her time here she had become quite good friends with many of the girls. Honey's music started and Melody sat on the stairs to watch. She loved the way the material of her see through outfit rushed around her legs as she moved to the music, and as she made her way to the pole and used it to enhance her movements Melody felt the joy of dancing rush through her.

While she danced as much as she could when she was at home, Melody knew deep down inside that there was nothing like the rush a dancer got when she was sharing her love of music and movement with the crowed in front of them. Melody snuck a little further up the stairs until she could see the front row of men who had been waiting all night for this moment. Melody smiled at their mesmerised looks.

Honey hadn't even removed her clothes and yet she still had them snared in her trap.

It was the dancer's magic that held them captive.

Melody watched for a little while longer, but as each piece of clothing came off she knew it was time for her to get back to work, the tips would be flowing freely soon. Standing up from the position she had been crouched in, Melody gave Honey a quick salute as she looked her way, all she got back was a secretive smile, one that only Melody would know the meaning of. As she slowly walked down the stairs and made her way back along the corridor, Melody marvelled at the bravery of the women she had come to know.

They each had their own reasons for dancing. Melody wondered if she would ever have had enough courage to do what these women were doing if the need called for it. Shaking her head she smiled to herself, of course she couldn't. Melody was just about to walk through the door that would take her back into the chaos of the bar when her phone chimed. Reaching down to pull it out of her apron where she kept it at night, she expected to see a message from Gabby demanding to know where she was. No doubt she was being run off her feet out there.

But the message was not from Gabby, if only it were.

The message that Melody read, was simple, yet effective and it had her blood running cold.

My dear Melody you thought you could hide; well you were wrong. I hope you get as much pleasure as I do with the thought of knowing, I am coming for you.

See you soon my sweet.

6

Taking a deep breath Melody tried to put the message out of her mind. She knew there was no way this guy could know where she had gone. No-one at school save the administration department knew about her hometown, then it was only so they could get a hold of her parents if they needed.

She was worrying for nothing.

He was no-one to be concerned with, Melody kept telling herself. He was just some tool who got his kicks out of scaring people, he would soon get bored with her and move on. Placing her phone back into her apron, Melody ran her hand over her hair to make sure that her ponytail was still in place. Once she was certain she looked normal, she placed a smile on her face and pushed through the door. Her ears were instantly met with the sounds of cheering that accompanied the entertainment each night. Glancing quickly at the stage Melody noticed that Honey had removed the outer layers of clothing and was working her way down to what the men wanted to see.

Here the women dancing got to choose how far they went, Honey was one of the few girls who left only the bottoms on. Although the see-through material her G-string was made out of left little to the imagination, it was more for the modesty of the girls. The men in the bar didn't seem to mind. They enjoyed the show regardless.

"Hey darling, can we get a refill." A voice called from her right, bringing her attention back to the room.

Melody smiled. It looked like she was back on it. "Sure, what would you like?" she asked pulling her order book from her apron pocket. When the table had finished ordering, she read it back to them like a pro making sure she didn't miss anything.

"Your drinks won't be long gentlemen," she offered as she turned to make her way to the bar.

She wasn't sure they heard her as their eyes had once again been captured by what was happening on stage. As the hoots and hollers became louder, Melody smiled to herself knowing that Honey had just made all their horny dreams come true. Melody continued to make her way through the crowded bar, she saw Gabby engaged in a conversation with someone at the bar. She could not see his face as his head was bowed so that he could hear what Gabby was saying, her hand was on his bicep and Melody could see the smile on Gabby's face from here.

That was not the surprising part though.

What surprised Melody was that Jax was standing just on the other side of the bar pouring some drinks for one of the other men sitting on the stools and he wasn't in the least fazed by what was happening in front of him. Melody continued to make her way over to bar and reached it just in time to see the man take Gabby into his arms and hug her tight. Leaning up against the bar and handing Jax her order she smiled.

"I'm surprised he still has his arms attached." She laughed as she tilted her head towards the two entwined next her. "What happened to all that 'we are innocent' crap you sprouted to me just before when I wanted to call one of those hotties?"

Jax smiled, but said nothing. Melody did notice however, that the man's back in question seemed to get a little straighter at the sound of her voice. Before she could say anymore he released Gabby and turned to her, "that's because Jax knows I would never go there and as for you remaining innocent, I must say I do concur. Now Jax tell me what in God's name is she doing working here as well?"

"How long has it been since you were here bro, you should know by now that I have no say over what these two terrors do. Trust me if I had my way they wouldn't be working here. But you know Warren, they have him wrapped around their little fingers. Unfortunately he is in charge of all hiring and firings. That simply leaves me with bodyguard duty."

Gabby laughed at that. "Don't act like you don't love it cuz."

The look Jax gave her told them otherwise. While Gabby and Jax bantered back and forth over how much he hated having them working here Melody took the time to take in Roman. She couldn't remember the last time she had seen him, it had to have been a few years ago, on campus. He had filled out since then. He still held the same charm and handsomeness that he always had, but it was less boyish, somehow he'd become more rugged. From the looks of him, Melody could tell he worked out. He filled out his polo shirt nicely. His biceps were practically bursting at the seams and Melody could see the sinewy muscle move each time he made a slight movement. Melody could see the bottom of a tattoo poking out underneath the edge of his sleeve and her mouth went dry. This man had always been a temptation for her, but here he was looking damn fine and it was all she could do to get her hormones under control.

Looking at his face was not an option.

His face was perfection, his nose straight, his jaw chiselled, and the five o'clock shadow that covered it had made her lose all sense. She had only looked at him briefly in those few seconds when he spun around, but it was enough to send her heart racing. Melody had yet to meet his eyes she was worried that if she looked into those blue depths all of her emotions for him would come flooding out. So, she kept her eyes on something safe. His arms. Licking her lips, she followed his arms down to his wrists hoping that she could gain some control back before she looked back at his face. But that was not going to happen. His arms were tightly packed the whole way down and when her eyes settled on his wrist, which housed a silver Rolex gleaming at her, she knew she was screwed.

The truth was undeniable.

Even after so many years apart she still wanted this man with every fibre of her being. Melody was trying to think of a way for her to get out of here and quick, she wished Jax would hurry up with her drinks, thankfully Gabby's next comment allowed her the time she needed to gain her composure. Her question drew all of Roman's attention back on her.

"So, Rome, you never did tell me what brought you back here? Why aren't you in Denver catching the bad guys?"

Jax placed her order on her tray and Melody knew she should probably take them to the men who were waiting. But a quick glance at their table told her that they were thoroughly engaged in what Honey was doing on stage, they wouldn't notice if she was a few more minutes. She needed to hear why Roman was home and how long for.

"There is not much to tell." Roman answered evasively.

Jax snorted across the bar, gaining him a glare from Roman. "Hey, don't give me that look, you know she will worm it out of someone eventually, you might as well tell her yourself and get it over with." After Jax imparted that piece of wisdom he moved away from the group to serve a few customers at the end of the bar. Roman downed the rest of his drink, before he groaned and turned to Gabby. Melody was still at his back put she could hear everything perfectly.

"Is there anything I could offer you to let this go?" he pleaded.

Melody smiled to herself. He should have known better. A comment like that would have only tightened the noose around his neck when it came to Gabby getting what she wanted. The shake of her head told Melody that she had been right in her assumptions.

"Fine. Let's just say that I disobeyed orders on a case one too many times which lead to me having to take an early holiday for a while." He offered turning back to face the bar. He picked up his glass and indicated to the other bartender that he wanted a refill.

Gabby laughed. "You were suspended! Damn Rome, I knew you were badass but you just gave me a whole new appreciation for law enforcement."

Melody turned to see if the guys were still interested in the show, she wanted to stay around to find out more, but they were signalling her letting her know they were ready. "I will have to catch up with you later." She said out loud to Roman as she picked up her tray and started away from the bar. She hadn't got far before his voice reached his ears.

"Hey Mello, make sure you don't leave before saying goodbye." The use of her nickname that was reserved just for him made her insides melt.

"I won't." she promised, before his attention was once again captured by Gabby.

Melody stood there for a few seconds more, before she turned and put her mind back into work mode. It looked like tonight was going to be a big one. She only had four and half hours left until the end of her shift, but she knew they were going to be a killer four and half hours. Just think of the tips she reminded herself as a new table grabbed her after she had placed the drinks down with the men she had served earlier.

Just think of the tips.

* * *

Melody looked down at her watch as she waited for the table she was currently serving to decide what they wanted. It had only been two hours since she'd talked to Roman, she still had one and a half hours to go. The last two hours had been hectic, more people had entered and more girls had danced, but throughout the night Melody could only focus on one thing. Her eyes drifted back to the man sitting at the bar. He hadn't moved from there all night, occasionally he would look around and her heart would skip a beat when their eyes collided and he gave her a smile. Right now he was laughing and joking with both Zeke and Jax. Zeke the middle brother of the cousins had come in once he'd heard that Roman was here. Although he was Jax's best friend, all of the brothers were close with Roman, they had all grown up together. Most of the trouble they got into involved the four of them. His laughter drew her eyes back to him once more. As he sat there joking, Melody wondered what he had been thinking getting suspended. With that came the thoughts of what case he would be working on. Her mind raked through the issues that were going on in Denver at the moment, then it hit her. He was obviously working the 'Denver Dancer' Serial Killer case. All the details of the past nine months and the murdered college students rushed forward and she wondered what kind of pressure he had to be under dealing with that kind of work day in and day out. While she didn't know any of the girls that had gone missing personally, just knowing that women who shared the same love as her were being killed sent a shiver up her spine.

"Hey Missy can I have my drink?" The older gentlemen at the table she was at, asked.

Melody looked down at him in confusion.

"My drink." he asked pointing at her tray. Melody looked down and realised she had been standing here doing nothing. The man must have thought she was daft. No matter how hard she tried to get her mind back on her job, it kept going back to Roman.

"Sure." She said offhandedly, while her focus was on the man at the bar once more.

"Here," she replied in the same distracted manner, she grabbed the drink and placed it on the table. The loud, "hey" and the crashing of glass managed to fix that. Through her inattention Melody had managed to catch the edge of the table with the glass causing it and its contents to go careening to the ground where it shattered on impact.

"Crap I am sorry sir; I will have someone come and clean that up immediately and I will bring you a fresh drink asap." Melody apologised, stepping her way through the mess.

"It's no problem at all Miss, you obviously have a lot on your mind." The elder gentlemen offered politely.

Melody could kiss that tip goodbye she thought sadly. On her way back to the bar she looked to see who had noticed her mishap, thankfully the one person she cared about was nowhere to be seen. The last thing she wanted to remind him about was how clumsy she had been as a teenager. While she had outgrown that quirk years ago, he would still remember. He had loved giving her hell about it back then.

"Not a word," she warned Jax as she reached the bar. Jax put his hands up in surrender and moved away to refill the order.

"Are you alright?" Gabby asked as she placed an order on the bar and waited. Melody looked at her friend, she had at least expected some smart-arse comment from her, but it didn't come. Leaning against the bar Melody really looked at Gabby, she didn't look well.

"I think I should be asking you that question."

Gabby gave her a quizzical look, until her brain finally caught on to what Melody had meant. She gave a slight smile before answering, "not really, I have a killer headache that is getting worse by the minute." Gabby's hand reached up and rubbed her temple to add credence to her tale. Melody could see the pain that was written all over her friend's face and the more time she spent here the worse it would get. It wouldn't be long before Gabby was no use to anyone. She might as well head home while she still could.

"You should go home." Melody ordered.

"But there is no-one to cover me."

Melody looked around the room to see how many tables Gabby had in her section, there weren't that many tonight as being a Friday the boys usually had extra hands on deck.

"It's all good I can cover your section. Go home."

Gabby gave her a relieved look, yet Melody could still see the indecision play out on her face.

"But…" she tried.

"Gabby there is no but's about it. Our replacements will be here at the same time, I am sure I can manage till then. Besides I could use the extra money anyway." At Gabby's look Melody shrugged her shoulders.

"What? Did you think I would give you the tips? I need the money more than you do."

Gabby gave a small pained laugh. "Okay I will go home."

"Good." Melody said as she leaned forward and placed a kiss on her friend's cheek.

Gabby was just about to leave when she stopped once more. "Damn I came here with Jax, he has to stay late tonight. I was going to give him a hand."

"Jax will manage just fine without you. Zeke is here I will make sure he stays and gives him a hand. As for you getting home you can take my car. The keys are in my locker, you know the combination. Just drop it back at my place in the morning."

"Are you sure?" Gabby asked.

"Positive."

Gabby considered it for half a second before she brought up a valid point. "Hang on, if I take your car how will you get home?"

Melody thought about that for a moment, she hadn't considered things that far, but at Gabby's wince she knew it didn't matter. Her friend needed to go home.

"I will figure it out. Now go."

"But Dee you need to be able to get home."

"I will take her." Came a voice from behind Melody. She didn't need to see his face to know who it was. His voice was like whiskey and honey and it filled her with warmth from the top of her head to the tips of her toes. The last thing she wanted to do was be alone with this man, but she could not deny her friend.

"See problem solved." Melody answered with false bravado.

"Okay I will go. Rome you're the best." Gabby added as she walked past Melody and engulfed him in a hug.

"You know I love a good damsel in distress. Now go home and rest."

With that Melody watched as her friend made her way out of the bar and into the back where to the locker room. She was grateful that her friend was going home to rest but that left her having to face feelings she was not sure she was ready to face.

"Don't look so worried Mello. I promise I will make it fun." Roman joked, as he sat back down on the bar stool.

When Melody looked at him, she could see the twinkle in his eyes. If only he knew what kind of fun she wanted to have with him, she wasn't so sure that twinkle would be there.

"That's what worries me." Melody offered instead. "You forget I know what you are capable of. Besides, I don't know how safe it is to take a disgraced cop home."

"Oh how you wound me." Roman held his hand to his heart.

Melody punched his arm. She remembered how easy it was to fall back into the playful friendship they had always had, once she put her sexual feelings aside that was. They were still there, lingering just under the surface as they always had been, but his openness helped her to harness them. He was still Roman; someone she had known her whole life. The man who had saved her.

Jax placed a drink on her tray, before asking about Gabby. "Well champ I will leave you to explain that one. I have drinks to serve and tips to make. Have to bring out the big guns after that little stunt." Melody picked up her tray, ripped out her pony tail and added a little swagger to her walk as she prepared to pass a table of young men who had just entered.

"Damn that girl is trouble." She heard Jax groan.

"Don't I know it." Roman added. Melody smiled to herself. If only they knew just how much trouble she was about to bring, they would have run in the opposite direction.

7

The rest of the night flew by. Melody didn't have any more time to talk to Roman, in fact the joint had become so packed that he himself was now working behind the bar. He had worked here a lot over the summer during their senior year, so he knew what he was doing. Melody let out a sigh of relief when her replacement tapped her on the shoulder.

"Can you let Milla know that Gabby went home. I have been covering her table."

"Sure can." Pam answered.

"Thanks." Melody grabbed the last set of glasses off of the table she had been cleaning and took them over to the bar. Roman was wiping the bar down with a cloth when she got there. Placing the cups on the bar so Sally, the other bartender, could take them out to be cleaned she placed her tray on the end of the bar and took a seat.

"Well my shift is finished, are you still good to take me home? If not it is okay I can always call an Uber."

Roman shook his head. "I will never get over why young women insist on getting in those things alone. Anything could happen to you I said I would take you home and take you home I will."

"Always the cop." Melody added with a warm smile.

That earned her a glare from him. It was meant to cower her, but it didn't. She knew he was a big soft teddy bear; he only saved his savage side for those who deserved it.

"Jax I'm out." He yelled across the bar. Jax was currently down the other end of the bar serving customers. He waved at Roman, "will catch you tomorrow bro." Roman nodded at him, before he came around the bar to her. "Alright let's go."

"I just have to get a few things from my locker first. I'll meet you out front. Which car is yours?"

Melody waited for him to answer, but he simply smiled and started walking backwards. "You can't miss it." He then turned around and continued out the door. Melody shook her head as she made her way into the staff lounge where she would find her locker. Upon entering she found Honey finishing her coffee and placing the cup in the sink. She leaned against the cupboard and smiled.

"What did you think Sweets?"

"You were amazing as always." Melody walked forward and gave her a hug.

"Are you in tomorrow?" Honey asked, moving away from the counter to place her left over dinner in the fridge.

"You know it. I am on open's tomorrow but I will still be here for your show." Melody winked at her as she walked over to her locker.

She never in a million years would have thought she'd be friends with a stripper, but as life was want to do, Melody once again found herself in a situation beyond what she had thought possible.

"Bye, you foxy woman." Melody threw at Honey as she pushed her way through the lounge door.

"Bye, Sweets. Until tomorrow." Honey blew her a kiss. It was hard to believe the woman in there was currently studying to become an Astrophysicists and had interned with

NASA. Stripping allowed her to do so without compromising her study time. It just went to show you really couldn't judge a book by its cover. Melody made her way through the bar, waving at Jax as she went. As she pushed through the front door, Melody took her first real breath for the night.While she loved working here, the stale, alcoholic smell that came with working in said bar, was one thing she would did not miss at the end of her shifts. Melody looked around the parking lot to see if she could spot Roman, she didn't see him right away and thought about going back inside to ask Jax. That was when she spotted it.

She knew it was Romans right away.

There at the end of the row was a Titan Truck, grey in colour but Roman in size and laying on the bonnet of said truck was the man himself. Melody chucked her bag over her shoulder, crossed her arms over her chest and made her way over to his car. Once she was there she leaned against the bumper and spoke. "I thought men didn't like it when people laid on their cars."

Roman sat up and smiled. "They don't, but since this is my car and I know my baby can handle it, I guess it's alright."

"I guess you won't mind if I join you then?"

Roman eyed her. "Don't even think about it."

Roman jumped down from his perch to land just in front of her. Now that he as standing close Melody remembered how tall he was. She had to take a step back and lean her head back a bit so she could look into his eyes.

He leaned forward slightly and whispered, "she only likes having me on top of her."

Melody had trouble swallowing, she knew the words had no sexual meaning behind them, but what they were doing to her body was anything but innocent. Roman was completely unaware of the affect he had on her, he simply hit the fob on his keys and walked towards the drivers side.

"So where do we call home when we are back in Pagosa Springs?" He asked opening his door and stepping up into the cab.

Melody did the same, except she had to step a little higher, while her legs were long, they were nowhere near as long as his. Once she was in the cab and putting her seat belt on, she answered. "The apartment over my parents garage."

Roman turned and smiled at her. "Still living at home with the parents huh?"

"No smart arse I live in Denver. I only stay there when I am back here."

Roman winked at her as he backed out of the parking lot. "Well then let's get you home shall we." With that he started down the road.

* * *

The drive only took twenty minutes and while Melody had worried that it would be made in uncomfortable silence, she was pleasantly surprised. He spent most of the time asking her about her time at DUA, and she found that she didn't have any trouble telling him about it. She loved the time she spent there, her passion for dancing shone through with each story she told him. At one point she was worried that she would bore him, but as he laughed along with her, she knew he was engaged. One story lead to another and before long they were reminiscing about the old days. Before she knew it Roman was pulling up outside of the diner.

"It hasn't changed a bit." He replied.

Melody smiled. "The one thing my parents can always be relied on for is their consistency."

"Well I guess I will be seeing you around." Roman stated as he got ready for her to get out of the car.

Melody realised she was not ready to say goodbye to him

just yet, before she could stop herself she found the next words pouring from her mouth. "I'm famished. Feel like some ice-cream?"

Roman gave her an odd look. "It's one-thirty in the morning. Don't you think it is a bit late, or should I say early for ice-cream? Besides what would your parents say?"

Melody laughed. "For one thing, it is never to early or late for ice-cream. As for the other, my parents are used to my midnight snacking, usually Gabby is with me."

Roman looked at the clock before looking at the diner. "I really should get going."

"Okay." Melody couldn't keep the disappointment out of her voice. She wasn't sure if he'd heard it or not but didn't really care.

"Oh what the hell, what is one more hour. But I refuse to eat ice-cream, I will settle for a coffee though."

Melody smiled at him. "That I can do." They quietly made their way into the diner, using the key Melody always had on her house keys. Her parents had given it to her when she was in high school just in case she had to open or close for them.

"Just sit anywhere. I will put on a fresh pot of coffee on and grab some food."

Roman chose to sit in one of the booths, she hurried as she put on the pot of coffee before going into the kitchen to find some ice-cream. Opening the freezer she found her favourite and dished herself a bowl. Once done she found fresh donuts on the bench ready for the morning rush. She grabbed a few and put them on a plate.

"I know you said you didn't want ice-cream, so I brought you these instead." Melody offered as she took his coffee, her ice-cream and the donuts off the tray she had grabbed off the bench. She quickly placed it back before she joined him. While she hated working the long hours here in her senior year, Melody had to admit there were perks to her family owning a diner. There was always yummy food on hand.

"What makes you think I will eat them?" He asked smiling at her.

"Because I know you couldn't turn down a donut."

Roman eyed her suspiciously. "Because I am a cop?"

Melody laughed. "No, because they have always been your Achilles heel."

Roman gave her a lopsided smile. "Oh yeah I guess there is that."

"So, tell me about you." Melody asked before placing a spoon full of ice-cream in her mouth.

Roman picked up a donut and ripped off a piece. "Where do you want me to start?"

"What made you become a cop?" She asked realising that she had never really known the story behind his career choice. Roman and Jax had graduated the year before them, and because they were older, they had gone their own ways. While Melody had missed them, she had been too busy focusing on her own dreams. Now four years later she had finally come to realise how far apart they had drifted.

"That's what you want to know?" He asked before popping another bite into his mouth.

"Yes sir, that is the story I want."

"Okay but be warned it is pretty boring." Roman took a sip of his coffee.

Melody wasn't letting him get away with things that easily. He had learnt all about her now it was time for him to repay the favour. "Noted, now start talking, Detective."

Roman smiled and started telling her about his life. They spent the next thirty minutes talking about his life in Denver. Melody was surprised they hadn't run into each other more. They often frequented the same coffee shops and practically lived around the corner from each other. Roman looked at his watch before stretching.

"Well it is now officially two in the morning. I guess I should make like a tree and leave. I still have to get back to the bar and get Jax's keys so I can crash at his house."

Before Melody could give any more thought to the words that were about to come out of her mouth she spoke.

"Why don't you just crash at mine?"

Melody was starting to regret her impulsiveness as Roman started back at her unblinking. She was just about to take it all back when he replied. "Are you sure about that?"

"What do you mean am I sure? Of course, I am sure and before you go ranting at me about letting men I don't know crash at my place, you are not men. You are Roman."

"Well, I don't know if I should be offended or not." He replied leaning back and crossing his arms over his chest. The sight of him sitting like that was doing all kinds of crazy things to her body and Melody was having second thoughts about having him in her house. Earlier she had been in a rush to get out of his company before she did something stupid. Now she was offering to have him in her house, in the place where she got naked. Her eyes roamed his body of their own accord thinking of what he would look like naked. As she felt the heat rise in her cheeks she knew she had to change the way her mind was going.

Get a grip of your self Melody.

"You know what I mean. You mean as much harm to me as Jax would. So do you want the couch or not? I have to work early tomorrow so I need to get to bed."

Roman narrowed his eyes and examined her closely before answering. "Thank you that would be great."

"Alright then let's go."

Melody closed the diner before she led Roman across the lawn to the garage, where they would find her apartment sitting above. As she climbed the stairs to her apartment four little words kept playing over and over in her head.

What are you thinking?

8

As Roman followed Melody up the stairs to her apartment he wondered for the hundredth time tonight when she had grown up. The last time he had seen her briefly on campus, she had still looked like the teenager she had when he left town. Now that teenager was gone and in front of him stood an amazingly built woman.

She had curves in all the right places and while she had the same blonde hair and blue eyes that she had in high school, with the dancer's body she now possessed, it was a look that men went wild for.

When he had first seen her tonight it had felt like he had been punched in the gut. While it had taken him a little bit to get used to the skimpy outfit on Gabby, seeing it on Melody was something altogether different. He had wanted to immediately tell her to go and take it off and put something decent on. While he had rained the impulse in, it had become harder as the night wore on to keep his protectiveness under control. As each member of the opposite sex smiled at her, hit on her or just flat out touched her, his anger grew. At one stage he wanted to break every bone in the body of a young male who had made a pass at her and offered her his number.

Thankfully though Jax was on the case. As soon as she had

come back to the bar with the number, he grabbed it and tossed it out. Melody hadn't been upset in the least. It was obviously a nightly ritual.

As the night wore on, he decided he needed to keep his hands and hopefully his mind busy to stop himself from doing something stupid. So, he offered his services to Jax. Thankfully it worked for a bit.

He had planned to stay at his parents, but when Jax had offered his couch, Roman had been thankful. While he loved his parents, he knew he would be more comfortable at Jax's, his friend didn't pry into the private details of his life. Roman had planned to leave early on in the night and go over the day's events. But that had not happened.

Instead he found himself staying at the bar to keep an eye on Melody. He told himself it was because he saw her as a little sister, but deep down he knew that wasn't the case.

The truth was Roman was no different to the rest of the leachers here. That was why he was so mad, he had no idea when he had started looking at Melody as more than just a friend. All he knew was that he had, because what he wanted to do to that body of hers was not something friends did at all.

As he sat across from her watching her lick the ice cream off of her spoon his lust was going wild, it was why he found it hard to turn down her offer. While he acted as though it was just like sleeping on Jax's couch he knew differently. Jax didn't look nowhere as good as she did.

"Here you go." Melody offered as she opened the door and moved aside to let him in.

He was still trying to reel in his treacherous thoughts when he walked past her and got a whiff of her perfume, and her arm brushed against his. Once more his emotions were sent into overdrive. He needed to get his mind on safer things. Walking further into the room away from her allure Roman took in the small apartment. It mimicked her personality to a tee.

The small apartment was split into three sections. The kitchen off to the left ran the entire length of the west wall of the apartment and had everything in its rightful place. A small island bench separated the lounge room from the kitchen, while leaving enough room at either end to enter either room.

While the lounge room itself took up at least half of the remaining space, it was cosy without being cramped. Roman noticed all of the Juilliard pictures that lined the walls and off to the south side of the room, behind the couch, just below the windows, rested a ballet bar. The area behind the couch and the two windows were completely clear of any clutter and he knew instantly this must have been the place where she practiced dancing.

Just off to the side of the windows was a door that opened up on to a full-length balcony. There was an outside dining set out on the deck and Roman could picture her sitting out there at night watching the sun sink down behind the horizon of the mountains that surrounded them. The final rooms that made up the apartment were her bedroom and the bathroom, each of which shared the east wall of the apartment finishing off the other half.

"I know it's not much, but it's home while I am here." She offered.

Roman turned around to face her, she was just placing her bag on the hooks above the cabinet that was to the left of the door, then she placed her keys in the bowl that lay beside the phone. No the place was not much, but it was her.

"The couch pulls out into a sofa bed, Gabby swears that it is comfortable, but who knows. I will just get you some linens and then I'll leave you to it."

Roman nodded his thanks as Melody went into the

bathroom. When she returned, he grabbed them off her. "I really appreciate this."

"It's no problem, really." She offered before heading back into her bedroom.

"Good night Rome." She offered as she shut the door.

"Night Mello." He answered using the nickname he had given her as a kid. He didn't use it to be disrespectful, it was his way of reminding himself who this woman was to him. The only problem was it wasn't working. Roman set about making his bed when he heard the water start in the bathroom. She must have had a connecting door to the bathroom from her room. Once his bed was made Roman crawled in as his mind pictured her in the shower as the hot water cascaded over her body. He sent up a silent prayer when the water finally shut off and all noises beyond the door ended. Now that she was in bed Roman closed his eyes and begged sleep to take him so that morning could come faster and he could get out of here sooner.

Half an hour later Roman found himself staring at the ceiling. At first his mind was on the woman only a few feet away, but soon his mind turned to the case. Now that was something he could focus on. He wondered what had happened with Neil. He had been made to leave the precinct before the little twerp had been released. He still couldn't believe that the captain had removed him from the case. Roman couldn't wait to nail that little arse hats balls to the wall. Roman just knew Neil was behind the murders, he just needed time to prove it. He let out a small sigh, he guessed he had all the time he needed now. Picking up his phone he noted the time and sent off a quick message to Shale, his partner. Roman set his phone down, he wasn't expecting Shale to answer him right now, he expected that he would talk to him in the morning. Roman just wanted to send it before he forgot. That was why Roman was a little shocked when his phone started vibrating on the floor where he had placed it. Picking it up the picture of Shale lit up to show who was calling. Sliding the bar over to answer Roman got up from the couch and walked to the kitchen so that he was far enough away from her room so that he would not wake Melody.

He looked at the door leading to the veranda and considered briefly going out there, but he instinctively knew the door sliding would wake her. The kitchen would have to do.

Roman made sure to keep his voice low as he greeted his partner. "What the hell are you doing up this late?"

A small chuckle came through the phone. "Well it turns out you were not the only one who is being punished for the incident with Solomon. Turns out Mummy and Daddy believe I had something to do with you going to the campus and claim that I was just covering so that you had time to harass the little turd."

"What a load of shit." Roman cursed. His voice rose a little, he couldn't help it. How could the captain let these people run his precinct? Roman hated how much power the rich had on the force.

"It's all good Fox. The captain knew it was a bogus charge and realistically, I got off lightly. I simply ended up on nightshift. Truthfully it's not that bad, it's actually quite at this time of the night. Not too many murders are reported during this time. It has given me a lot of time to go over the case actually. Hence the reason for my call."

"And?" Roman asked.

"Nothing. Nudda. Zip. As Always there is no evidence to nail the bastard."

"Damn it. Have you checked every case again?" Roman knew it was a stupid question.

"Do you really want me to answer that?" Shale shot

through the phone.

Roman leaned up against the counter and pinched the bridge of his nose with his forefinger and thumb. Closing his eyes, he sighed. "No. At least tell me something new has come up." There was a pause on the other end of the phone. "Shale!" it was more of an order rather than a question.

"The ransom just came in for Erica Hatchman."

"Fuck." Roman swore as he pounded his fist against the counter top. His head was now resting on the cupboard which was attached to the roof.

"Rome?" Came a sleepy voice from the room behind him.

"Shit." He whispered into the phone.

"Now I don't remember you telling me you had a sister and I am sure that woman sounds too young to be your mother. So pray do tell partner who exactly is that sexy voice I hear coming thorough your phone?"

"Shut up." Roman whispered into the phone as he turned to face Melody.

He was going to apologise as he turned to face her, but all that left his mouth was a groan of pain instead. She was standing at her doorway rubbing the sleep out of her eyes dressed in nothing but a soft pink satin cami and shorts set which left little to the imagination. To make matters worse Shale heard the groan and was currently laughing his arse off on the other end of the phone. Roman moved the phone away from his mouth a bit to answer Melody.

"Sorry I didn't mean to wake you. Everything is fine just go back to bed and get some sleep." He silently prayed that she would do as he said, turn around an take her tempting arse back to bed.

Instead she walked right into the kitchen, pulled a cup out of the cupboard beside him, filled it with water and proceeded to lean against the bench right next to him and drink. The heat from her body was radiating off of her and the skin of her arm that was just touching his was sending electrical waves the whole way through his body. He needed to do something and fast.

"Shale just give me a sec." Roman hit mute and laid the phone on the bench. He could see that Melody was still half asleep as she drank her water yet he needed her to realise the situation she was currently in.

He was a man of honour, but currently that honour was in serious jeopardy. He was not a monk after all.

"Excuse me." He stated right before he turned and placed his body flush against hers and reached above her head to get a glass. In doing so he made sure that every part of his body was in contact with hers.

He knew he was doing it for a good reason, but right now he was having a hard time remembering what that reason was. Her breasts, that were just covered by a thin piece of satin, were making it hard for him to think, he had to work fast. Once he had his glass, he placed a little space between them. He was pleased to see that she was now wide awake. Her glass was poised on her lips but her eyes were wide and they were staring at him. He could see the lust there but he could also see the recognition of what she had done.

Roman took another step back until he was resting against the island on the other side. He grabbed hold of the edge of it to stop himself from reaching forward and grabbing her. Slowly Melody removed the glass from her lips and licked the remaining water off of them. She was slowly killing him.

"Well I think I had better get back to bed." She commented her voice a little husky, before she turned and placed her cup in the sink. The sight of her arse cheek peeking out of her pants made him groan once more. It was supple, pink, tight, and the sight of a tear shaped birth mark only added to her allure. The idea that he knew something about her that no other man probably knew turned him rock hard.

He wanted her with a need that scared him.

Roman turned his eyes skywards and prayed for patience. He was being punished for something he just knew it.

"Did you say something?" She asked turning to face him once more. Roman didn't even bother looking back at her he simply shook his head no. With that, she said one final goodnight before her soft footfalls could be heard. Roman didn't bother looking again until he heard her door shut. Only then did he let out the breath he had been holding.

"Fox you still there?" He heard through the phone.

Taking one last deep breath Roman picked up his phone, hit the mute button and answered.

"Yes, I am still here."

"You know that was mean right?" Shale wined.

Roman just shook his head. Normally he would have shared the incident with his partner, but with Melody it was different. It was that whole protective thing he had going.

"I'm sure you will get over it. Now about the ransom, you have to find a way to stall the family from paying it. You know what will happen if they do."

"Yes I do, but we have no idea what the bastard will do if they don't."

Roman thought about that for a minute. "True, but it's a risk we have to take. Sooner or later the bastard is going to slip up and when he does we will be there to catch him."

"Alright I will see what I can do. It is going to be a little tougher now though."

"I have all the faith in you partner."

Shale laughed once more. "Alright I will leave you to whatever it is you are doing there. Talk to you soon Fox."

Shale hung up after promising to keep him updated on what happened. Walking back to the couch Roman laid down and placed his phone back on the floor. Running his hand over his face, Roman hoped this family would listen to them and wait. His mind wondered from the case to the woman who was currently sleeping in the next room. What had she been thinking wearing those kinds of clothes to bed? As Roman's mind gave in and allowed him to go to sleep, his conscious thought became that of his dreams. Instead of letting her walk away though, his dream self did everything he had wanted to do, and more, and even though he only got a few hours' sleep, they had been the best few hours he'd had in ages.

9

Melody awoke to the sound of her alarm. Reaching over she shut off the offending noise, before she rolled over and stretched, releasing all the pressure of sleep from her muscles. As her arms came to rest back on her blankets, she took a moment to wake fully and take in the events of the night before. Most of the night had been wonderful, normal in fact, but she couldn't help shake the feeling that something else had happened.

Something she could not remember.

Throwing her blankets off and shaking loose the cobwebs Melody made her way to her wardrobe and took out a clean uniform. She had one hour to get ready and make herself functional before she had to be at work. Turning her head towards her bedroom door she wondered what the man on the other side was doing. She assumed he would still be asleep, they hadn't made it to bed till well after two in the morning and God knows how long he had been up before that. Opening her bathroom door she made her way to the shower and started it. Looking in the mirror Melody took note of the bags under her eyes and decided to make a note to add a little extra coverage today.

She told herself that the need to look nice had nothing to

do with the said male in her living room, but everything to do with the façade she had to portray while she worked.

Men wanted to see perky, happy waitresses in the bar, not sleep deprived ones who were barley functioning.

It took Melody about half an hour to shower and dress. Taking one last look at herself in the mirror and happy that her look was good as it was ever going to get, she made her way out of the bedroom and into the lounge area.

She had expected to find Roman still in bed, instead she found the lounge as it had been the night before. Her open notebook on the bench caught her eye. Walking over she saw a note from Roman. The handwriting was just like him, bold, strong and masculine.

Mello,

Thanks for the use of the sofa last night. Gabby was right it is comfortable. Much better than Jax's beat up old futon. You are probably wondering why I didn't hang around. Well Gabby showed up this morning with your car, so I decided to give her a lift home. I had a few things I needed to do anyway. The keys for the car are in the bowl and there is a fresh pot of coffee in the coffee machine. Enjoy work today. If I don't get to the chance to see you before I leave make sure you grab my number from Jax so that we can have coffee in Denver one day.

Rome.

P.S. Get something more sensible to wear to bed.

She smiled at the smile face he had added to the end. His last comment confused her for a moment, that was until her mind finally registered what he was talking about.

"Oh my God." She mumbled as Melody fell onto the stool that was just off to her right and laid her head down on the bench. "How am I ever going to face him again." She mumbled to herself.

Melody's dream from last night came rushing back to her in full. Only it hadn't been a dream. She had really been standing in her kitchen, drinking water, with Roman staring at her in her, 'not for visitors' sleepwear. It was a well-known fact that when extreme exhaustion took over, Melody could often be found having conversations with people, while seemingly awake, and yet have no recollection of it the next morning. It was for all intense purposes like having a dream. She had lost count of the amount of times her mother had asked her to do something as a teenager thinking she was coherent, only to find out later that Melody had thought it was all a dream, so the said thing never got done. It was why her parents, even to this day, made sure she was fully awake and functional before they ever gave her any information or instructions. They also left her notes just to cover all bases.

There was nothing she could do about it now.

From the last words in his note, she assumed that he would be heading back to Denver soon and that meant she would not see him for a bit. Melody still had a couple more weeks here before she went back, she had to get as much money together as she could. Melody couldn't help the little rush of disappoint she felt at the thought of not seeing him again. Standing she made her way over to the coffee machine and poured some into her travel mug, she didn't have time to mess around as she only had forty minutes before she started work, and as it took twenty minutes to get there, that left her with twenty to get her mind in gear and her stuff ready.

Grabbing her keys Melody opened the door to her apartment and started to make her way out. Before she closed the door however she looked back over to her lounge, it was as though he had never been there. Melody knew differently of course, she knew her little space would never be the same again, she only wished the night had turned out differently.

Oh the memories they could have made.

Shaking the lustful thoughts from her mind, Melody shut and locked the door behind her before racing to her car. She needed to get a grip. Roman was gone and she had more important things to focus on like getting the money she needed to attend this program, that would never happen if she showed up late and lost her job.

Jumping into her car and turning it on, Melody sped out of her parents drive way and made the twenty-minute drive to the bar. The only problem with driving was it gave you time to think, unfortunately her mind wondered to the twenty-minute drive last night. Groaning, Melody sped up.

God let this drive go quickly she prayed as she raced down the highway to a place that would take her mind off of her troubles, even if only for a short while.

* * *

Melody let out a sigh of relief when she drove into the parking lot of the bar. Her job was safe. Not that she ever doubted it. She knew in her heart that Warren would never fire her. Still she was a stickler for holding up the rules. Well that is what she thought.

Grabbing her bag and personal items from the seat beside her, Melody jumped out, locked the door and rushed inside. Even though the bar wasn't open for another hour there were a few people inside setting up for today's crowd.

"Hey Zeke." She shouted to the cousin behind the bar, he looked up and waved at her as she zoomed through the area where the seats and tables would be set up, to the door that would lead her to the back room.

Just as she was about to reach it Gabby came rushing through almost collecting her.

"Whoa slow down there." Melody teased.

Gabby laughed and hugged her. "Glad to see you are feeling better today." Melody offered as she made her way past Gabby to the door.

"Much, now hurry up so we can get the party started and get this joint ready for business."

With that she marched off to the Jukebox and chose a song. Warren didn't switch the jukebox to payment mode until the bar was open. That allowed his employee's the enjoyment of music as they cleaned. Melody quickly dashed into the employee's lounge and dumped her stuff into her locker. Grabbing her apron, she tied it around her hips and then made her way out to help Gabby. Gabbing another mop she stared to the clean the floor so that they could set up the tables. Melody didn't mind this kind of work, it allowed her time to chill and she got to listen to music.

As it was want to do, when music was around, her body took over and before long Melody was dancing while she moped. Gabby cheered, before she ran over and put on a hip hop song, they both loved.

Melody laughed. "What are you up to Gabs?" She laughed.

Gabby walked towards her a smile playing on her face. "You know perfectly well what I am doing. It's time to show us them big moves you got. You know the moves that the hot shot school wants."

"You're crazy." Melody chimed in as she continued to mop.

"Come on girl, you know you can't deny your body when that beat is around."

Melody could only stand there and shake her head. Gabby was right, if there was one thing Melody could not deny, it was her passion for dance and who was she hurting by dancing now. Grabbing the mop Melody started dancing as though she was in class. The song that was playing was the perfect blend of hip thrusts, pelvic moves and hip-hop floor moves that allowed her to showcase everything she had learnt and before she knew what was happening Melody was on the stage with Gabby both of them showing off their moves.

Zeke was leaning against the bar caterwauling and whistling, encouraging the two girls as they danced, and Melody loved every bit of it. Her body felt as though it was one with the music and with each twerk, drop and pelvic thrust, Melody felt the world around her disappear and all of her troubles seemed to melt away.

This is what she loved. This was what she had been put on this earth to do.

Looking over at Gabby, Melody was drawn back into their innocent childhood. There were no issues of money, no stalkers and no choices to make, it was only them dancing and having fun. Melody smiled as Gabby grabbed her hand and started to dance against her, she was defiantly the wilder of the two.

"You're a bad influence." Melody yelled over the top of the music.

Gabby smiled and grabbed hold of the pole, "you ain't seen nothing yet." With that she pulled a stripper move. Melody couldn't help herself; she danced her way over to the other pole and joined in the fun.

They were laughing so hard tears filled their eyes, even Zeke had joined in. He was currently behind the bar pumping away to the beat. Looking around at the joy that filled the room Melody had the sudden urge to let loose and be like Gabby. Looking at her friend she whistled. Gabby didn't stop dancing, she simply moved around the pole so she could see her friend.

"You ready to see what I'm made of?"

Gabby winked. "Give it to me girl. Show me what all you fancy girls learn at your academy."

Melody smiled a wicked smile and thought back on some

of the moves she had seen Honey make and she added a few of her own dance moves from the piece she was working on. The results were magnificent.

Gabby was standing there mouth wide open as Melody went in for the kill. Dipping low, Melody sunk into the splits while her body worked its way down to the pole. She was almost done and about to put the icing on the cake when the music stopped. Melody let go of the pole and turned her head to the area where the jukebox was.

Her eyes widened briefly before her mischief gene set in.

There stood Jax, arms crossed, brows furrowed, a menacing look gracing his face.

Melody looked to Gabby who was laughing, then to Zeke who was suddenly busy wiping the bar. She knew she could stand up and act as though nothing happened or as usual she could play with Jax. The last option won out, he made it too easy. Leaning forward until her left was on her bare leg, she rested her chin in her hand so that her breasts were almost falling out of her top, she then wiggled her eyebrows and waved at him with her other hand before asking, "what's up Jax?"

To her disappointment he didn't bite, he simply shook his head then pointed at both her and Gabby before saying, "what did I say? Innocent, that is what you are."

Gabby sat on the side of the stage and laughed. That was all Jax said before he walked off, but he wasn't even half way across the room when he yelled, "Rome." That was when Melody noticed the other person in the room. She wasn't sure how she'd missed him. There he was, leaning against the wall near the Jukebox; arms folded over his chest, ankles crossed, staring at her with a smile that could melt butter. His eyes were like fire, warming her from the inside. Self-conscious all of a sudden, Melody straightened as much as she could and watched as he pushed himself off the wall before he walked across the room towards Jax, his hands in his pockets. Melody kept his eye contact but couldn't help the laugh that escaped at Jax's next comment to him.

"Nothing but trouble I tell you. They will be the death of me, mark my words Rome."

"We keep you young." Gabby yelled.

"You keep me grey." He shouted back as he pushed through the door. Melody took the opportunity of their distraction to get up from her position. Once standing she brushed her butt off, then looked back at the door. She was just in time to see Roman push through it but before he did he looked back, his eyes travelled the length of her, before stopping briefly on her breasts. It wasn't long before they were tangling with her own eyes and that was when he winked, smiled and then went through door. That one gesture sent a flood of feelings coursing through her. Her blood rushed through her veins, her heart beat faster and her body flushed as thoughts of what she would like him to do with that mouth of his flowed through her.

Damn she was in trouble.

10

"I'm back from my break. You can take yours when you are ready." Gabby said as she rushed past Melody to the bar. The lunch rush had been insane. After Jax and Roman had passed through the door and disappeared, Gabby and Melody had finished playing around and set up for lunch. That had been the last ounce of peace she'd had. Today was Saturday and the lunch rush was always a mad house on Saturdays. Not only did all the regular families come in, but the bar also had the influx of tourist that were journeying past.

"What can I get you?" She asked the family that was currently sitting in front of her. She would take this last order and then head out to take her lunch break. Even though it was four in the afternoon, Melody would be here to well after midnight, so technically it was still lunch for her.

"We will have three buffalo burgers, one chicken burger, a large fries for the table and four cokes please." The father of the family ordered for everyone.

"No problem, I will be back with your order soon." Melody answered as she finished writing down the order. She then rushed it over to the bar, before taking back some complimentary bread rolls for the table. If she hadn't worked here after nine, she would swear that working here was no different to working in the diner for her parents. The tips were the same, as was the work. The bigger tips didn't come until after dark when the fun began.

Thinking of fun, Melody's mind wandered back to the morning she'd had with Gabby, that memory brought with it Roman. She hadn't seen him or Jax again since they had disappeared, they must have left while she had been busy. Her eyes scanned the bar of their own accord once more looking for him. But as it had the previous times, the search revealed nothing. He was not here.

"Order up." Came the shout from the kitchen.

Melody made her way over to the pass and picked up the order. Once she delivered it to the table she nodded at Gabby to let her know she was taking her break. She had half an hour to gather herself, her longer break was at nine. Pushing through the door she made her way to the employee's lounge. Walking in she put the kettle on, grabbed her food from the fridge and chucked it into the microwave. Once that was done, she made her way over to the lockers and pulled out her phone. Turning it on she was relieved to see that there were no new messages. She felt a little less stressed about her stalker's messages, while they were coming more frequently and a little more intense, he still had not shown up as he had bene promising. This proved to Melody that it was probably some freshman who was trying to rush for a fraternity. She just happened to be the lucky girl he had picked. Yet even though the thought passed through her mind an ominous feeling filled her stomach.

If that were the case, why had he gone to so much trouble to find her number once she'd changed it.

The news reels and articles on the 'Denver Dancer' Serial Killer were running through her head.

What if this was him? What if she was his next target?

Melody shook her head; she was being silly. It was nothing

more than a prank gone array. She was not rich like the other girls who had been taken so there would be no reason for him to hunt her. Melody sent up a prayer for small favours. She gave a startled yelp as the phone in her hand started to vibrate, looking down and recognising the number she immediately answered.

"Professor, to what do I owe the pleasure."

Melody heard her professor laugh on the other end of the phone, but it was not a laugh of humour. The ominous feeling was back in Melody's stomach.

"I wish it was with better news I am afraid. I just got off the phone with the academy and they are needing an answer by no later than Monday as to whether you will be doing the course or not."

Melody took a sharp intake of breath. They were meant to give her until the end of the summer to decide. That was still three weeks away. She needed those three weeks to determine how much money she could earn. As it stood, she was nowhere near having enough. That meant that her dreams would not be fulfilled after all.

"Oh and before you answer, they have also changed the payment date. They will need the money within two weeks of you accepting."

Melody's head was reeling. Two weeks.

That was not enough time. She barley had four grand and two weeks was not enough time to get the other six grand.

"Professor Kline, while I really…."

Before she could finish her sentence her professor cut her off.

"Melody before you say anything that I can't undo, I advise you to accept the placement."

"But what about the money?"

"Don't worry about that for now. Your official acceptance will not go in until Monday and from then you have two weeks to get as much as you can."

Melody thought about what her teacher was saying. She knew there was no possible way for her to get that much money in so little time, but she also knew that if she said no she would not be given another chance like this.

Juilliard was all she had dreamed about since she'd found her love of dance.

Looking around the staff kitchen Melody's mind raced. It raced with all the what if's and ideas of how she could get more money. It rushed with what she would be giving up if she declined and what she ultimately discovered was that she was not ready to give up on her dream.

"Okay, tell them I am officially in." Melody found herself saying into the phone.

Melody had never felt such a rush of excitement and dread all at once.

"Good choice Melody. All right I will go and get the paperwork ready for Monday. I will send you through all of the details for when and how to pay and I will give you a call in a few weeks to see how much money you have and what we need to do to make sure this happens. I look forward to seeing you soon Melody."

"Thanks Professor. Talk to you soon"

With that Melody disconnected her call, placed her phone on the table and just sat there staring at it for a few minutes.

What the hell was she going to do?

Where the hell was she going to get just under six grand from?

Question after question rushed through her mind as she tried to take in the extent of what she had just committed herself to. Melody tried to crunch some numbers in her head, but there were too many questions floating around in there for her to focus. Looking around the kitchen she noticed the note pad and pen sitting in the middle of the table, it had been left there from one of the other waitresses. Grabbing it

Melody started to crunch some numbers. She looked at how much she'd earned with her job here and at the diner and combined it with the average tips she got. She then tried to figure out how many more hours she would have to do to get the almost six thousand she needed. But no matter how much math Melody did, it all pointed to one thing. There was no way she was going to be able to get that amount in two weeks. Every way she worked it she was always a couple of grand off.

Her phone dinged and without thinking Melody picked it up to read the message. She assumed it was from her professor, how wrong she had been.

One, two I'm coming for you. You tried to run and you took my fun. One, two I'm coming for you. You think your smart, you tore out part of my heart. One, two I'm coming for you. You can't run, you can't hide, Melody mine soon I will be by your side. One, two I'm coming for you. One, two I'm coming for you.

As Melody let her eyes roam over the message twice more, she was filled with fear. This was no message from someone pulling a prank. This was someone who wanted her to fear him. She didn't for a minute believe that he was on his way here. Yet his words sent a shiver of fear racing through her.

"Watcha looking at so hard there?"

Melody screamed and her hand went to her heart

"Sorry Sweets, didn't mean to scare you." Honey laughed as she took Melody's lunch out of the microwave and placed her drink in there.

Melody gave a quick half hearted laugh as she looked around the room. She knew that her stalker wasn't there with them, yet his message left her feeling exposed. "No, I'm sorry I didn't hear you come in."

She quickly placed her phone in sleep mode before she stood up and got her lunch. Looking at her watch she noticed she only had fifteen minutes to eat before she had to be back out in the bar. They would have an hour to clean up after lunch and get the joint ready for the dinner crowed of truckers, young guns and anyone else who came for the nightly viewings. Grabbing a fork, she went back to the table and started eating as Honey joined her.

"Why are you here early?" Melody asked realising that Honey wasn't due to be on stage for several hours yet.

"I came to help out in the bar for the night." She answered.

"Oh." Melody replied. She vaguely remembered that some of the strippers came in early to earn a few extra dollars. Money. It was always about money. With that thought in mind, Melody's eyes returned to the piece of paper where she had written all of her calculations and ideas. It was hopeless, short of robbing someone, there was no way she was going to get the amount of cash she needed in the time she needed.

"So you on a double tonight?" Honey asked as she sat down at the table.

"Mmmm, oh yeah double, right." Melody answered.

"Girl what has you in a funk?" Honey asked reaching for the paper that Melody was focused on.

"Damn what's with all the math?"

Melody let her fork drop into her food. "It's nothing, other than my dreams disappearing right before my eyes." Melody wailed as she dropped her head into her hands.

"What's going on girl?" Honey asked all humour gone from her tone.

Melody looked up into her eyes and was not surprised to see concern lacing them. Over the past four weeks of she had become quite good friends with some of the girls. Melody spent the next five minutes explaining to Honey what was happening.

"Damn girl." Was all she said as she sat back in her chair.

"I know. I'm screwed."

"I wouldn't say that."

Melody leaned back in her own chair and gave her friend a calculating look. "Then what way would you say it?" she asked. Melody did not like the look that came over Honey's face. It was the same look Gabby used to give her before she roped her into one of her cockamamy plans.

"You're right, the plans you have written down will not gain you the money you need to save in time. However, you are missing one thing on your list. A sure-fire way of getting at least one third of that amount in one night."

Melody looked at her as though she was crazy. "I am not going to do anything illegal Honey, no matter how much I want this dream."

Honey laughed and grabbed the pen that was back in the middle of the table, she then scribbled something on the page and turned it back to Melody. Melody's eyes became as wide as saucers when she read what was on the page.

"You can't be serious?"

"Dead serious. It is legal and a guaranteed minimum two thousand dollars."

Melody looked back down at the page. This was something that could be done, the question was indeed how much she wanted Juilliard. Melody shook her head, there was one catch. "It will never work. There is no way I would ever be allowed to do it."

Honey smiled and tapped the side of her nose a few times. "You leave everything up to me. If you want to do it, we can come up with a plan. I already have an idea in mind."

Melody looked at her smiling friend. Her heart was racing with excitement. Just the thought of getting away with the plan sent thrills rushing through her. She looked down at the paper once more and quickly added the new amounts to her calculations. Honey was right, this was the only way. At least that was the excuse Melody told herself as she opened her mouth to speak.

"What's the plan?"

Honey's smile widened as she leaned forward.

"Well first we need to…."

Melody's mind wondered off as Honey laid out the plan. She knew she should have been paying better attention, but the thrill of what the night was about to bring was far more superior than any of the details. This was going to be a night she would remember for the rest of her life.

Yep she was in deep, deep trouble.

11

"So, you know what you have to do?" Honey asked Melody as they placed their dirty dishes in the sink. Melody washed her hands and then wiped them on the towel that was hanging from the cupboard door.

"I think so. I guess we will know when the times come." She jested weakly. Melody gave Honey a quick hug before she headed towards to the door. "Well I guess I had better get back out there and act normal" she laughed as she pushed her way through the door and started to walk down the hall.

"Hey Sweets, don't worry so much you will be great." Honey said grabbing her attention.

Melody looked back at her friends as she shot her a wink. She smiled at Honey before saying, "I hope you're right for both our sakes."

Honey laughed and continued further down the hall to the bathrooms. Melody shook her head, she wasn't lying if this blew up they were both in deep trouble. Pushing her worries out of her mind Melody made her way back into the main area and over to the bar. She had hoped to see Roman, but he wasn't anywhere to be found. Melody knew that she should be thankful for that and yet her heart felt a little emptier.

"About time you got back to work." Jax joked as he placed

a drink on the bar for the man in front of him. Melody shot him the middle finger as she picked up her note pad and pen.

"Here take these drinks to table four while you go can ya?" Jax asked as he set four drinks on tray on the bar.

Melody shot him a sassy smile. "Only if you say please *really* nicely."

Jax glared at her. "Please take these drinks with you and I may just pay you this week."

"Fine, but only because I need the money."

Melody loaded up the drinks and then turned to see where number four was. She noted that it was full of young men, probably from one of the local lumber yards. They were quite rugged looking. "Well, it won't be such a chore after all." She replied as she picked up the tray, sent Jax a wink and sashayed over to the table.

"Women, they will bring you nothing but trouble." The man at the bar announced to Jax.

"Don't I know it." He replied.

Melody smiled to herself, she loved getting his goat and she did it so well.

As she neared the table she wondered what Jax's reaction would be if he knew of her plan tonight. She could just picture him having a heart attack and locking her in her room for the rest of her life. That image brought a wider smile to her face. It was a dangerous feeling she was feeling, knowing she had this secret over everyone. A secret they were never going to know about. The men were all smiles and laughter when she dropped the drinks off and as was customary, she ended up with a few phone numbers being added to the napkins.

"Never fails." She boasted as she placed her tray down on the bar and lifted the napkins.

"Oooo, which table are these from?" Gabby asked as she commandeered the napkins from Melody's hands.

"Table four." They both turned and looked at the men again. A few of them were watching them. Gabby gave a wave to one at the same time Jax highjacked the napkins.

"This is a place of business not a brothel." He grouched. "Now get back to work."

"You're no fun." Gabby pouted.

"I am your cousin; I am not meant to be fun. I am meant to protect you." Jax replied. Not letting up.

Melody laughed at their antics and proceeded to do as Jax ordered. She had to remain busy to keep her mind off of what was coming. Looking at her watch she saw that she was already an hour closer to her fate. In just four hours Melody was going to finally find out what she was made of. She just hoped that what she was made of would get her the dreams she wanted.

Only time would tell.

* * *

"I'll have a rum and coke and my friend will have a beer."

Melody wrote down the table's order and as she did so she looked at her watch. Yep it was eight twenty-five, time to get the show on the road. She nodded her understanding to the two gentlemen and then headed back to the bar. She made sure to make herself look as pitiful as she could, every aspect of this plan had to be pin point accurate otherwise it would not work.

"You look like hell," Jax commented as she placed her order on the bar.

Bingo Baby

"Yeah I have a cracking headache. I'm sure I will be fine."

Add a few dramatic sighs for effect.

"Do you want to go home?"

Like candy from a baby.

Melody knew that Jax would offer that first. His concern for her was heart-warming, she knew he wouldn't question it as Gabby had had a similar thing last night.

"No, but I think I might go and lie down in the back for a bit. It is almost time for my break anyway. Is it okay if I take a little longer tonight? I will make it up at the end of the night."

Melody almost smiled at how quickly Jax gave in. He should have listened to the old man at the bar earlier. Women were trouble all right. She kind of felt bad that she was lying to him, but it was only a little white lie. She was going to make the time up so it wasn't like she wasn't earning her money and knowing what was coming she kind of did feel a little nauseas.

"Go ahead. I will make sure no-one disturbs you."

Just what she had been hoping for.

"Thanks, Jax you're the best."

Melody placed her notepad and pen in the pocket of her apron and left Jax to wiping down the bar and pouring drinks. Thankfully she made her way through the crowed and out the back to where she was meeting Honey without seeing Gabby. She was not sure she could lie to her best friend as easily as she had Jax. They shared everything and Gabby was the one person who could tell when she was lying. Melody held her breath until she had reached the door to the room where employees sometimes slept. Before she pushed her way through though, she took a deep breath and considered once more if this was the right move. She thought about her parents, her friends, her career, and then she thought about Juilliard. She thought about how much she wanted it. That was all the confidence she needed to push through the door taking away that last bit of hesitation. She could do this in her sleep.

"There you are, I was starting to think you had backed out." Honey cooed clamping her hands together. "I can't tell you how happy I am that you are here. You are going rock this. Now lock the door and sit down, it's time to get you ready."

Melody did exactly as Honey ordered and as each part of her costume was added to her body the thrill that Melody felt earlier returned.

This was really happening.

She was really going to do this.

"All done, you're ready. It's almost curtain time Swan Song." Honey announced.

Melody stood up and looked at herself in the mirror that was at the far end of the room. Occasionally on really busy nights the strippers used this room to get ready. The cot had been added later to be used for those times people needed a place to lay down. Melody couldn't get over what she was seeing, she didn't recognise herself. Gone was her blond hair and in its place was a fiery red wig with curls that reached her butt. Her face was concealed by a mask that covered everything but her eyes and lips, and the outfit that she wore left even her speechless. Melody felt deliciously sexy and knowing that she was being bad sent waves of electricity through her whole body. This was what it felt like to have adrenalin running through you. It was exhilarating.

"Okay time to go. I can't go with you as I have to stay here and pretend to be you if someone knocks. I know you will do great. You have seen my show enough times to know the routine, no-one will even know it is not me up there. Just remember you only need to take off the top half, the bottom stays on. Only if you want it to of course." She winked as she gave Melody her final instructions.

Melody's heart raced as Honey checked that the hall was free. When she gave her the all clear signal Melody quickly snuck out of the room and made her way to the edge of the stage. She could hear the men getting wound up as the announcer introduced her. She tried to listen to what he was saying but her mind kept on racing over what she had to do. "It is just like being on a normal stage." She whispered to herself. "You are simply playing a role."

"……give it up for Hoooooney." The announcer's loud voice was drowned out by the cheers and the music that started to play over the PA.

Melody took the stairs up to the stage and smiled as she made her way out onto it. The song that was playing was one of her favourites to dance to and she had seen Honey preform it a million times. In that moment Melody let all of her stress go and promised herself that she would enjoy the moment. Her body needed no reminding of what to do, as soon as she started feeling the music her body followed. It was a freeing feeling to be someone else for the night and as the money started being placed on the stage she knew that she had made the right decision. For one night Melody was going to be someone else, she was going to be the girl all men wanted. As she started to take off the first layer of clothes, her eyes shot to the bar to see if anyone had noticed the difference and as she did her eyes collided with the blue of the man she had loved for years. It was as though he was staring straight into her soul and although Melody should have been worried that he would figure her out, his attention only added to her boldness. In this moment she could allow everything she'd ever felt for him show.

As he continued to stare at her Melody's moves became more sensual, her clothes kept coming off and her eyes only saw him. In her mind she was dancing for him. It was the most erotic feeling Melody had ever felt. As the music continued she fell deeper into the hole and every fantasy that she had ever had about Roman seeped its way into the dance. She only hoped that at the end of the experience she would be able to dig herself out of said hole because this feeling was becoming an addiction.

An addiction she wasn't sure she wanted to give up.

It was a dangerous dance she was playing and one she was not sure she could give up.

12

Roman entered the bar and noticed immediately that Melody was not in the main area. He couldn't explain the need he had to find her in any room. All he knew is that when he knew she was close his eyes automatically sought her out. Glancing down at his watch Roman noted that it was nearing the time she normally took her break. He was surprised that it had only taken him a few days to learn her schedule, but considering he found himself watching her more times than he liked, perhaps it wasn't so surprising. Roman made his way through the throng of people waiting for the nightly entertainment to start and headed for the bar. He didn't sit down in his usual spot however, instead he walked around the edge of the bar and lifted the ledge that separated the area from behind the bar to the patrons on the other side. He poured himself a quick shot before he turned and started taking orders.

"About time you got here." Jax quipped throwing a cleaning towel at him.

Roman caught the towel with one hand and then used it to wipe up the spillage that was in front of him.

"I do have a life you know."

Jax laughed at that. "How are the folks?"

"They are good. They said to say hi and asked me to remind you that you are to come to dinner with me next time I go." Roman grabbed the order that had been placed on the bar and started making the drinks.

Jax stopped what he was doing and leaned back. "Did you get a chance to have a look at the paperwork Ren gave you?"

Roman thought back on his meeting from this morning. When Jax had rung him this morning asking him to come into the bar, the conversation that followed had not been expected. It turned out someone was stealing from the bar and Warren had requested Roman's help to try and figure out who the perp was. Roman didn't even have to think twice about accepting. It was great to be doing some real detective work again. Warren had piled him up with all of the company's ledgers leading back until the time the money started going missing. It didn't take Roman long to figure out where and therefore possibly how the money was going missing, but he wanted to check a few things out before he voiced his suspicions.

Roman looked over and saw Jax watching him expectantly. He laughed and shook his head. "Yes I did, and before you even ask, yes I have some ideas about what is going on but I need time to check somethings out. I will tell you and Ren at the same time once I have all my ducks in a row."

"Always the detective." Jax grumbled.

"It is called gathering evidence, it's how we catch the bad guys," Roman shot back.

Jax threw him the middle finger and then turned to serve another drink. Roman grabbed the next order that was placed on the bar and started to fill it.

"Where's Dee?" Gabby asked as she came up to the bar and put her order in.

Roman shrugged his shoulders, he had been looking for her himself but he didn't want anyone else to know.

Gabby whistled grabbing Jax's attention. "Dee?" she asked in the form of a question when Jax looked her way.

Jax placed the drink he was holding on the bar in front of a customer and walked over to where Gabby was standing. The music was starting to get louder which meant that any minute now the nightly festivities would start.

"She took her break early. She had a headache, so I told her to rest. I promised no-one would disturb her." Jax answered, warning Gabby to leave her be. Roman made sure to keep his façade neutral, although he was worried about her he couldn't let it show.

"Did she say anything to you this morning?" Gabby asked.

Roman shook his head. He had gone before she rose, but he did know she didn't get much sleep last night.

"Maybe I should check on her?" Gabby contemplated as she looked at the back door.

"Gabs just leave her be. It is her break time anyway; I promise I will go and check up on her if she does not come back after her break. Until then let her rest."

Gabby looked at Jax, then at the door once more. Roman could see the indecision play out on her face. The extra people coming through the door though helped her make that decision.

"Fine, but if you don't go then I will, do you hear me?"

"Loud and clear."

With that Gabby went to serve the new customers that were being seated. Roman couldn't blame her for her concern, he wanted nothing more than to go back and check on Melody himself, but he couldn't. Roman didn't like how protective he was becoming of her. Since the moment he saw Melody that first night his feelings for her were leaning into the realm of not friends and that he could not allow. He had known Melody practically her whole life, and he would not do anything to risk that friendship.

It was going to be hard though.

With events like last night clear in his mind, mixed with the woman he saw dancing like she had this morning, his libido was becoming harder to settle. He had seen many women dancing throughout his life, but none of them had the impact on him that Melody did this morning.

When Jax had opened the door to the bar, they had been just in time to see Melody use the pole as her own personal weapon, her body moved in a way that he could picture her doing while she was straddling him, and as she came down into the splits giving him a view of her supple breast he had felt himself harden. He was grateful that he was wearing his jeans. Melody of course didn't know he was there and the way she was acting with Jax gave him an idea of the kind of person she would be in bed. She was playful and erotic all at once.

It was the sexiest thing Roman had ever seen.

Roman could feel himself hardening once again and he knew he needed to get his mind of the minx and quick. Remembering why he was here also reminded him of something else.

"Hey, did you ever get a hold of your buddies up in Denver?" He asked as Jax poured a drink beside him.

"Oh yeah I did. One of my buddies who owns a strip club next to the university said he heard a few guys talking about the incident on campus the other day. Seems like you're famous." He laughed.

Roman threw his cloth at him. "I meant about the case?"

"Na, nothing yet. But they did say they would keep their ears close to the ground and if anything came up they would give me a call."

"Barkeep." A man yelled from the end of the bar.

Jax left Roman as he went to serve the customer. It was not a lot but at least it was something. People talked in bars all the time; they often thought no body was listening. Little did they know bartenders took in everything of interest. All Roman needed was one little piece of evidence that could help them break the case. One little clue to lead them to Neil.

"……Honnnnney."

The sound of the announcer's voice introducing the first talent of the night broke through Roman's inner thoughts. Most of the men at the bar turned to face the stage and Jax came to stand by his side once more. They both leaned against the back of the bar to watch. It was not like they were interested in the show, once you had spent many a night here, the show became like any other. No they were more interested in making sure the men in the room behaved. They both had a two-way on their hips ready to call the bouncers if anyone got grabby.

The music increased in volume and the curtains to the back of the stage opened, revealing the luscious body of Honey. Roman had watched her dance last night and he had to admit she was good, but as he thought about Honey, another dancer's face entered his mind and while he watched Honey dance and sway to the music, it was Melody's body he was seeing. It was why he was so entranced in her movements.

His eyes fell to her hips as they swayed to the music and then they slowly made their way to her supple breasts. Her body was currently using the pole to keep her balance as she slid down and opened her legs to the men in the front row, her red flaming hair touched the stage, before she slowly snaked her body back up the pole. He was not sure if it was the memories of Melody doing that exact thing this morning, or the lust she'd crated in him that had him hardening once more. For some reason tonight Roman couldn't take his eyes off the stripper on stage. Without realising it he leaned forward on the bar and continued to stare, it was in that moment that his eyes connected with the stripper's and electricity surged through him.

She was staring straight at him. Her eyes burned into his as though she knew something he didn't.

He couldn't tear his eyes away and as he continued to stare so did she.

Her movements became more sensual and when her top finally came off and her supple milky white breast spilled out Roman sucked in his breath. Thankfully Jax had moved away from him to serve a new customer, he didn't know how he was going to explain his sudden interest in Jax's stripper. Roman himself could not explain it. He was not sure what was different about Honey tonight, but different she was. Before long the dancer was down to her final piece of clothing, he could see her hesitate as she put her fingers in the side of her G-string trying to decide what she would do. Roman held his breath, while he wanted to see what was underneath, he wanted her to keep them on. He felt a connection to this woman he couldn't understand.

It wasn't until she did her next move that it hit him.

Some detective he was.

Roman stood up straight. Lust no longer filled him, instead his body filled with rage.

Surely he was wrong.

Roman raked his brain to try and come up with reasons as to why what he was thinking was ludicrous, but when she mounted the pole upside down and slid slowly down it, turning as she went, the heart shaped birthmark slapped him in the face.

"Fuck!" He exclaimed under his breath.

Roman wanted to jump on the stage and rip Melody off, but that would give away her identity. He could not let that happen under any circumstances. He also knew that he could not let her get away with this either. He needed her to know how stupid this plan of hers had been. Looking back at the stage he was once again greeted with her porcelain white skin glistening with glitter. Her breasts were perfect and while he wanted to take them into his mouth, he also wanted to rip out the eyes of every man here who had seen them.

He couldn't stand here and watch this anymore, his restraint was hanging on by a thread.

"Something caught your attention there stud." One of the waitresses asked as she placed her order on the bar.

Roman tore his eyes from Melody and faced the girl. "Not really, just marvelling at how flexible the girls are." Roman turned away and started to pour the drinks the waitress was waiting on. He needed to get out of here, but he also wanted to have a word with Melody. He needed a fool proof plan that would not blow her cover. Then the waitress' comment gave him an idea. Looking around the bar he tried to figure out what to do, when he saw the hallway leading out to the rooms that could be hired for personal parties. Turning to Jax he set his plan in motion.

"Hey, I have an idea on how I am going to get the information I need."

"How?" Jax asked giving Roman his full attention.

Roman nodded towards the dancer on the stage, he chose not to look back at her as he didn't know how much more he could take of seeing her up there like that.

What in the hell had she been thinking?

Jax's eyes widened. "What? How?" Jax couldn't seem to put two thoughts together.

"Think about it. Who would know the ins and outs of this place? Who would most people feel comfortable talking around without worry that they are going to get caught?"

Realisation dawned on Jax and Roman laughed as his lips formed an O. "But won't the guilty party become suspicious when you start asking those kinds of questions. What if it is one of the strippers, what will you do then?"

Roman leaned against the bar and faced Jax fully. He crossed his arms over his chest and got ready to lay out his plan. He would of course eventually talk to the strippers as he was suggesting, but for now the reasoning behind his next suggestion had little to do with finding the thief and more to do with the minx on stage.

"First off, I have already told you I am pretty sure I know who it is, so no, questioning the strippers will not expose one of them. Secondly as for keeping suspicions down, what if I pretend to hire out one of the rooms for a private show? That way I can question them freely and they will feel comfortable answering me as there will be no-one there to point fingers at the information I gain."

Jax turned to look at the rooms. They were currently empty as most men waited until the first few shows were finished before they went back there. "That could work." He stated. "Who do you plan on questioning first?" he asked as an afterthought when he went back to wiping down the bar.

"How about her?" Roman had to keep the edge out of his voice as they both turned back to the stage where Honey aka Melody was once again on the pole. Roman had to admit she had skills. None of the men in the front row had been able to take their eyes off of her and with the amount of money that was piling up on the stage it was obvious that she was the star.

Jax looked at him then raised one eyebrow, "you sure this isn't your way of getting some private time with her?"

Roman shook his head. "If I had wanted that I would have asked for it last night."

"True." Jax looked at Honey one more time before he nodded.

Roman let out the breath he had been holding. He knew he didn't have much time as the set was almost over.

"Okay head back to room number six, it is the furthest

from the bar it will afford you the most privacy. I will have one of the bouncers grab her as she comes off stage and bring her to you."

Roman nodded before he lifted the divider and headed towards the hall. Thank God that worked. Roman was not sure what he would have done if it hadn't. Roman was just entering the hall when he ran into the waitress from before. She looked at him and then down the hall and laughed. "Well I guess you couldn't resist after all."

Roman hated the idea of everyone thinking that he ventured into private shows with strippers, but it was important for the ruse he was upholding to agree.

"Well you know what they say, why resist what you want."

Roman turned from the girl so that he did not have to explain any further. Before long he had made it to room six. Opening the door Roman took in the room trying to figure out where the best place would be for him to make his move. The room was full of mirrors and along the far wall sat a leather couch that wound around the room, it was perfect for a party of one or seven. In the middle of the room was a single round stage with a pole that reached to the roof. On one wall that was just off the side of the door was a bench with food and champagne. Normally the men who paid for these rooms paid well, so it was not unusual to see a smorgasbord of food.

Roman was not here for fun; he was here for business. With that in mind he walked over the lounge and sat in a position that placed him right in front of the pole and the door.

He made sure that he would be the first thing Melody saw when she entered.

He couldn't wait to see how she got out of this. A small smile spread across Roman's face, perhaps he would have a little fun with her before he gave her secret away.

Stretching back Roman placed his arms across the back of lounge, spread his legs wide and waited.

He waited like a lion waited for its pray.

Pray that he couldn't wait to taste.

13

The blood was still pumping through Melody's veins as she made her way off the stage. She didn't have to worry about the money as Warren was there collecting it. It was one of the measures he took to make sure that the girls were never felt up by the gentlemen who entered the bar, as well as making sure none of their hard-earned cash was taken by someone else. Melody had seen this process a million times. Once Warren had collected the money, he would place it in an envelope with the strippers name on it and place it in his office until they collected it. Honey would of course collect hers; she would then pass it on to Melody. When Honey had explained the plan to Melody, she had offered to give Honey some of the tips. Honey just laughed.

"Sweets I will make it up tomorrow night, don't even fuss about it."

Now that the dance was finished Melody was starting to feel a bit cold. She was still only in her G-string. She couldn't believe that she had almost taken it off, it had been all Roman's fault. The intensity with which he had been watching her had made her bold. It had also made her a little crazy. Jealousy had reared its ugly head and Melody could only wish that he would look at her with that same intensity.

She knew it was a ridiculous thought, how could she be jealous of herself. But she knew deep down that he would never look at her they way he had looked at 'Honey' tonight, and that was what made it hurt so much.

As she got to the bottom of the stairs there was a bouncer waiting for her with her robe. It was not unusual, Honey warned her that this would happen. It was precaution that was taken in order to keep the strippers safe. He would walk Melody back to Honey's dressing room and from there Honey would help her change back into her work clothes and no-one would be the wiser.

Melody smiled to herself. She couldn't believe their plan had worked.

Apart from the extra attention Roman had paid her, no-one else had even battered an eyelid in her direction. Not that there would have been any reason too. As far as anyone knew it had been Honey up there dancing. Melody reached the bouncer and took the robe, she nodded her head as a way of thanks. She wasn't sure if the bouncer knew what Honey sounded like, so she decided to keep talking at a minimum. Once Melody had her robe on she started to follow the bouncer down the hall, only five more feet until she was safely in Honey's room. Only five more feet and she could breathe easy knowing that she would have some extra money to add to her pile. She couldn't wait to see how much she'd made. Melody had only committed herself to doing this one time. She was wanting to wait to see how it went before she decided if she would do it again. Although, if she had to make that decision right now, she would defiantly do it again. The rush of having a dirty secret that only she knew awakened the bad girl that lurked down deep in her soul.

The bad girl that lived inside of us all.

Melody frowned as the bouncer continued to walk past Honey's door. She wasn't really sure what happened next as she had never seen this part of it. Honey had told her that he would walk her to her door, but beyond that there was no more instruction. Melody assumed that he had something else to do so she paused and opened the door. The bouncer stopped and spoke just as she was stepping in. She could see Honey pressing against the far wall trying to stay out of the line of vision of anyone walking past.

"Honey, you will need to follow me." The bouncer spoke up.

Melody looked at Honey for an answer, she simply shrugged and shook her head.

Great not even she knew what was going on.

I'm busted.

Melody's heart rate picked up as that thought crossed her mind. What other reason would the bouncer have for not letting her go into her room?

"Could I freshen up before we go any further Hun." Melody asked, hoping that he didn't catch the slight shiver in her voice. She tried to make herself sound as close to Honey as she could. The bouncer didn't seem to notice the change he simply shook his head and answered. "I am afraid not; your presence was requested in one of the private rooms. The boss made it clear that I was to take you there right after the show."

Crap. She was dead.

She looked at Honey and mouthed the word, 'help' but there was nothing she could do. She looked as guilty as Melody felt. If it was Warren waiting for her there, both her and Honey would be in trouble. Honey would lose her job for sure. On the other hand if it was another paying customer, well that brought a whole new set of troubles coming her way. Honey hadn't informed her of what to do in that situation as neither of them even considered it coming up. Honey snuck her way over to behind the door where she could whisper to Melody. "Don't worry, just keep playing your role. They are not allowed to touch you and the bouncer will be right outside the door so you can scream for help at any time."

While that made Melody feel a little better, it still did not move the large pit that was sinking to the bottom of her stomach. This was bad, but there was nothing she could do. Straightening her shoulders, she closed the door and continued to follow the bouncer down the hall past the offices and over to the other side of the bar where the illustrious private rooms stood. Gabby had filled Melody in on what they were for, but she had never been allowed in them. Jax had informed her and Gabby on their first days that the rooms were off limits. They had special cleaners come in and tidy up so that none of the waitresses had to step a foot inside.

Melody would have to remember every detail about the rooms so she could one day fill Gabby in on them. She would not tell Gabby about this escapade until well after the fact, but she knew one day she would and Gabby being Gabby would want to know every salacious detail. The music was quieter down this end of the bar and as the bouncer drew closer to one of the rooms Melody could hear her own heart beat in her ears.

She hoped that this would not take long and that the person inside only wanted to see her dance. Some of the strippers were known to give lap dances of their own accord for more money, but it was never expected.

"There you go; remember I will be right here if you need me." The bouncer announced as he opened the door.

Melody took a deep breath, pulled her robe closed a bit more and made sure the persona of Honey was back in place before she entered the room. Thankfully she was still wearing her mask, it was the only part of her costume other than her

G-string and wig that still had on. Melody's heart rate picked up a beat when she heard the click of the door shut behind her, her eyes closed of their own accord and she simply stood there for a moment waiting to hear anything that would alert her to how many men were in the room.

When she didn't hear anything, she assumed that they were waiting for the show to start. They had paid money to see her dance, she guessed talking was not on the agenda. Opening her eyes she focused all of her attention on the platform and pole that was sitting in the centre of the room. She could do this; it was no different to dancing on stage, it was just less people. She would think of it like an audition.

With that thought in mind she walked over to the stage before she opened her robe and began sliding it down her arms. As the robe was just about to completely drop off to reveal her breasts someone cleared their throat on the lounge in front of her.

"There is no need for that." His gruff voice followed.

Melody's eyes flew to the gentleman on the seat of her own accord, she knew that voice. She heard it every night in her dreams.

Oh God. This was it. She was in deep shit now.

Melody slowly pulled the robe up over her shoulders as she watched Roman squirm in his seat. She knew she should be in full panic mode right now, and she was, but she was also filled with jealousy like nothing she had ever felt. Roman had paid to see Honey in a private show. She wondered how many times he had done this before and from there more questions and images filled her mind until she found herself wanting to rant at him.

She knew it was ridiculous. He was not hers and he was free to do as he pleased, but that didn't stop the hurt that was filling her soul. What would it take for him to look at her the way he was looking at the supposed Honey?

While these thoughts were rushing through her mind Melody stood there waiting to find out what Roman wanted from her. If he did not want Honey to strip, then why had he paid to have her brought her.

"You can hop down from there if you like." He offered as he stood and went to get a drink. Melody watched as he filled a glass with champagne and downed it in one gulp. He then poured himself another before turning around and leaning against the table. Melody had yet to move so he must have understood her confusion.

"I didn't bring you here for a show I brought you here to ask you some questions if you don't mind?"

Melody's mind was racing. What questions would Roman need to ask Honey? She wasn't sure that her voice would hold up so she simply nodded her head. Now that she knew the real reason she was here she was able to get off the stage. As she did her robe slipped open a little once again showing her inner thigh and part of her breast.

Melody heard Roman's groan right before he downed another drink. A small part of her felt pleasure at knowing she held this power over him, even if he didn't know it was her. Once on the floor she made sure her robe was secure and took the drink he offered her. He had refilled his own and poured her one as well. Once he took sip and was happy that everything was in place he asked his question.

"I was wondering if you could tell me if you have heard of anyone bragging about any extra money they might have come into. Or if any of the employees have started buying up big?"

Confusion set in once more. This was not where she had been expecting this conversation to go, but that was a good thing. She could answer these questions quickly and without speaking. She would be back on her way to Honey's room lickety-split and everything would go back to normal. With that in mind Melody took a sip of her drink and acted as though she was pondering the thought. After a short amount of time she moved the glass away from her lips and shook her head no. Roman almost looked disappointed. Was it because their time here was being cut short? Or was it because he didn't get the information he wanted? Either way she knew that it was best that she got out of here asap. She would have to remember to ask Honey the same questions and fill her in on what happened so that if faced with the situation again she could lie her way through it.

"Well that's a shame. I guess I am back to square one. I will have to check with the other girls. If you do hear of anything, please let me know. We need to find out who is stealing from the bar."

"Someone is stealing from Ren?" Melody asked in shock.

She couldn't believe that someone would be that low, as well as stupid. While Gabby's cousins were law abiding citizens and had a heart of gold, they didn't take too kindly to people ripping them off. They had a unique way of ruining people's lives without even getting their hands dirty. Melody looked at Roman and saw his eyes had widened slightly, it was then she realised her slip up. Her only hope now was that he would pass it off as something else. Surely others in the bar called Warren by his nickname. Melody held her breath for a few heartbeats as she waited to see what Roman would do. The relief she felt when he finally took a drink and said, "well thank you for your time *Honey*, please let me know if you hear of anything. If you wouldn't mind can you keep this to yourself, we don't want to let the perp know we are on to them," was overwhelming.

She didn't like the way he said her name, but this time Melody was smart enough to keep her mouth shut and simply nodded. He mimicked the nod letting her know they were done, she quickly made her way to the door. Freedom stood a few feet away, she could almost smell it. Melody laid her hand on the knob of the door and pulled, but when it didn't budge she tried it again. It was only then she felt the presence behind her. Looking up she saw that Roman was holding the door closed with his arm, he was standing just behind her.

Her heart picked up in speed and her blood turned to fire when he leaned down so that his lips were close to her ear. He used his other hand to move her hair away from her ear and as it brushed against her skin it became electrified. She closed her eyes and held in a groan as lust filled her to the core. She could feel the G-string she was wearing soak through as the lust reached her centre. God how she wanted this man. Her lust went into overdrive as he placed his lips near her ear and she could feel his breath on her neck. The lust soon died and his words were like ice cold water being splashed over her body.

"Did you really think you could get away with it?" He whispered low.

Melody took a moment to gather her wits. She was starting to panic. Surely he didn't know, there was no way he could, if he had there was no way he would have ever let her finish her dance. Then it hit her. He thought Honey was the one stealing the money. Melody did not like where this was going. She knew Roman would keep her here until he got the answers he needed, she would have to play dumb and scared so that he would let her go.

"I......don't know what you mean." She stammered out, her voice catching at the end.

"Don't play coy with me, you are no good at it. You know exactly what I am talking about." He whispered once more leaning closer, causing her panic to mix with lust once more.

Damn she wished her body would pick one emotion and stick with it. It was taking all Melody had not to lean back into Roman's strong arms and suck in his warmth. But that would not be what Honey would do. Or was it?

Women were known for using their wiles to get what they wanted. Testing her theory Melody slowly pushed her arse back until it was leaning against him. She noticed that he was hard and again she felt the rush of excitement knowing she had this power over him.

"I really don't," she replied again, only this time she moved slightly so that her rear end rubbed his cock.

She heard his sharp intake of breath and a groan right before he grabbed her waist to stop her moving. He then growled in her ear the words that made her blood run ice cold.

"Damn it Melody this is not a game. Do you have any idea how much trouble you are in?"

Melody spun in his arms until her back was pressed against the door. She looked up into his lust filled eyes.

He knew.

"How?" Was all she could get out.

Roman stepped away from her and ran his hands through his hair.

"Come on give me a bit more credit than that. I am a detective you know."

Melody swallowed hard and rung her hands in front of her.

"When did you figure it out?" He was once more sitting on the chair with his head in his hands. She knew she should be worried about him telling the others about it, instead she was more worried that this would change his opinion of her.

"I kind of knew from the moment you locked eyes with me that something wasn't right, but it wasn't until I saw you do the splits that the inkling hit me of who was up on the stage. I of course didn't know for certain until I saw your birthmark."

"Birthmark?" Melody asked in confusion. Roman laughed

and leaned back on the couch.

"Oh this is precious. Yes your birthmark it is right there on your arse cheek. I saw it last night when you were bending over the kitchen sink and that is what lead me to believe it was you. Then of course your little slip up with Ren's name sealed your fate."

Melody looked down at her locked hands. She didn't know what she had been thinking. How could she ever think she could fool this man. She had thought it had been too simple.

"Does anyone else…." Before she could finish her sentence, he was shaking his head.

"Are you going…."

"That depends." He cut her off once more.

Melody was just about to ask him what he meant when there was a rap at the door.

"Rome we need you back out at the bar." Jax yelled.

Roman stood up when the knock sounded. Before she could stop herself, Melody found her hands gripping Roman's shirt. This of course meant that her robe was open showing her stomach and the front of her G-string as it hung from her breast. She however did not notice it as she was too worried about gaining Roman's promise.

"Please don't tell him." She pleaded.

Roman looked down at her body and groaned right before he pulled her in and kissed her. When he pulled away, he called back.

"I am almost done here."

"Right." Jax answered. They listened as his footsteps fell back from the door.

"I will not say anything, *yet*. I have to get back, but this conversation is not over, we will finish it tonight at home."

"Tonight?" she asked confused.

"Yes, I will be staying at your house again. Jax's couch is uncomfortable and I am sure you would rather have this conversation in private."

Melody nodded her head. While she was happy that Roman would be staying at her house again, she was not sure she would be happy with the lecture that would come with that.

"Right, go and get back into your normal work clothes and get back to work before Gabby comes looking for you."

Melody nodded and started to walk out of the room. She was stopped mid stride when his next words met her ears.

"Mello, don't think of leaving without me. I will be watching you for the rest of the night."

Melody didn't say a word, she simply opened the door and started back down the hall, her bouncer in tow.

She knew he had meant his words as a warning, but what he didn't know was that they had the opposite affect on her. Knowing that he would be watching her all night sent the lust that had died off shooting right back to all the right places. Touching her hands to her lips she remembered his there. She knew he probably did it to shut her up, but nonetheless it had felt magnificent. Melody had waited a lifetime to feel his lips on hers and knowing that he had been lusting after her, not Honey sent the bad girl in her reeling once more.

It was a dangerous feeling he had awoken in her, and she wasn't sure she was ready to bury it once more. Perhaps she could use the bad girl within to her advantage tonight. As Melody made her way back to Honey's room she ran through every scenario that could play out tonight, and with each one her inner bad girl screamed with glee.

It was then she realised it was a dangerous and slippery slope she was heading down but she wasn't quite sure she wanted to stop it.

Only time would tell how far she would be willing to go.

14

Moving into the bar he looked around in search of the perfect seat. He needed one that would allow him to blend into the background and go unnoticed, while still being able to see what was going on. His eyes scanned the dark interior and it only took moments before his eyes found the table he wanted. It was off in the corner yet faced the entire room. He had a great view of the stage as well as the bar area.

The strip show that had been on when he'd entered the bar was just coming to an end. His eyes stayed on the dancer for a brief moment, while she was tempting, he was not here for that. Normally the woman on the stage would be the type that he would add to his plan, she had all the right parts and the way she danced was magnificent.

But tonight, he only had one prey in mind.

This time Melody would not get away.

He stood leaning against the wall, waiting for the right moment to nab his spot. There were still people at the table but he could see them paying their bill. Putting his hands in his pockets he pulled his hat down lower over his eyes and causally walked through the throng of people. By the time he reached the table the other members had left. Their empty glasses were still sitting on the table and the remnants of the drinks that had missed their mouths covered both the table and the floor.

"Pigs," he muttered to himself as he pulled out the chair closest to the wall and sat down. Now it was time for him to find his prey. This was the exciting part. While the staking from a distance was fun, it could not beat the rush of adrenaline he got knowing that he was only a few feet from his intended victim. Watching their eyes and body full of life turned him on, especially since he knew that he would soon snuff that life out like a candle in the night.

Just thinking about the pleasure, he would gain from having Melody trapped in his own little tale had him reaching under the table to shift his manhood. He was as hard as a stone and his jeans did not give any lei way when it came to a hard-on.

He had to get his mind on something else. Just then a waitress came over to take the empty glasses and wipe down the table. He hoped that she would leave him be, but as luck would have it, she didn't. Even with his hat on people could tell that he was a good-looking man. Especially when he wasn't trying to hide the fact. Most of the time during his normal day he spent his time not trying to hide who he really was. It allowed him the ability to go around without anyone giving him any trouble. But days like today, when he was being his true self those good looks became tiresome. They also allowed him to be recognisable, something he did not want to do. He watched as the waitress placed the tray she had been holding on the table and pulled out her note pad and pen.

Her name tag read *Gabby*, and like the dancer on stage she was rather desirable. Perhaps after he finished with Melody it might benefit the plan to move to the outer reaches of Denver, like perhaps Pagosa Springs. There was no shortage of females here that would fit right in with the plan.

He would have to give it some thought, but right now he just wanted to be left alone so he could watch Melody. He would watch her for a bit and then when the night was done, he would send her another text. This one would let her know that he was here. He just needed the right ammo to add to the message. He wasn't hungry or thirsty, but he'd learnt over the years that in order for him to stay under the radar he needed to blend in, and one did not come to a bar without at least drinking.

Picking up the sticky menu from the table he browsed it quickly. "Rum & coke and some Nachos please." He ordered. His tone had been a bit harsh but at least it got the waitress to leave. He was sure he heard her mumble

Jackass to herself under her breath, but it didn't bother him in the least.

Leaning back in his chair he spread his legs out, crossed them at the ankle and then relaxed to watch the nightly going ons. It didn't take long for his order to reach his table, thankfully after that everyone left him alone.

He slowly ate his nachos and drank his drink as he waited. Twenty-minutes had passed and still no Melody.

Shit did I get the night wrong.

He was down to his last few Nacho's and was trying to decide what he would do when another wrench was thrown into his plans. *What the bloody hell was Detective Fox doing here?* For a brief moment he considered that the detective was on to him and had followed him from Denver, but as he watched the detective go behind the bar and talk to the gentlemen there he knew differently. The way they were in deep discussion and the way in which the waitress joked with them told him that the detective was here for personal reason.

It was just a coincidence. Nothing to worry about.

Maybe it was time for him to go. The last thing he needed was for the detective to see him, Detective Fox would recognise him instantly. He hung his head a little further and leaned both of his arms onto the table, if anyone looked over here all they would see would be a loner, hanging out in a bar. Picking up the last Nacho he placed it in his mouth and then decided to go. Standing up he scanned the room once more to see if Melody had reappeared and as if on cue, she opened the door on the far side of the wall and walked through.

She was here.

He watched her fix her apron, he sat back down and took in all of her beauty.

It had felt like ages since he'd laid eyes on her. While she was gorgeous at school, it was nothing compared to how she looked in the skimpy outfit that the waitresses wore here.

He had to admit it fit her so much better than it had Gabby. As though his thoughts conjured her up Gabby was once again standing at his table.

"Can I top you up?" She asked a little less perky than she had earlier.

He did not want another drink, but he knew that if he didn't he would have to give up his table. Choice made he picked up his glass and handed it to her.

"Same." He simply put.

Gabby grabbed his glass and stormed off. As she passed Melody, she whispered something into her ear which had her glancing his way. As her eyes landed on him he lowered his head a little more so he could watch her from under the brim of his hat. Although her eyes were only on him briefly it was enough to set his blood on fire.

He knew he had to stop staring at her otherwise it would draw unwanted attention, so he turned and watched the stage, making sure to keep Melody in his peripheral vision at all times.

It was time to lure her in.

* * *

* * *

As the hours ticked by he learnt all he needed to know and all he could say was that his excitement only grew as the night went on. Over the course of the night he had come to learn that not only did the detective know the owners of the bar, he was also quite friendly with Melody and while this might have pissed others off, it had the opposite reaction for him. He saw it as an opportunity not only get the woman he wanted, but also as a way to pay the detective back for his interference.

He should have listened to his supervisor and just left things alone, now he was going to pay and in knowing Melody the detective had unknowingly added to the misery he was going to cause her. Looking down at his watch he noticed the time, while he wanted to stay and put his plan into motion it was clear that Melody was not going anywhere anytime soon and he knew that if he wanted to keep a low profile the last thing he needed was to get done with a DUI.

Emptying his glass, he placed it back on the table and took one last look at Melody as she passed through the same door she had entered earlier. Yep it was time to go. He left some extra money on the table as a tip for the waitress, he had fixed up his bill on the last order and made his way out of the bar. There were less people in here now as the last of the strip shows had finished a little over half an hour ago, so he was able to get out quickly.

Once outside he took in a deep breath of the fresh air, put his hands in his pockets, turned left and started to make his way down to his pick-up truck that he had hired. He had his own car of course, but it would not have been wise to bring it down here. He needed to make sure there was no trace of him after dealing with Melody. He had just put his key in the door, when raised voices exiting the bar drew his attention.

"Don't argue with me Melody."

"I am not arguing with you, but you don't have to drive with me. If you drive your own car it will make it easier for you when you leave in the morning."

"Or easier for you to lock me out."

He heard her give a short laugh before she answered the detective. He could not see what they were doing as he did not want to give away that he was eaves dropping, instead he pretended that he was simply getting into his car.

"Why would I want to do that Rome?"

He heard the detective growl at the humour in her voice. He had been right earlier; the detective did know Melody. He could not stand here much longer without drawing suspicion, thankfully the detective finally agreed with Melody and they made their way off to their own cars.

Opening his door, he got in, turned his truck on and headed out of the car park.

It was time for him to go back to his hotel and put his plan into motion.

In a week's time he would take her.

In a week's time Melody would learn how much she meant to him.

Next Saturday was going to be the night that Melody's life was extinguished for ever.

"I hope you are ready my love? I am here and I am coming for you."

An evil laugh filled the cab of the truck as he sped away to get things ready.

15

Roman watched the tail lights in front of him as they sped down the highway towards Pagosa Springs.

What was he going to do with her?

When he had let her know that he was on to her secret Roman had expected Melody to at least be a little worried, but it had been the opposite. For the rest of the night she acted as though nothing had happened. She continued mucking around with Gabby and even flirted and got the phone numbers of some of the guys. To make matter worse for every glare he sent her way, she backed it up with a sassy smile. Roman continued to seethe well up until they pulled into the driveway of her parent's diner. They both pulled around to the back of the house where they could enter her garage apartment. Roman parked beside her and expected that she would wait for him, but she simply got out of her car and made her way up the stairs.

He could tell by the way she was stomping on the stairs that she was as angry as he was.

Good! It was about time she realised the trouble she was in.

Roman got out, locked his car and slowly made his way up behind her. He was just in time to walk through the door and see her throw her keys on the bench. Then she spun on him. "Who the hell do you think you are telling me what to do?" She practically spat.

Roman was a little taken back. He had expected her to be mad but not about that. She was not sorry about what she'd done, no she was mad that he had the audacity to watch out for her. That only got his own temper riled up. If she was not going to take her safety seriously it was about time that he showed her just what could have happened to her tonight. Taking a menacing step forward he was pleased to see that she finally realised he was also angry. Removing his jacket he placed it on the back of the chair he passed as he continued to hunt her down. She moved back other step and only stopped when the wall blocked her exit. She looked to the side to see if she could make it to the kitchen. Deciding to make a move she side-stepped but only made it to the end of the bench before he stopped her. Placing his hands on the bench either side of her he effectively stopped her from moving. Now it was his turn to make her see reason.

"I am the person who is worried about your safety. It is clear you aren't," he bit off.

Melody tried to shove him away, but he wasn't budging.

"Would you stop being over dramatic Rome. I was not in any danger."

His eyes widened. How was it that she couldn't see what he saw? "Not in any danger, are you kidding me? What would you have done if it had been someone else in that room tonight?" He asked.

He could see that she knew he was right, but Melody being Melody she was not ready to give him the satisfaction of knowing that. "I would have been fine; the bouncer was just outside. I knew what I was doing Rome. Besides I needed the money and I got it."

"You needed money." He spluttered. "That is the excuse

you are going to use for putting yourself in danger."

"I told you I was not in danger; the bouncer would have…"

"Saved you, yes I heard you the first time. You, however, are under the illusion that he would have been able to hear you Melody."

She tired once more to move him, but he had news for her. Roman was about to teach her a lesson that she would never forget. Being a detective he knew things that would curl her toes and she needed to know that no matter the contingencies that were put in place things could still go wrong. She finally gave up trying to move him and crossed her arms over her chest. Looking down he noticed that her breasts looked as though they were inviting him to taste them. His mind wandered back to her on stage with her breasts free for all to see. The anger he had been feeling bloomed into full blown rage. He didn't know what he would have done should someone hurt her.

"For God sake Rome, of course he would have heard me. If someone tired anything I would have screamed my head off."

"What if they had spiked your drink?" He asked reasonably, gaining her attention as he took off his belt.

It was time for Melody to learn just want men were capable of. As she pondered what he said Roman grabbed both of her wrists with his free hand and raised them above her head.

"What are you doing?" She asked in shock.

She tried to rip her hands free but his strength was too much for her.

Before she could even consider what he was doing he'd taken his belt, rapped it around her arms and then secured her tightly to the metal pillars that connected the bench to the above cabinets.

Melody looked up at her hands and then brought her

surprised eyes back to his. He had placed his hands back on either side of her on the bench.

"Wh..a…tt? she tried to get out of the restraints as she looked back up at her wrists. Roman watched as she once more tried to wriggle her way out of the makeshift restraints.

"Don't worry it is just my way of making sure you can't leave. I want you to take notice of what I am going to tell you."

Melody's eyes shot back to his. "Was the belt necessary? You could have just asked me to stay put."

Roman leaned back against the wall and admired the view. "You're right, I could have, but we both know that you have a tendency to storm off. As for the belt, it was the best I could do since I didn't have my handcuffs."

Melody shot him a glare for that remark. "Fine, would you hurry up and make your point so I can go to bed."

She turned her head and looked out over the lounge room. He knew she hated being disabled but he needed her to be in order to show her just how much danger she'd put herself into tonight. He would start off with the basics, Roman was determined that he was not going to let her go until she understood.

"Right, well as I said he could have spiked your drink and then you would have been unconscious. What would you have done then?"

Melody's eyes shot back to him, they were full of fire and he knew she wasn't going to go down easily.

"Well firstly, I would never have taken the drink that was offered, I'm not stupid. Secondly the bouncers check everyone who enters the room for contraband, they also bring in the champagne."

Her eyes were filled with defiance. She thought she'd made a good argument.

"You took the drink I gave you." He pointed out.

"What?" Roman knew she was trying to play dumb, but it wouldn't work with him. Leaning forward once more so that his nose was almost touching hers, he repeated slowly, "you took the drink I gave you."

Melody's eyes shot around the room as though trying to find the answer to his argument. "That was different and you know it. Besides that choice doesn't count, you made me nervous on purpose so that I would take it." She breathed in deep as she once more squirmed in the restraints. "Besides my statement about the bouncer was correct. They check everyone that goes in and all the drinks that go in."

Roman leaned back again, it was time for the next part of his plan.

"Are we done here?" she snapped at him. Roman knew she was not angry because she was afraid of him. She was angry because he had bested her. She hated not being in control of things, he had learnt that about her a long time ago.

"Not quite. You didn't answer me about what you would do if you could not yell for your bouncer?" During his speech Roman had once again placed himself in front of her so he could reach the bench.

"For God sake Rome, how in the world would they stop me from yelling out for help? It's not like they could sneak a gun in there."

Roman gave her a sly smile as she finished her sentence. He did not reply he simply gave her a calculated look before he pulled the scarf that had been sitting just behind her and covered her mouth with it. Melody was trying her best to stop him from doing it, but as her arms were tired she was defenceless. Once his masterpiece was finished he stood back and looked at her. She was still trying to free herself and the scream of rage that came from her when she couldn't move sent a rush of satisfaction through him.

"I'm sorry did you say something? I can barely hear you."

He joked putting his hand near his ear to make his point. Melody stopped struggling and shot daggers at him. Now that he had her full attention it was time to move in for the kill.

"Now that your last argument has been proven mute, do you concede that I was right about tonight?"

Melody didn't answer she simply shot him some more daggers before she turned her head away from him and ignored him.

Roman ran his hands through his hair in frustration. Stubborn girl. He did not want to push his point any further but if she did not concede he was worried that she would do something foolish like this again. She needed to see the errors of her ways. Her life may depend on it one day. Grabbing Melody's face Roman turned it back until she was looking deep into his eyes.

"Come on Mello, I have you dead to rights. You know that everything I have told you tonight is the truth. Just conceded that you were wrong and promise that you will never do anything so foolish again and I will finish this." Roman hoped that reason would break though her stubbornness, but he should have known better. She simply narrowed her eyes and shook her head no.

"Damn it Melody, conceded."

Again she shook her head, this time with more vigour.

"You are not going to like what comes next. I am not going to give up until you realise just how much danger you put yourself in tonight."

Roman had expected her to fold, but the look she gave him was one that declared war. Her eyes were snapping fire at him and her face told him that she was not going to back down no matter what. Roman growled before he placed his nose right up against hers. His breathing was ragged and he was having a difficult time keeping his frustration under control. He needed to keep a calm head for what came next, he was not doing it for pleasure he was doing it to show her just how low down and dirty men played. That was what he told himself anyway. Calming his racing heart, Roman looked her deep in the eyes and placed a wicked smile on his face before stating, "remember I gave you the chance to end this. I am giving you one final chance to concede."

He waited for her to nod, instead her muffled voice came through the scarf, "bring it."

Roman shook his head before stepping back. He looked her up and down slowly before a full smile spread across his face.

"Let the fun begin." He said as he took a step closer.

It was time for the real lesson to begin.

16

Melody was fuming. She wasn't scared that Roman would take advantage of her, no she was pissed that he was using his superior strength to get her to agree with him. That was something she would absolutely not do. She was not some naïve little girl who didn't know what crap awaited her in the world, and she wasn't clueless either. Her and Honey had spent hours making sure that every contingency had been planned for. Well almost every contingency. She hadn't planned on Roman figuring out that it was her dancing on stage. Still, that did not give him the right to decide what she could and could not do. The moment this gag came off she was going to tell him just that. Melody watched Roman as he planned his next move. He thought he had her cornered, little did he know that there was nothing he could do to her that would make her change her mind. She would not give him the satisfaction of winning. Melody knew that in the end he would give up and let her go, she just had to hold out till then. It wasn't going to be hard; the restraints were not tight enough to cause her discomfort and he had made sure that she had enough slack in her arms. It was actually quite comfortable. Melody could have easily stopped him from tying her up, if only she hadn't been surprised, but surprise her he did. Never in her wildest dreams would she have pictured Roman being capable of going to these extremes to make his point. That was why she hadn't registered what was happening until it was too late. Her brain simply couldn't comprehend it. If she had to admit it, apart from hating the fact that she was being bested, being tied up by Roman was exhilarating.

Of its own accord her body filled with lust as she felt him tighten the belt. It showed her a whole new side of Roman. A side that excited the bad girl that had been let lose tonight. While she was fighting his overbearing male ego, she was secretly excited to see how far he was willing to push his point. The problem was he was taking to long for her liking. Melody decided to move things along. The sooner this ended the sooner she could go for a cold shower to cool down her libido. She waited for his eyes to once again reach hers before she did the one thing guaranteed to piss him off. She gave him a look that stated, 'well what are you waiting for?'

Bingo.

Melody watched in fascination as Roman pushed himself away from the wall and stalked towards her. "Are you really going to make me do this?" he whispered. Melody rolled her eyes.

God when had he become so dramatic.

That was probably the worst thing she could have done. Rolling your eyes at a male was equivalent to flashing a red flag in front of a bull. With his nostrils flared and his eyes flaming he kind of looked like an angry bull getting ready to charge. The image that was provoked in Melody's mind caused her to let out a laugh. Again, the wrong thing to do

"Damnit Melody this is no joke." She knew she should be serious but she could only laugh again. She didn't mean to, but she couldn't get the image out of her head. Her laughter soon died however when Roman pressed his full body up against her.

"You know Mello you really should not push a man who is on the brink. That is another lesson I am going to have to teach you today."

Melody sucked in her breath as he leaned in close and whispered that in her ear, at the same time he had placed his hands on her waist just under her shirt. He had yet to move them, but the heat alone was enough to take away her humour.

"You should have given up earlier." He continued to whisper as his hands moved up over her shirt, along her rib cage and stopped just at her shoulders.

"Do you still think you had everything under control in that room?" He asked before nipping her ear.

Melody swallowed as she tried to get some moisture back into her mouth. It had not disappeared from nerves or the gag in her mouth. No, it had disappeared in fear that he would stop what he was doing. She knew he was right, but she was not willing to risk him stopping. So once again she shook her head no. With that Roman placed his head on her shoulder and let out a sigh right before he ripped the front of her shirt in two, right down the middle. This effectively had her breasts bare once more. The cool air had nothing to do with the puckering of her nipples, that was entirely Roman's doing. Melody could only watch as his eyes shifted down to take in her body. Her eyes didn't stay open long however when he placed his palms on her bare breasts and started to kneed them. He pinched one nipple which had Melody drawing in another breath.

"Would you have been able to stop a man from doing this to you in that room?" Roman asked in a husky voice.

Melody knew that his question was meant more for himself than her. She could see that he was doing his best to try and keep the situation in his control. Melody was not going to have it. She had wanted this man for far too long and finally, even if he hadn't meant it to happen, she was going to have him. Melody looked him right in the eyes when he looked at her and nodded.

"This is a dangerous game you are playing Melody." She continued to look at him and shrugged. Her body screamed with glee as she felt him flip the button on her shorts and further still when both hands moved them down over her hips, before they finally fell to the ground. Melody was sure she finally knew what ecstasy felt like.

Oh, how wrong she was.

Melody looked Roman right in the eyes, the question of 'what next?' played in hers.

Roman shook his head before saying, "one way or another Mello I am going to get you to concede that I am right. One way or another I will get a promise from you that you will not risk your life as you did tonight."

Then his mouth was on her breasts sucking and licking them until they were hard peaks. Melody's head fell back against the bar behind her and her eyes closed allowing her body to feel every delicious movement he made. As his lips moved from her breasts down over her ribs and further south she could no longer hold in the groan that was welling up inside of her. Then she felt his hot breath near her core, but nothing happened. She opened her eyes and looked down at him questioning why he had stopped. Her eyes clashed with his right before he said, "that's better." Then he took her into his mouth. His tongue worked its magic as it shot inside of her over and over again. Then he swirled it around her clit before he sucked on it hard. With each movement his tongue made, Melody felt herself nearing the edge. Her body felt as though it was about to shatter into a million pieces, her legs clenched his head keeping him locked in place and she silently begged for him to go faster. It was in that moment she wished she had her hands free so that she could touch him, but this would have to do. She was almost there, she could feel it, Melody prepared herself for the climax she knew would come.

But it never did. Roman stopped. He stopped and stood up.

Melody could not believe it. Surely, he was not going to leave her hanging. She wanted to scream at him, she wanted to claw and beg him to continue but she was still tied up and gagged.

Dropping her head back on the bars behind her she asked.
Why me?
She had been so close and yet so far.

* * *

Roman ran his hands through his hair, he could still taste her on his tongue, damn she was sweet. He had only meant to teach her a lesson, he'd had no intention of touching her like this, but once her breasts had been bared and that defiant look entered her eyes he had not been able to resists. It had only meant to be a lesson.

Who was he kidding?

He had wanted Melody from the moment he knew it was her on that stage and from the moment he had kissed her in the room his lust had been on full alert. Looking back at her he was once again hit with the sight of her that drove him wild. Her breasts were rising and falling with each breath she took and her legs and core shone with the evidence of her lust for him.

Screw it.

She obviously wanted him as much as he wanted her and she knew where this had been leading and had egged him on anyways.

"Screw it." He said out loud this time. That brought Melody's eyes open and back to his. The excitement he saw there only drove him on harder. Reaching up he ripped the belt off of the railings and from around her hands before removing the gag so he could kiss her. He had not been expecting the onslaught that followed. Melody practically jumped into his arms and smashed her lips to his. That was the only green light he needed. Roman was not finished what he had started. Walking over to the couch he pried her arms and legs from his body before placing her feet on the floor and stripping himself bare. Melody did not move as she took in his body. The lust that filled her eyes as each piece of clothing came off had him stripping faster. Once he was naked, he laid down on the couch and used his finger to call her over. Melody was just about to climb on top of him when he stopped her.

"Turn around and place your legs on the arms of the couch by my head." He ordered.

He was pleased to see recognition fill her eyes. She did not argue, she simply followed his instruction. Soon her core was right where he wanted it and he went back to administering the same love he had earlier. He loved the way she tasted and the way her body moved as his tongue pleasured her core, it drove him wild. His cock pulsed as he felt her tighten around the two fingers, he had just entered inside of her and the scream that ripped from her throat as he sucked her clit almost sent him over the edge. But it was her warm soft mouth which she placed over his cock that had him sucking in his breath and increasing the speed in which he pleasured her.

Soon she was coming all over his fingers and tongue and moments later he found himself unloading her mouth. He had expected her to pull away when she felt him tighten, instead she had sucked him harder and continued to suck until every last drop of his ecstasy had been taken. Giving him one final lick, she lifted her leg over his head and stood up. He sat up on the couch and grabbed her by the hips before she could leave.

"Rome?" she asked in a husky voice that sent all of the blood rushing back to his cock.

He gave her his cocky smile before answering, "I know you didn't think it was going to end there. You still have yet to concede," and with that he pulled her down onto his lap so she was straddling him and entered her in one movement.

They groaned in unison and it didn't take much to get her riding him as though she was a seasoned rodeo rider. Grabbing the back of the lounge Melody moved her hips as only a dancer could, taking the whole of him in until it met her womb. Soon they were once again in a frenzy and Roman was certain that the scream that left Melody's lungs when she came once more could have been heard as far as the bar. Moments later Roman joined her, grabbing her hips he thrust up, hard and his head feel back against the lounge as he felt himself eject inside of her. Melody collapsed on top of him and he could feel her heart beating in her chest as he final shots of his seed dissipated.

He leaned forward and kissed her shoulder before saying, "do you concede now?"

Roman had expected her to agree and that would be the end of it. So when she bit his shoulder and shook her head he groaned.

"Damn it, it looks like it is going to be a long night."

Melody laughed at that. "Well we had better get started." She quipped before laughing into his shoulder.

"You little brat. I am going to make you sorry you ever played this game with me." Roman added as he picked her up still attached to him and walked her to her room. Melody came once more before they even reached the room as his cock rubbed on her clit and moved inside of her with his moments. Roman threw her on the bed once there and climbed on top of her before saying, "well?"

"Well Detective, I guess I am going to learn just how good your interrogation skills are after all." She joked.

Roman groaned and buried himself inside of her once more. It was going to be a long night alright he could feel it, he doubted they would get any sleep, but it was going to be well worth it when he got her to concede to him. Now it was no longer about proving he was right; it was about wining and making sure that no matter who she was with her body would always remember his.

He wanted to ruin all other men for her.

17

Melody stretched her arms out above her head and looked over at the clock. It was eleven in the morning. Thankfully she did not have to be at the bar until four this afternoon. She wasn't sure what time it was when her and Roman had finally fallen asleep this morning all she knew was that she had lost count of how many times and ways they had made love. She did know however that after the last time in the shower they had fallen into and exhausted sleep curled up in each other's arms. Melody smiled to herself, Roman still hadn't been able to get her to concede that he had been right, but it was not through lack of trying.

"What has you smiling?" Roman asked leaning up on his elbow. Melody looked to the side and her smile became brighter. She had not expected him to still be here. She had expected to find a letter as she had yesterday morning. Melody gave him a sideways glance and a cheeky smile.

"Oh nothing, just last night and how I am superior to you in all ways."

Melody laughed as he raised his eyebrows. She then turned over and matched his position.

"Superior hey?" he asked.

Melody nodded her head. "Oh yes by far. You see men

think they are smarter than women, but more often than not it is the woman who leads the man to do what she wants while letting them think it was their idea."

Melody smiled at the confusion that crossed his face. Then it dawned on him what she was saying. "Is that so?" He said in a dead calm voice.

Melody nodded again. "How can you prove this?" Roman asked moving a little closer to her. Melody should have realised something was going on, but she was too busy teasing him to notice.

"Well let's see, even after all of your *lessons* as you called them, I still came out the victor. Hence I am more superior."

"Who said the fight was over?" Roman asked before he pounced on her and started tickling her. Melody tried to fight him off, but he was too strong. He simply straddled her legs and kept on tickling. Soon Melody couldn't breath and she knew there was only one way out.

"Mercy." She screamed before she wet herself.

"Do you concede?" Roman asked stopping briefly, but when Melody didn't answer quick enough he started tickling her once more.

"Okay I concede."

Roman stopped and placed his hands either side of her head and leaned in a little bit closer.

"You concede what?"

Melody paused, but as soon as he sat up, she put her hands up in a surrender gesture. "I concede that you were right about last night. I should never have put myself in that position. Happy?" she asked as she wiped the tears from her eyes. It had been so long since she had laughed like that, she didn't even care that he had bested her.

"And?"

Melody looked up at him. She wasn't sure why, but he looked even more delectable to her this morning. It probably had something to do with the intimacy with which she'd gotten to know his body last night.

"Melody!" Her name was said with a hint of warning behind it and was enough to bring her back to the matter at hand. She had to think back to their conversation last night and then she got it. Shaking her head to clear it from all of her lustful thoughts she added, "and I promise I will not put myself in that position again."

"Good, now we should probably think about getting up." He said as he rolled off of her.

"Melody did not move as quickly, instead she sat back and watched as he stood and put his boxers on. She had to admit she could get used to a view like that.

"I hope you know that if I don't get in to Juilliard it will be all your fault though."

Melody laid back on her pillow and pulled the sheet up to cover her breasts. Now that he was not beside her, she felt a little self-conscious about her nakedness. After Roman finished putting on his boxers he kneeled back on the bed and crawled over to her.

"I am sure I will live." Was all he said before he kissed her.

The kiss was a quick coming together of their lips and before Melody could deepen it he was once again off the bed just in time for his phone to ring. Roman picked it up, checked who was calling, then answered.

"Hey what have you got?" He asked as he made his way out of the bedroom.

"I am sure you can live with it, but I can't." she yelled after him just as he made it to her door. Roman turned to her and offered her a smile before he continued out of the room. She vaguely herd him say, "it's nothing," before he went back to listening. Melody lay in bed for a few moments more, listening to Roman's voice as she decided that she should get up. It was not because she wanted to, or had to, Melody just realised that she was in desperate need of some coffee. A night full of passionate sex sure could make a girl thirsty.

* * *

After getting dressed into her normal bedroom wear Melody splashed some water on her face and made her way out into the kitchen. Roman was leaning against the bench, legs crossed at the ankle, one hand resting on the bench, while he talked to whoever was on the phone.

It seemed like it was a one-sided conversation as Roman wasn't doing much of the talking, he simply agreed or aha'd when he needed to. Melody shot him a smile when she noticed that he had started the coffee pot. While Roman continued to stand there talking she searched for her coffee mug, normally it was in the top cupboard, she even had to stand on her tippy toes to look, but it wasn't there. Weird. Then she remembered that she had stacked the dishwasher before she left yesterday and hadn't had the chance to empty it. Opening the dishwasher, she pulled out the bottom rack and saw her cup all the way up the back, leaning over she retrieved it before standing and placing it on the bench. She was just pouring the coffee into her cup when she felt the warmth of Roman's body at her back, without even thinking she leaned into him and instantly felt his need for her poking her in the back.

"What else did they have to say?" she heard him ask into his phone. At the same time, he reached around her, opened the cupboard above her head and pulled down another cup, placing it next to hers. This only served to push his manhood deeper into the crevasse of her behind. A groan left her throat of its own accord and when she tilted her head back she saw him looking down at her with lust filled eyes.

She could see that he was doing everything in his power to

stay focused on the conversation with whoever was on the phone. Melody however had other ideas, she saw this as the perfect opportunity to get some payback for his underhandedness with her this morning. After she poured some coffee into his cup she put the coffee pot back in its cradle, but as she did so she made sure to stick her arse out a little and move it so it rubbed him just the right way.

Melody had to laugh a little when his hand grabbed her waist to stop her from moving and when she looked at him, he mouthed the word 'behave.'

He should have known better than to say something like that to her after last night. Melody mouthed the word 'what?' back at him acting all innocent before she stood up straight and took a sip of her coffee.

Melody pressed forwarded into the cupboard to place a little room between them and waited for him to reach around and grab his coffee, once he had she removed her free hand from her coffee cup and slid it behind her back to take his manhood in her palm. Once she had it, she began to massage.

Roman almost dropped his coffee mug he was holding, so he placed it back on the counter. He then pushed her forward into the cupboard to stop her administrations.

Melody almost laughed when he spoke next, "no I didn't growl at you. I simply spilt some coffee. Just continue with what you were saying. What did the captain do about it and what have the parents decided to do?"

Melody was a little peeved that her plan hadn't worked and, although she tried, she could not move her hand that was now wedge between them. Her disappointment soon turned to joy when his free hand, which was no longer holding his coffee reached up and started to massage her breasts.

Melody tried not to make any noise from the pleasure he was giving her but it was becoming harder as his hand moved down her body until it reached the band of her shorts. She assumed he would stop, but Melody sent up a prayer of thanks when he continued. Soon his fingers were at her core, massaging and teasing her until she was riding his fingers as though it was his cock.

There was something erotic in knowing that he was giving her so much pleasure and yet she could not make a sound as it would give them away to the person on the other end of the phone. Melody's hand had been released from behind her and she threw it over her shoulder and grabbed onto his hair as her body convulsed around his fingers. Her lips were tingling from where she had bitten down on them to stop herself from screaming.

Melody had assumed that Roman would take his coffee and move away from her, instead she heard him say, "I'll have to call you back. Give me about half an hour."

He didn't wait for an answer he simply hung up his phone and practically threw it on the bench in front of her. Without so much as a word, he spun her around before placing her arse first onto the bench.

Capturing her mouth his tongue entered to dance with hers, at the same time he pulled her shorts to the side and sheathed himself in her heat. Melody groaned into his mouth and he pulled her forward until she was sitting on the edge of the bench.

Tilting her head to the side she deepened the kiss as their lovemaking intensified. Soon she could not help it, she broke their kiss and reached up so she could hold onto the cupboards above her and rode out the storm he was creating in her once more. It didn't take long for Melody to reach the brink and Roman leaning forward taking her breasts into his mouth through the satin of her cami sent her tumbling over it. Melody let go of the cupboards and grabbed his shoulders as her legs squeezed him tight and once more a scream was ripped from her throat.

With a few more thrusts Roman joined her over the precipice, before he placed his head on her shoulder to catch his breath. It only took him a few minutes before he raised his head and looked her dead in the eyes, "you wanna hope that everyone in the diner is deaf."

Melody looked at him for minute before she burst out laughing. "Maybe you should be worried, they might think you are murdering me."

Roman pulled out of her and helped her down from the bench before he went and got his coffee, just as he was walking out of the kitchen he shot back, "honey that was no scream of pain, that was pure pleasure."

He sure was cocky, but then again he had a right to be, he sure did know how to pleasure a woman. Grabbing her coffee Melody followed him out to the lounge room, she would deal with the fallout of her screaming later, for now she just wanted to sit with him and talk. It was time she found out exactly what was going on in Denver, it was time to get back to real life and she needed to know once and for all how dangerous her stalker was, because if he was the 'Denver Dancer' Serial Killer, Roman would have bigger fish to fry than her stripping on stage.

That was if she told him of course.

18

Melody sat on the couch next to Roman. He was currently surfing the channels of the T.V. probably trying to find some sports to watch. It was a male thing. Pulling her legs up underneath her, she put her arm on the back of the lounge and leaned her head into her palm. She stared at the channels randomly changing and tried to gather her thoughts. Melody knew that she couldn't just jump into asking him questions about the case he was working on in Denver or he would instantly become suspicious about why she was asking about it now, she had to slowly work her way up to it. She couldn't even ask him what it was his partner was calling about as that would alert him to the fact that she had indeed been eavesdropping on his phone conversation and her ploy for taking her time making the coffee had been just that. She raked her brain for some way to broach the subject, but for the life of her she couldn't think of one. Lost her own thoughts Melody didn't realise how deep she had gone until his hand rubbing her leg brought her back to the present.

"Melody?" His voice finally reached her braincells.

She turned her head and looked at him, "did you say something?" she asked.

Roman simply shook his head and laughed. "I asked you

what you were thinking so hard about?"

Melody gave a quick short laugh, if you could call it that and came up with an answer. Taking a sip of her coffee, she answered. "It was nothing, I was just thinking about how much money I still needed for Juilliard."

At the mention of last night's antics Roman's eyes narrowed dangerously on her and she thought it might be prudent to calm him down.

"Don't worry I am not considering anything, should we say, that you don't approve of."

Melody could see that he didn't buy it, he was still looking at her with narrowed eyes.

"I promise." She added making a cross over her heart to hammer home her point.

"Good." He closed his eyes and laid his head back on the couch as he listened to the T.V. There was a sports recap on from the last night. Melody looked down to where his hands still rested on her leg. He was moving one of his fingers around drawing patterns on it and she wondered briefly if he was even aware that he was doing it. Not that she was complaining, it was nice to know that he felt completely comfortable with her that his actions came naturally. Their talk only moments ago did give her the in she needed however to steer their conversation into the realm of the stalker. She needed to know just how dangerous her situation was.

Once she had all the information then she could decide if she would let Roman in on her problem or not. She knew it would be the smart thing to do as he could probably have her stalker figured out in a day or two, but she did not want to bother him if it turned out to be nothing.

"Speaking of last night," She let out a laugh when his head shot up and he was frowning at her again.

"Would you care to explain what is going on at the bar?"

"Oh that." Roman said as he placed his head back on the couch. He quickly filled Melody in on what had been going on. She was hoping that it had been a ploy he'd used to get her in the back room, so she was surprised to find out that it was for real.

"I can't believe someone is ripping off Ren." She commented before taking another sip of her coffee.

Roman smiled a small smile before he sat forward on the couch, drank the rest of his coffee, then stood and went to the kitchen.

"That reminds me, I should probably call my partner back."

Melody smiled a small smile to herself. She didn't need to hound him, he had just given her the right to ask the question she needed to ask. "Oh, so that was who was on the phone. Do you have him working on the case for you?" She brought her own coffee cup back into the kitchen, acting as innocent as possible. Roman was once again leaning against the island bench the same way she had found him this morning, he was currently reading through his messages. He looked up from his phone at her question. It took him a moment to register what she'd asked. "No, that one I have figured out all by myself. Shale was calling to let me know how our other case was progressing."

Melody smiled that was the first time she'd heard him use his friends name. Shale and Fox, it sounded like it would be a good cop series name.

"Oh yeah, Gabby mentioned something about that a while back. Stalker right?"

Melody turned around and proceeded to rinse her cup so that she didn't look like she was too interested. She hoped that he would not give her the simple answer. She needed him to talk about it, but it had to be of his own volition.

"I wish it was just a stalker." He grumbled as he shot his

partner a message. He then sat his phone down on the counter and ran one of his hands through his hair. Melody turned around and leaned against the edge of the sink. She didn't say anything she let him lead the conversation. She was starting to give up hope that he would but then he asked, "how much do you know of the 'Denver Dancer' Serial Killer?"

Melody shook her head, "not much. Just what I have seen on T.V. Do you really not have any leads?" She asked. Again, Roman ran his hand through his hair. She was starting to realise he did this whenever he was frustrated. It was one of his quirks. She liked knowing that about him.

"It's true. The bastard leaves no trace of himself. He uses a burner when he is stalking the girls, he kidnaps them at times that are noisy and full of distractions and he waits until the parents have paid the ransom before he sends their daughters back to them and during the whole thing he goes by undetected."

Melody was dying to ask about the stalking part, but she had to be patient. She had to work up to it. "Do you have any theories or suspects?"

Roman nodded, "but as it is an ongoing investigation, I cannot discuss them with anyone. Other than Shale of course. Trust me I would if I could, but I'm already in enough deep water."

"Ah yes the incident that lead to your suspension. Do you think the guy you arrested is responsible?"

Melody laughed when Roman narrowed his eyes at her. Putting her hands up in surrender she added, "sorry. It was worth a try."

She let the silence fall between them for a few minutes and acted as though she was thinking. Then it was time to go in for the kill, so to speak. "Surely you could get something from him during the stalking stage. Normal stalkers spend months texting their victims, don't they?"

Roman looked at her in an assessing manner.

Damn his detective nature.

"How would you know that?" He asked in a low tone.

"I watch cop shows," she answered off handily hoping to draw away his suspicions.

Roman groaned. "God I hate those shows. They make our lives so much harder. Half the time the crap they are betraying isn't even close to what is real. It's the reason everyone thinks that forensic evidence can be used to solve a murder in a week."

Melody laughed at how riled Roman was becoming. "Whoa there. I am sorry I even brought it up. So, I'm to assume this stalker of yours is not like those on the shows?"

Hand through hair again.

"No, he only sends a few texts over probably a week before he switches up his ammo. The texts turn to presents being delivered, all of which he orders over the phone, once that has been done the letters start. Letters that have been personally written. The girls normally find them somewhere personal and the most disturbing part of it all is there is usually something ultra-personal of the girls, like her hair attached to the letter."

Melody shuddered, while she felt better knowing that her stalker was not linked to the 'Denver Dancer' Serial Killer, of that she was certain, she did not like that this mad man was getting around her university. She certainly felt less safe now, even with her own stalker.

Roman must have seen the look of terror come over her face, thankfully he linked it to what they were talking about. He stepped forward and took her into his arms. "Those poor girls." She whispered into his chest as he rubbed her back.

After a few minutes he stepped back to the bench. "Anyway, that is why I was talking to my partner."

The way in which he said the words let her know that the subject was closed, which was fine with her. She had what she needed and if she never heard of this lunatic again, it would be too soon.

"Please be careful Rome." She never thought of it before but hearing about the guy he was after brought home just how dangerous his job was.

"Always am." He answered.

Melody stood there for a moment more before glancing up at the clock. Seeing that it was now almost twelve she decided she should probably start getting ready for the day. Pushing off the counter she started to walk out of the kitchen throwing over her shoulder, "I'm going to go and have a shower." Roman smiled at her and slapped her arse as she walked past him. Melody placed her hands on her arse and shot him a death glare, which only gained her his laughter. As she entered her bedroom she heard him rinsing his mug, she could get used to this domestic kind of life, she thought to herself as she stepped out of her Pyjama's and stepped into the shower.

She turned the shower on and waited for it to warm up, as she waited she pictured what life would be like if she got to spend the rest of her life with Roman and as she stepped into the hot water that was now streaming down her body, she realised how dangerous thoughts like that were. As much as she had thought she'd loved Roman before, it was nothing like what she felt now.

Now she was worried that she would do anything to get that life, even give up Juilliard.

19

Roman listened to the shower running as he refilled his cup with coffee, he was going to need a few more of these if he was going to make it through the day. He'd gotten very little sleep last night, with that thought came the memories of the night before and his mind conjured up the image of Melody and himself in the shower before they'd finally fallen asleep. Instantly his body stood to attention. Roman gave a self-deprecating laugh. He had lost count of the amount of times he'd had her last night, then again just now, still his body was yet to be sated.

He worried that it might never be.

Sex with Melody was unlike any he'd had before. Yes, he had reached his climax with his other partners, as had they. But with her it wasn't just his body that had been involved in the act, it had been his whole being. He felt connected to her in a way that he'd never thought possible. Leaning back against the sink Roman considered how he had let it get so out of hand. He had simply meant to teach Melody a lesson.

When he'd first tied her up the thought of sleeping with her had never crossed his mind, in fact he had assumed that the moment he opened her shirt she would give up. Deep down in his heart he knew that from the moment she walked through the door and into that room last night he'd wanted her. All night as he watched her flirt with he young men in the bar he had wanted her. Then following her home last night while he conjured up the plan, he knew he wanted her. Then the moment her eyes filled with lust, when he'd tired her to the bench, he knew he'd only been fooling himself. He hadn't been trying to teach her a lesson, he was simply fighting what he knew was inevitable.

Of their own accord his eyes shot to where he'd tied her up, one thing Roman had come to learn about Melody over the last few days was that she had a wild streak. Growing up, whenever Melody and Gabby would get into trouble the boys had all assumed it had been Gabby that had started it. Everyone in town knew that Gabby was wild, but what they never expected and what he was only just learning was that deep underneath the prima ballerina façade that Melody wore, beat the heart of someone even more wild than her best friend.

The only problem was, Melody's type of wild was a lot more dangerous than Gabby's. The problem with Melody was that when she was struck with this wild streak all sense of safety and logic went out the window and it usually dragged the person she was with down with her.

Last night had been a perfect example of this.

From the moment Roman realised that it was Melody on that stage every sense of responsibility seemed to have vacated his brain and he didn't find it until sometime early this morning in the shower. Only then as he sat washing Melody, after having her once more, did he realise that not once during their lovemaking had he worn protection. Roman was always packing so there was no excuse for not wearing it, and *never* in all of his sexual life had he'd engaged in sexual intercourse without protection.

Until Melody.

There was just something about her that made him lose all sense, and that was dangerous.

Once they were in bed Roman had hinted at their lack of protection to try and see what her reaction would be. He hadn't wanted to freak her out, but she missed his point altogether and simply kissed him, snuggled in to his arms and fell asleep. Roman was hoping that it had more to do with her being tired and not understanding his hints rather than her lack of concern. He would have to remember to stock up on protection and place it in the bedside table. There was no use tempting fate. Roman was making a mental note of all the things he had to accomplish today, when he heard Melody call out from the bathroom.

"Rome could you grab me another towel from the top of the duchess in the living room please."

"Sure." He yelled back. He didn't know if she'd even heard him, but he thought it was rude not to at least offer some sort of reply. Locking eyes on the duchess in question Roman started to make his way out of the kitchen. He was just passing the bench when his phone alerted him to the fact that he had received a text. It had to be from Shale.

Picking his phone up he swiped it up to open it as he continued to make his way over to the dresser.

He was silently cursing his phone when the damn thing wouldn't open. As he reached the dresser, he pushed the home button thinking that would at least light it up so that he could see what was going on.

Roman stopped mid-step and just stared at the screen.

No wonder it wasn't opening, this was not his phone.

"Rome." He heard from the bathroom once more.

Ripping the towel from the draw and slamming it shut he marched into the bathroom. Melody had a lot of explaining to do. He hoped to hell that this was just a friend playing a prank on her, but deep in the pit of his stomach he knew what the truth was. Roman thought back to her behaviour over the last couple of weeks and tried to figure out if anything had been out of the ordinary, that is, more out of the ordinary than stripping for money. He was trying to deduce how long she might have been getting these messages for, but over all her behaviour had been the 'usual' Melody. That was all except for their conversation this morning.

Son of a bitch.

At the time Roman had felt that something was a little odd in the way she asked about the 'Denver Dancer' Serial Killer, but he just put it down to curiosity. Shale had just called and the attraction he'd felt for her and their morning activates had drained all of his normal brain activity to his lower regions, but now his detective skills were back in full force and could finally see what the premise behind their conversation had been.

"Rome, are you making that towel or what?" Melody called once more.

Roman looked at the towel and then to the phone. It was time he and Melody set some things straight and one of those things was going to be about her keeping things from him. Walking into the bathroom he handed Melody the towel before he leaned against the wall. Her phone was still in his hand, but it was now covered by his other arm. He waited for her to wrap the new towel around her head, before placing another one around her body. He was thankful that she had covered up before stepping out of the shower he didn't need the temptation of her body in this moment. Melody looked at him as she removed the towel from her head and started to dry her hair. She walked past him into the bedroom. Roman stayed in the doorway of the bathroom, still leaning against the wall he simply moved his body around so he was now facing her. Melody was facing him still drying her hair, but she stopped when she noticed him just staring at her. He could only imagine what she was seeing. He was seething inside.

"Is something wrong?" She asked looking at him with concern.

Roman pushed off the wall and stalked towards her.

"Well that will depend on what you have to say next." He answered in a clipped tone.

Melody crossed her arms over her breasts and frowned at him. "What are you on about?" she asked confusion lacing her words.

"Do you trust me?" He asked.

"Are you seriously asking me that now?"

"Melody?" His tone was low and controlled. She must have noticed, her look of concern was now replaced with annoyance. He knew he was being overbearing, but he didn't care. All he cared about was getting the truth from her.

"Of course, I trust you." She bit off.

He could see she was getting annoyed with him, by the way she went back to drying her hair. Her movements were angry, full of frustration.

"And what is it that I do for a living?" He calmly asked as he took another step towards her.

She stopped drying her hair again and rolled her eyes at him. She seemed to do that a lot around him, he kind of found it endearing, and he would have laughed if the situation they were in wasn't so serious. He needed to know how deep into the situation Melody was and only then would he know what to do next.

Roman had expected her to answer him, instead all he got sass. Melody threw her towel on the bed before answering, "for God sake Roman do we have to go over this again, I told you last night…"

"What. Do. I. Do. For. A. Living?" He asked again, making sure to enunciate each word. He had stalked his way towards her until he was now standing right in front of her.

Her breasts were rising and falling with each ragged breath she took, he could see her pulse beating in her neck just above her collarbone. Looking deep into her eyes he had expected to see a little bit of fear, instead he found excitement and lust. Her heart was racing, not because she was scared, but because she was turned on. Shaking his head and stealing his feelings towards her Roman knew he had to keep a level head. If he even so much as let her know where his feelings were headed, he knew where this would end, it wouldn't be with the answers he needed. Thinking of the danger she could currently be in worked at effectively cooling down his libido.

"Rome..." she started.

"Just answer the question Melody." He ordered.

Melody's jutted her bottom lip out in a pout and all he could think about was how he wanted to take it between his teeth, but that would have to wait.

"You're a detective." She snapped.

"And what does that entail Mello." He asked sarcastically. He was not asking for clarification on his part, he was simply making it more effective when he drove his point home.

"I suppose it means that you solve crimes and capture the bad guys." Placing her hands across her chest once more she stared at him with defiance. Yes, Melody was defiantly one who liked to be in control.

Yet her body told a different story. She also liked to be dominated. "So you trust me and you know what I do for a living, am I correct?"

"Oh, for God sakes Rome, yes I trust you and I know what you do for a living. So what gives?"

Roman gave her a minute to stew before he pulled the phone out from underneath his arm. Pushing the button on the home screen he turned it so it was facing her before dropping his final bomb.

"Then care to explain this?" He asked.

Roman had expected her to blow up, instead she sunk into her bed, her faced paled and she whispered, "Oh God."

It was then he knew this was no prank. Melody was in serious danger. Nothing else mattered but her in that moment.

Even though he had no solid evidence to the contrary, he felt it in his bones. This was the work of the 'Denver Dancer' Serial Killer, and he was after Melody.

20

Melody reached for her phone, opened it and read the text.

I told you I was coming, now I am here. Did you feel me last night? Did you feel my eyes as they watched you prance around in your short shorts, and white top? Did you feel me as they watched you flirt and laugh? I hope you have fun Melody because soon I will be the only one you will be laughing and flirting with. Soon I will have you all to myself. Not even your detective can save you this time. He can't be by your side all of the time and when that time comes, I will be there to take his place.

I am here and soon I will have you.

Melody wanted to believe that he was bluffing, but there were too many accurate details in the text for it to be a bluff. She had hoped by ignoring the maniac he would go away, but it looked like that plan had backfired.

"So?" Roman asked. "Care to explain?" She could hear the edge in his voice and she didn't blame him.

"Why did you have my phone?" she asked lamely.

She was not mad that he did, in fact it was kind of a relief knowing that someone else was aware of what was going on.

It especially helped that that someone was a detective who dealt with this kind of thing all of the time. No she was not mad, she was just trying to buy herself some time so she could gather her thoughts.

Why hadn't she told him sooner?

She knew the answer. Melody did not want to make him feel as though he *had* to protect her. She wanted him to be around her because he wanted to be, not because he had to be. Now that would all change.

"Really? That is all you have to say?"

Melody glanced up at his sarcastic tone. She could see the pulse in his neck beating with his rage and she wasn't sure what he was maddest about, the message or her keeping something like this from him. When she didn't answer he spoke once more.

"Fine, I will answer your question, but then you will answer mine. Got it?" His tone gave no room for argument. Melody simply nodded. It was not like she was trying to hide the facts from him anyway.

"I was distracted when you called out to me, I heard the phone and assumed it was mine. Shale is sending me some information. Now how long has this been going on?"

Melody folded her legs up underneath her and started to roll her phone around in her hands. She thought back to when the messages started. Had it really been that long. "About eight weeks." She finally whispered in a low tone.

"Eight weeks." Roman's roar was the complete opposite to her own. She was just so tired of the whole thing and now she had to face facts that this was no longer a situation she could ignore. If the stalker was for real, he was here. In her home town.

Roman was pacing back and forth in front of her. He was once again running one of his hands through his hair as he mumbled something to himself. Melody was in no rush to disturb him as that would only bring his anger back to her.

"Why the hell haven't you gone to the police before now?" He asked.

Melody shrugged. That only seemed to add to his ire. He stopped and narrowed his eyes on her and she thought it would be prudent to answer him. "Honestly I have been hoping that it was just a prank. You know collage boys completing a dare. It never crossed my mind that it was anything more serious." She looked down at her phone again. Now she was not so sure.

"Okay that I understand, but damn Melody haven't you heard of changing your phone number?"

Melody narrowed her eyes on him this time. She really hated it when men treated women as though they were simpletons. "Now why hadn't I thought of that?" She answered in a tone that denoted she was a bimbo.

Roman growled low in his throat and took a step towards her. Melody decided that she would rather get this grilling over and done with so she could figure out what she was going to do about her stalker. It was now clear that was exactly what he was. "I did change my number about a month ago and all was fine until I came here. I am not even sure how he got my new one."

Roman began pacing once more. "It is easy if you know how. Besides there are too many ways for him to have gotten it to narrow the field. We just need some kind of break to...."

The rest of what Roman was saying was cut off when he started mumbling to himself as he paced. Pulling her legs up underneath her and crossing them she watched on silently as Roman continued to pace and talk to himself. His body flexed with each movement and the way his brows furrowed as he worried over the problem made her smile. She wondered if he looked like this all of the time when he was solving a case. It was something she hoped to find out. She remained silent until he stopped and pulled out his phone.

"Who are you calling?" She asked but was cut off when he put a finger up and spoke into the phone.

"Shale, tell me you have something?" She watched as he nodded and offered yes or no answers to whatever was being said. Leaning back on her hands Melody waited to see what his plan was.

"Well I may have something here." Pause as Shale spoke. "Not sure yet, but Melody has been getting messages from someone. Messages similar to those of our last victims."

Roman's eyes shot to hers as he shared that last piece of information. Melody was no longer relaxed.

"It doesn't matter who she is, I just need to know if a particular someone has been acting suspicious lately or has left town."

Another pause, with some nodding. "No, it's all good for now. If you come down here it will raise the suspicions of the captain and we don't need that. Besides I need you there keeping an eye on things. I will call you if anything happens. So has he left town?"

Roman began pacing again as he listened to his partner. Melody couldn't help wringing her hands, her heart was pounding and she felt like she had the night the messages started again.

Please don't be the 'Denver Dancer' Serial Killer.

"Will do. You too." Roman finally said before he hung up the phone.

He was busy doing something on there, but her next statement had him pausing in his administration. "You think it is him, don't you?"

Walking forward he crouched down beside the bed so that he was eye level with her. "Honestly, I don't know. All signs are pointing to yes, but we can't say for certain."

Melody hung her head as tears started to fall down her

face. As if she didn't have enough on her plate to worry about, now she could possibly have a deranged killer after her as well. She thought back to the news stories of what had happened to his previous victims and shuddered. She didn't want to end up like those girls, she wanted to live.

She wanted to dance.

She wanted love and the life that came with that.

Roman placed his hand against her cheek and rubbed a tear away with his finger. Melody's tongue darted out to catch one that just fell from the other side. She hated showing any weakness in front of anyone. Especially this man. She wanted him to see her as a force to be reckoned with. She hated reminding him of the weakling she had been back in school. Roman deserved a strong woman, not a woman who needed him to fight her battles.

"I will not let this guy, no matter who he is, hurt you. Understand? I will find him and I will see him prosecuted to the full extent of the law."

As Melody looked into his eyes she once again saw the same determination he wore the day he saved her from being raped. He was forever her protector and there was nothing she could do about it.

"I want to believe you." She said in a small whisper, "I'm just not sure how you plan to do that?" Melody was waiting for the explosion to come.

Instead he smiled and shook his head, "how is it you always forget what I do for a living?"

She knew he was trying to bring levity to the situation and despite herself it worked. She smiled a small smile.

"That's better. Now all I need for you to do is trust me. Trust that I can protect you. Can you do that?"

Melody nodded. She didn't even hesitate because no matter what else happened, that she could do.

"That's my girl, now I have to get to work." He replied as

he leaned forward to kiss her.

It was in that moment that she realised how deep her love for this man was. She had always thought she loved him, but right in this moment she knew for sure that her life was empty without him and that her heart would never love another. Grabbing his face she deepened the kiss, she was not ready to let him go just yet. Another few minutes would make no difference to anyone's lives but theirs. Roman broke away from the kiss and stood up. "I have to make these calls Mello." He groaned.

Melody decided to fight fire with fire and give him something she knew he could not deny. Unwrapping the towel she leaned back, rested on her elbows, bent her legs at the knees and then opened them so he got a full view of her core. She was already wet with need for him and the moment he saw it she knew he was lost. Running a hand through his hair, Roman cursed, threw his phone on the bed, pulled down his pants and impaled himself on her. Melody moaned as the tip of his manhood reached her core. Throwing her head back and laying the rest of the way down on the bed, she prepared herself to ride out the storm. Melody didn't think it could get any better then it had last night until he lifted her legs up over his shoulders and deepened his movements. She was shot straight to heaven and came twice more before he reached his climax.

As his climax finished Melody released her legs from his shoulders and he collapsed on top of her, both of their breathing ragged. They lay entwined for few minutes, Melody happy feeling Romans heartbeat, until he rolled to the side. Melody turned to her side and ran her fingers through the hair on his chest. She loved that he was still manly like this and didn't succumb to the dictates of modern society that saw men waxing and shaving off all of their hair. It only added to his sex appeal. Her hands continued on their journey and were soon skimming his six pack. She was lost in thought, thinking about everything they had done together.

"Son of a bitch, you did it again."

Melody's eyes shot up to his, wondering what the hell he was talking about.

"Excuse me?" She asked, thinking surely he wasn't talking to her.

"Every damn time you get near me I forget all my senses." Melody frowned at him. He sounded mad, but at himself not her. She didn't have a clue what he was on about. She simply raised an eyebrow at him, the same way he did when he was asking her a question. Sitting up Roman ran a hand through his hair before he turned and looked at her. Melody decided to sit up so that she was on the same level as him. Well close enough anyway.

"Do you know that in the entire time we have been engaged in, …… well this." Melody smiled at the way he couldn't get the words out. He simply swiped his hand wide encompassing the bed.

"In sex." She filled in for him laughing. That did not go over well, he narrowed his eyes on her.

"It's more than sex and you know it, but that is beside the point. Not once have we used protection."

Melody's eyes shot up in surprise. Not because he was right, but because the thought of protection hadn't even crossed her mind and that was unusual for her. Melody had only slept with a handful of guys and she made sure she had protection with all of them. But not with Roman. The more Melody thought about it the less concerned she became. This was Roman after all.

"Melody, did you hear what I said?" he asked bringing her back to their conversation.

"Yes I heard you, and so?"

Roman shook his head and leaned back, it was his turn to

look surprised.

"SO. What the bloody hell does that mean?"

The concerned look on his face told her that 'So' was probably not the best word she could have used, but it fit.

"Come on Rome, it's you and me. I am pretty sure neither of us have any STD's am I right."

Roman's eyes were closed and he was running his index finger down the bridge of his nose as though he was trying to fight off a headache. Reaching out she ran her hand down his arm and tried to sooth him, "really Rome. It is all good."

With that his eyes flew open and his hand dropped to the bed. "All good you say, well what about an unwanted pregnancy? Did you stop to think about that? I thought you wanted a dancing career?"

This time Melody did smile. She couldn't help it. "Trust me Rome, an unwanted pregnancy is the last thing you have to worry about. I made sure a long time ago that there would be no chance of that happening until I was ready."

Roman looked at her and narrowed his eyes.

"How can you be certain?"

His voice had mellowed and he looked a little more relaxed, she knew they were past his panic attack. She knew she should have been just as concerned as he had, but for some reason she wasn't. She had never wanted to share that kind of intimacy with someone before, but with Roman it felt right.

"I just am. This is where you have to trust me. I did not spend my youth working on this body to lose it before I even made it to Juilliard." She added as she stood up.

Leaning forward she grabbed his face in her hands and kissed him before she once more headed into the bathroom for another shower. She would see if she could coax him in for one more round before they got to work on solving the mystery of her stalker.

"Okay, but from now on we will use it. Do you hear me?" he yelled over the water she had just turned on. Before she stepped in she looked over her shoulder and smiled at him.

"Why bother now, the horse has already fled the barn, so to speak. Now are you coming to join me?"

With that she stepped into the shower and smiled when he stepped in behind her. Pushing her up against the wall, he spread her legs and entered her from behind as he whispered in her ear, "you are dangerous do you know that?"

Melody moaned, "and you love it." Soon her moans and screams could be heard throughout the apartment as she lost herself to him once more. He was right, she was dangerous because the thrill she got from being bad was becoming addictive, as was he.

21

"Hello, my name is Melody and I will be your waiter today. Can I start you off with some drinks?" Melody listened half-heartedly as the family placed their order. Thankfully they had already chosen their meals so she would not have to come back again.

It was Thursday after lunch, so the diner was not too busy, which was a good thing as it gave her time to think. Ripping the order tag from her notepad, Melody went behind the bench and placed in on the shelf of the kitchen window for the cook. She then prepared the drinks and took them back over to the family.

"Just give me a shout if I can help you with anything else." No-matter her mood or where her mind was she always made a point to be pleasant to all she served, the tips she gained here were still helping to pay for Juilliard.

Especially now, since she didn't know when she would go back to the bar. On Sunday before Roman had left he'd made her promise that she wouldn't work at the bar unless he was there. Normally she would have been pissed at being given an edict such as that, but she couldn't deny that the stalkers last message had left her feeling unnerved.

Even here in the diner she felt on edge. She was constantly

examining the behaviour of those that came in, wondering if they could be the person stalking her. Melody was wiping down the counter when the door jingled and someone walked in and sat at the counter.

"Order up." Cook yelled at the same time.

"I'll be right with you." Melody shot over her shoulder to the newcomer as she picked up the order from the kitchen window and placed them on a tray.

"Take your time." Gabby smiled. Melody rushed over and placed the orders on the table for the family and asked if they wanted their drinks refilled. The little ones of course did, and once that was done she reminded the family to call her if they needed anything. She checked that everyone in the diner was happy before she finally made her way back to Gabby.

"Hey Bitch, where have you been I haven't seen you since Sunday night at work." Gabby whined.

Melody smiled at her, "the usual?" she asked. Gabby nodded.

Melody put in her order of fries and a chicken burger with the lot. Placing a coke down in front of her she answered. "I have been working here. Mom and Dad needed me this week."

Gabby took a sip of her drink. "I guess I can't argue with that. At least tell me you are coming in on Saturday and Sunday? I have missed you. The bar is not the same without you."

Melody laughed. "Yeah right, you would be loving all the extra attention." Gabby shrugged at that and took another sip of her drink.

"Order up." Came from the window once more.

Melody turned to get the food, "back in a minute." She shot to Gabby as she went to the take the order to a couple at the back of the room. Their drinks also needed refilling and as she was walking back to the table with them she heard the door jingle once more. More customers meant more tips, but it also meant less time with Gabby. Melody had missed seeing her friend this week, she had been busy working at the bar, while Melody had been working here. As for Melody's spare time, the last few days had been spent with Roman. Except for yesterday and last night, that he had spent with his parents. She smiled as she thought about him and their clandestine relationship. They weren't keeping it from anyone because they were ashamed, it was because neither one of them wanted to admit what it was that was between them. Melody knew that once she got back to Denver her life would once again revolve around dancing and she had a feeling that Roman felt the same way about his job. So for the time being, it was easier for them to continue pretending they were just friends around everyone else.

Melody was fine with that.

Well that was what she had to keep telling herself, because deep down she knew that if she didn't keep reiterating that fact she was going to allow her true emotions to come out and that would not end well for either one of them. The truth was she was head over heels in love with the man. Melody placed the drinks she was holding on the table in front of her, but before she could go back to the counter she took care of other customers who were ready to leave. She placed a bill on one table and then cleaned another table near her as she waited for the previous table to pay. They thanked her as they walked out past her.

Melody walked back to the table and smiled when she noticed they had left her a 20% tip, it was a good tip, but she would still need a lot more of these if she was going to get the money for Juilliard.

Placing the money in her apron she grabbed the tray with the dirty dishes and headed into the kitchen for the cleaning crew to grab. She had just walked out the doors when "order up," sounded throughout the diner. Knowing this would be Gabby's order, she smiled as she made her way over to the order window. Her feet became glued to the floor and her hand grabbed the bench when she saw who had entered the diner earlier. Sitting with Gabby, laughing and joking, was Jax and Roman. Roman's eyes shot up over Gabby's head and landed on hers. He winked at her and gave her a secret smile, before he turned back to Gabby and continued teasing her with Jax.

Melody took a deep breath in and tried to get her emotions under control. Over the last week, this guy had seen her naked, broken down all her barriers and learnt her most private secrets, and still he had the power to make her knees weak and her heart flutter. She wondered if she would ever get used to being near him. Forcing her feet to walk once more, she grabbed Gabby's order from the window and placed it in front of her.

"Hey, get your own!" she ordered, slapping Jax's hand away as he reached for one of her fries.

Melody laughed. "Are you staying long enough to eat?" she asked Jax and Roman. They looked at Gabby's food before nodding and placing their own orders.

"Make sure you spit in his." Gabby yelled out to Conrad the cook, while pointing at Roman. Conrad laughed at her and shook his head as he went about making their meals. Thankfully, everybody currently in the diner were regulars and knew that Gabby was only joking and that the cook would never do that. A few of them were even chuckling along with Jax.

"Hey, what did I do?" Roman asked, before stealing one of her fries. He was faster than Jax had been. Before she could say anything he popped it into his mouth and smiled wickedly at her as he chewed it. Gabby moved her plate out of his reach while she glared at him. This in turn however, allowed Jax to steal one.

"Hey!" She hissed, before she yelled out to Conrad once more. "Hurry up with their orders Conrad before they eat all of my food. As for what you have done, you, much like Melody here have not been around this last week. Both you and she have left me alone with this oaf." She continued as she elbowed Jax in the ribs.

"More like they have left me with you." He countered as he stole another Fry.

This time Gabby growled, before she smothered her fries in BBQ sauce.

"Now why did you go and do that? You ruined perfectly good fries." Jax grumbled. Gabby smiled and popped one in her mouth. Conrad yelled out that Roman and Jax's order was ready and Melody grabbed them and placed them in front of the boys. The next few minutes were sat in silence as each of her friends enjoyed their meal. Melody took that time to clean off some more tables and close out more customers. Soon she was back at the counter with her friends who were once again joking.

"Don't ask me, I haven't seen him either. Apart from a couple of nights before I went to work, he comes in after me and is gone before I'm up." Jax was saying to Gabby.

Gabby turned to Roman and raised her eyebrow. Melody held back her laugh when he simply mimicked her and took another bite of his burger.

Jax on the other hand let his out. "I know you don't think that will work brother? You know she will wait until you are done with your entire meal. You might as well answer her."

Gabby hadn't taken her eyes off of him and she was currently rapping her fingers on the counter. Roman finished his mouthful, wiped his mouth and then looked at her once more. "What am I supposed to be answering?"

"Where have you been?" Gabby asked once more through

gritted teeth.

"Ah yes, well that is an easy question to answer." Roman replied before once more taking a bite of his burger.

While Gabby's frustration grew, Melody's heartbeat picked up. Surely, he wasn't going to tell her the truth. She knew Gabby would be hurt if she found out about their relationship from anyone else but Melody.

"I have been visiting with my parents and helping with the business at the club." Roman answered as he wiped his hands on a napkin. Gabby narrowed her eyes at him for a brief minute then nodded. Melody smiled and shook her head, her friend could be a real ballbuster when she wanted to be. Roman didn't have to answer Gabby, but as Jax said they all knew it would be easier on everyone if he did. Roman would have been out of the deep end if Jax hadn't snorted. That sound brought Gabby's eyes flying straight to him.

"What?" he asked realising to late what he had done. Roman was shooting daggers across Gabby's head. Jax smiled apologetically.

"What do you know?" Gabby asked with the same perseverance she'd aimed at Roman.

"I don't know anything. Really." He added when she punched his arm.

"Then why did you snort?"

"I snorted because I don't believe a word of it. Like you I have been given the same answer for the last week when I ask where he has been. If you ask me I think he has a bit on the side and just doesn't want to share it with us."

It was Roman's turn to snort this time.

"Melody can you go to the storeroom and grab me a few things." Conrad asked through the order window handing her a piece of paper at the same time. Melody was torn, she wanted to stay and see how this conversation played out, but she knew that the diner took precedence.

"I'll be back in a minute guys." She informed her friends as she made her way to the far side of the counter where she would come to the side of the diner that led to the toilets and storeroom.

Melody was nearly to the end of the counter area, when she heard, "where are you going?" from Gabby. She didn't need to be told who she was talking too, as the next voice gave him away.

"Well if you must know, I am going to the bathroom. Do you want to follow to make sure?"

Melody's lips curved up in a small smile as Gabby mumbled her answer. Her nerves settled a little knowing that nothing would be said in her absence that would give her away. With her steps a little lighter Melody made her way down the hall to the storeroom, she punched in the code and then opened the door. She grabbed a basket from beside the door before she used her foot to jam the wedge in under the door to keep it open. She then made her way around the front shelves to the back shelves and started to place some of the items that Conrad needed in there. She was completely engrossed in what she was doing she didn't know that someone had entered behind her until she heard the click of the door shut.

Thoughts of her stalker rushed through Melody's mind. Her heart raced, she closed her eyes and tried to stay quiet, until she heard, "Melody?"

Her fear turned to happiness in beat of second. Placing the basket on one of the shelves she fixed her hair and then walked out from her hiding place. Leaning against the shelf she looked Roman up and down, "what brings you here?" she tried to ask coyly. But her husky voice gave her away. Roman was on her in the next minute. Her mouth was meshed with his and he had turned her so she was now pressed up against the wall.

"God I missed you last night." He whispered raggedly as his mouth moved from her mouth, down her neck to the top of her shirt. His hands had moved from their place on her hips, to under her shirt where his fingers were now playing with her nipples through her bra. She wanted nothing more than for him to take her, but she knew they didn't have the time.

"God I wish we had more time." He spoke her thoughts as his lips travelled up her neck once more.

"Tell me you can come over tonight." She begged grabbing his face between her hands bringing his lips back to hers where she kissed him passionately before bitting his lower one.

Roman growled deep in his throat. "I will make the time." Removing his hands from her shirt he grabbed hold of her hands and placed them above her head, capturing them in one of his strong ones.

"Until then I want to leave you with something to tie you over." He then deepened his kiss at the same time as he ran his hands down her stomach to the top of her shorts. There he flipped the button open.

Melody turned her head to the side, breaking the kiss before trying weakly to make him see sense. "Rome, we really don't have time…" But her words were cut off and replaced with a moan as three of his fingers entered her core. He used his thumb on her clit to drive her wild. She could feel her tension building within seconds and just as she exploded his mouth was back on hers capturing her scream. Roman removed his fingers from her then let her hands go. Grabbing his face she kissed him softly on the lips.

"You know you should think yourself lucky that I talked my parents out of putting security cameras in here." She joked.

Roman looked around the room just to make sure they

hadn't, before he placed his forehead on hers. "I guess I had better actually go to the bathroom and then get back out there before they come looking for me."

"Probably for the best. Gabby is already suspicious." Roman leaned forward and kissed her once more, before he started to make his way out of the storeroom. Opening the door he looked both ways, before he looked back at her and winked. "See you to tonight." He stated resolutely before he walked out of the room.

Melody leaned against the back wall and placed her fingers against her lips. She loved the taste of him, along with everything else. She could not deny it any longer. She had fallen so deep into the hole, just as Alice had, and she didn't see anyway of climbing back out.

Her heart was now in charge and it was leading her on a very dangerous dance indeed.

22

Melody was pulled from her dreams on Saturday morning by the incessant ringing of her phone. Turning over she groaned as she looked at the clock noticing that it was only nine. Thinking it was Roman calling she picked up the phone and answered without checking, "good morning handsome, about time you called."

"Well if I knew you were waiting on me to call I would have called much sooner. I thought seven would be a bit rude though."

Melody sighed as Jax's strong voice rang through the phone. She knew she had to play along otherwise he would be asking a million questions as to who she thought was calling. She really should remember to check her caller ID in future.

"And you know I would have killed you if you did." She sat up and leaned against her headboard.

Rubbing her hands over her face she waited for him to tell her why he was calling. "It's consideration like that, which makes me appealing to all the women." He joked.

"Oh and here I thought it was your prowess in the sack." Melody joked back.

Jax laughed before finally getting to the reason for his call, "look I was hoping I could steal you away from your family today to work a double shift. Two of our waitresses just called in sick and I could really use you."

Melody was wide awake now. The only reason she wasn't going into the bar was because Roman wasn't going to be there this weekend. After their little rendezvoused in the storeroom, he had informed the group that he was heading back to Denver the next morning for the weekend. Then later that night in bed he'd filled her in on the lead one of Jax's friends might have for him. He was going to meet up with his partner and they were going to go and check it out. Off the books of course. If anything came of the lead his partner would follow it up. It was then Melody promised Roman she would not go into the bar while he was not there. At the time she'd made the promise without even thinking. She knew he was just being cautious, but the truth of the matter was her parents didn't need her and she needed the money. Before she could change her mind she answered, "sure, what time do you need me there?"

"The normal. I will need you to help set up for the lunch rush, that is why I am calling so early."

Melody smiled. "Sure, I'll be there soon. Now let me go so I can get ready."

Jax didn't even offer a reply he simply hung up the phone. Melody laughed at that. He really must have been desperate. Throwing the blankets off she was about to get out of bed when her phone rang again.

"I promise I will be there on time." She answered into the phone.

"Okay, but who are you meeting?" Roman's sexy voice travelled through the phone.

Melody slapped her hand against her forehead. Hadn't she just gotten through berating herself for not checking caller ID before answering. Slowing down her racing heart she tried to think of a good excuse that would not involve lying to him. She was just going to omit some details.

"I am meeting Gabby and you know how she gets about punctuality." Roman laughed at that. Thankfully he didn't ask any more questions.

"So I guess this is a bad time?" Melody would have loved to have said no, but the truth of the matter was, she had to get ready for work.

"I'm sorry. I would love nothing more than to stay and talk to you, but you know what she's like." Melody made her way to the bathroom and turned on the shower. She heard his groan through the phone and smiled.

"Tell me you're naked." He whispered huskily.

"I can do you one better." She answered right before she stepped out of her nightie, took a photo and sent it to him.

"That should hold you over until you get back on Monday night." She teased.

"God woman, if you keep sending me pictures like that I will be back sooner."

Melody laughed. "Well maybe that was my plan. Now I really do have to go."

"Okay but give me a call when you are free."

"It probably won't be until tomorrow. Gabby has something planned for us."

There was a pause on the other end of the phone and Melody worried that she'd gone too far with her explanation.

"Mello."

The way he said her name was like a caress. She closed her eyes and answered.

"Yes."

"Be careful."

Her heart swelled with love. "I promise." She answered. She knew she was wishing for too much, but when he showed concern like that she could almost believe that he loved her as she loved him. She had no idea why a lump formed in her throat, but she knew that if she didn't get off the phone to him soon, she was in jeopardy of telling him exactly how she felt. Swallowing, trying to get rid of the lump she spoke once more. "I have…" her voice came out squeaky though, so she cleared it and tired again.

"You okay?" He asked concerned.

"Yeah sorry, just a frog. As I was saying I have to go Gabby will be texting me soon if I don't get a move on."

"Alright, talk to you soon Sweetheart." With that he hung up. She knew he used the term Sweetheart as a general greeting to most of the women close to him, but when he said it to her she liked to think of it as an endearment. Stepping into the hot water, she let it flow over her body and wash away all the romantic feelings she was having towards him. In a few weeks they were going to go their separate ways and it was time that she started to focus once more on her career. It was the reason she'd chosen to work tonight and even though she was not following Roman's request to a tee, she was not going to dismiss his concerns.

No she was going to make sure that even though she was going into work, she would never let herself be alone. As Melody washed she made a plan to always be in sight of Jax and she would even get him to walk her out after her shift. She knew he would not question her as to the reason why, he had done it many times before. Finishing up her shower and turning the water off, Melody grabbed her towel and stepped out. Now that she had a plan in place she could go to work feeling a little safer. Nothing was going to happen to her as long as she stayed near people. What Melody didn't know was that she had not counted on a decision being made that would do the exact opposite.

One decision that would change her world forever.

* * *

* * *

As was the norm the Saturday lunch rush was hectic. Melody had made it to the bar with plenty of time to help Gabby set up. She had been ecstatic when Melody walked through the door and let her know that she was working the double with her. They had even made plans for Gabby to go home with Melody and spend the night.

Melody was happy about that as it would add some credence to the lie she'd told Roman and it would give her the extra protection she needed. It was now four o'clock and Melody was in the lunchroom on her break. Her and Gabby never took their breaks together as Jax preferred to have at least one of them on duty at all times. As he put it they were his best two waitresses.

"Hey Sweets, it's good to see you back." Honey stated as she walked into the lunchroom and hugged Melody where she sat. Melody hugged the arms that was currently wrapped around her upper torso and patted it with her hand to let her friend know she was also happy to see her.

"Missed you too Girl." Melody replied. She had expected Honey to sit down with her, instead she walked over to the lockers while mumbling. "Oh before I forget I have something for you." She opened her locker and reached up to the top shelf pulling down an envelope. Once Honey's locker was closed she walked back to the table and placed the envelope with Melody's name on it in front of her. Melody looked at the envelope with confusion, before she picked it up and opened it. What she saw had her mouth dropping open.

"Where? How? Why?" she couldn't get a sentence out. Melody didn't even know where to start.

Honey laughed. "That is the money from last Saturday night. I didn't get a chance to give it to you. So I put it in my locker. I have been waiting all week for you to come in. Don't worry, if you hadn't come in this weekend I was going to bring it to you."

Melody looked back at her friend, her eye's still wide, before she once more looked back at the money. "Are you sure this is all mine." She asked as she pulled it out and started counting.

"Sure is Sweets, you did good." Honey sat across from her and winked.

Melody finished counting the money and placed it back in the envelope. There was two and half thousand dollars there. Some of the men had tipped as big as one hundred-dollar notes. "Is this normal?" she asked Honey, still unable to take her eyes off the envelope.

Honey stood from the table and walked over to the sink. "Sure is girl. Some nights you might even get more depending on how big the crowed is. Tonight seems to be one of those nights." She leaned against the bench and looked meaningfully at Melody. When Melody didn't hear any more from her friend she looked up and noticed the way she was looking at her.

"Oh no, I am not doing that again. Last time I almost got busted."

She wasn't going to let anyone know that Roman had indeed busted her. That was going to be their little secret.

"Suite yourself. Just think though, one more night like that and you would be one step closer to that dream."

Melody hated how Honey was playing her. She couldn't do it even if she wanted to. She had promised Roman that she would never do something like that again. On the other hand Honey was right. Another night like that would almost guarantee her the spot at Juilliard and with only a few more days left before the money was due, Melody was having a hard time saying no.

"You know you want to." Honey coaxed as she walked

over to the table.

Melody looked down at the money once before meeting her friends stare.

"Come on, live on the edge a little, you know you like it."

Melody didn't say anything, she knew she couldn't argue with her friends comment. The truth of the matter was, she was right, Melody did enjoy living on the edge. Looking down at the money once more her conscience wrestled with the what to do. She needed the money to go to Juilliard and she enjoyed dancing. Yet, she had made Roman a promise never to strip again.

You also promised you wouldn't work here without him.

"Alright I will do it." Melody decided. Roman would never find out that she'd done it as he was currently in Denver.

"Oh yay." Honey cheered as she jumped around the room.

"What has you so happy?" Gabby asked as she walked into the lunchroom to grab something out of her locker.

Honey winked at Melody before answering, "just excited that Melody is working here again."

"Hell so am I. Tonight is going to be crazy I can feel it already." Gabby answered as she made her way back to the door. Melody laughed at her not so subtle way of telling her that she needed her help now. "I am glad I am here too. I'll see ya back out there soon."

"Don't leave it too long. I could use some experience out there."

With that she was gone. Melody shook her head at Gabby's dig at the inexperienced waitresses that were called in on busy nights like tonight. They were not bad, it was just that they could only handle a few tables at a time so Jax usually placed them on the smaller areas. The larger areas were left to Gabby and her.

Melody stood up and placed the money in her locker

before making sure it was well and truly locked.

"So I will see you in my dressing room at eight-thirty?" Honey confirmed.

Melody placed her head against the locker. "This had better be the last time. If I keep feigning headaches I am sure Jax and Gabby will have me at the doctors before you can say 'stripper.'"

Honey laughed before she left the room. As the silence of the room fell around her Melody let the knowledge of the decision she had just made settle in. She should have been feeling fear and guilt, instead she was feeling excitement. The memories of her last dance and what it had led to fuelled that excitement and before long all the worries had left her and she was now looking forward to the night ahead. As she walked out of the room and back into the fray of the bar, the little devil on her shoulder kept on convincing her that she was doing the right thing. It had even convinced her that hers and Roman's worries about the stalker getting to her were not confounded.

Little did she know that the little nagging voice in the back of her head that was trying to warn her of the danger, was the voice that she should have been listening too. Because tonight, unbeknownst to her, the choice to ignore that voice was going to get her into more trouble than she'd bargained for.

<h1 style="text-align:center">23</h1>

It was hard to find good help. 'The plan' was not working this time. The parents of the current 'Denver Dancer' kidnapping were not playing ball. Normally within twenty-four hours of the ransom being made the parents of said girl would pay and then her misery would end. In this instance that damn detective and his partner had gotten to them first. Now a decision had to be made.

The decision to take Melody all rode on whether to wait for the ransom or to kill the girl.

For 'The Plan' to work and for him to stay under the radar he needed to make sure that everything he did was constant. One wrong move is what would get him caught. He was already risking things by being here. Looking down at his phone, he sent off a quick message. There it was done. The parents would have one last chance to pay the ransom and if they didn't she would die. She was going to die anyway, them not paying the ransom sooner only prolonged the inevitable.

Maybe this time if the ransom didn't get paid he would make sure that the body was never found. That would send a message to anyone who thought they were smarter than the 'Denver Dancer' Serial Killer. He was already ahead of the game and knew something that the Police had never suspected.

With that thought in his mind and a smile on his face he walked into the bar and went straight to his usual seat. He had been coming in her for over a week now, scoping out all of the exits and security cameras. He had planned out Melody's kidnapping down to the wire. Now he just had to figure out a way to get her outside by herself. The bar had a lot of camera's inside, but for some reason they had none outside.

What he had planned would change all that.

Sitting down he waited for the young waitress to come over and take his drink order then he got ready for the show. He had enjoyed watching the dancer Honey last week, she had stirred things in him that only Melody had before. So he decided that he would treat himself again and then finish with Melody. Tonight was going to be a good night. He licked his lips and rubbed himself to relieve the hard on that was now pressing against his pants just from thinking about what he would do to her. He had planned to remove his hand, but the lights dimmed and the dancer was introduced. Turning himself deeper into the booth he gained a little more privacy and continued to rub as the dancer started moving.

His eyes never left her, even when the waitress brought his drink. He did however have the mind not to draw attention to himself as a perv and removed his hand from himself when he noticed her approaching out of his peripheral vision. As the music continued and the dancer shed her clothes, everything around him faded away and all he noticed was her.

He became mesmerised the way he did when he watched Melody and as her top came off and her breasts swayed to the music, he could almost invasion that it was Melody on stage and she was dancing just for him.

At one stage in his fantasy he even imagined that her eyes met his across the room and the way she was dancing was her way of beckoning him to take her and make her his. Never before with any of the other girls had he felt this strongly for someone. Melody was not like all of the other victims, no she had become his own little fantasy.

Oh she would die like the rest of them, but first he would relish hearing her scream his name. When the music finished and the dancer left the stage, he could no longer contain his excitement. Soon it would be time to have her. Licking his lips he decided he would go and get the tools he needed out of the car and that would give him time to settle his need. His manhood was aching with how hard it was.

Standing he made his way out of the bar. Walking out into the night air, he took in a deep breath and smiled a wicked smile. His body was tingling with excitement, he knew she was here tonight he'd heard her name mentioned when he walked in. Now he just had to wait for the perfect moment.

Walking to his car he opened the passenger side door, reached into the glove box and retrieved the cloth he had already soaked with chloroform. Closing the door he leaned against the car for a few moments and went over 'The Plan' in his head. He had everything ready to go, all he needed now was to get her outside on her own. Once he did that the rest of the night would fall into place.

His heart beat with excitement as he moved away from his car and started to walk back into the bar, his step a little lighter. Then as if it was meant to be, the object of his desire, walked out of the bar and straight into his arms.

It was as though God was gift wrapping her for him. Someone was letting him know that he was on the right path.

Melody had to die.

Now it was time to go all in. Lifting his head up he plastered on his award-winning smile and let the rest of his charm work for him. He loved being him, he thought to himself as he looked into the smiling eyes of the woman who had just sealed her own fate.

Life was grand indeed.

24

As Melody rushed off the stage and down the hall to the room where Honey was waiting for her she half expected to be caught once more. The whole way through the dance, Melody had scanned the bar for Roman, but as it had been earlier he was not there. Pushing the door open she was greeted by the open arms of her friend.

"See I told you everything would be alright this time." Honey cooed as she helped Melody remove the wig and makeup.

"I still can't get over how much fun that is." Melody whispered as she stared into the mirror.

"You know you don't have to stop." Honey offered.

Melody laughed as she stood up from the seat she had been sitting in and proceeded to get back into her uniform. Honey readied herself for her later show. "I think I have tempted fate enough to last me a lifetime. From now on I will get the rest of the money I need through tips."

Honey shook her head and smiled. "It's a shame, you are really talented and could make a lot of dough."

"I'll keep it in mind if Juilliard falls through." Melody quipped back as she opened the door. She checked both ways before turning back to her friend.

"Thanks for everything Girl."

Honey blew her a kiss, "anytime Sweets. Now get out there before someone comes looking for you."

"Copy that." Melody shut the door behind her and headed out to the main room once more. Her heart was still racing when she reached the bar and she realised that she hadn't had a moment to catch her breath. She couldn't go back to the lunchroom as that would raise suspicions. Looking around trying to figure out what she was going to do, her eyes landed on the door as a new customer entered.

That was it.

"Hey Dee, you ready to swap over?" Gabby asked coming to stand beside her.

Melody knew that if she wanted a moments break she would have to take it now. "Do you mind if I quickly run out to the car? I realised that I was supposed to text Mom that I was staying late tonight and my phone is out there. You know she won't go to sleep until she's heard from me."

Gabby smiled, "sure, but be quick I am starving."

Melody thanked her friend, promised to be as quick as a flash and then headed for the door. Melody sighed in relief as the fresh cool night air hit her skin. The sounds of the bar behind her melted away to a din when the door closed.

"Excuse us Miss." Two older gentlemen commented as they waited for her to move out of the way of the door. Stepping to the side she offered them a smile before looking towards the end of the building. She guessed she had about five minutes before Gabby came looking for her, but that was fine, five minutes was all she needed to get her nerves under control.

Placing her hands in the pockets of her apron, Melody walked towards the end of the building to the left, her plan was to move out of the way of people entering while she gathered herself. Reaching the end of the pathway Melody looked out into the darkness of the carpark, this brought back Roman's warning. Melody shivered, she had been so focused on calming her nerves that she'd completely forgotten about where she was. Looking around, her nervousness came back but for an entirely different reason.

Out here, she was alone.

Although she could still see the door, very few people were now entering and leaving and it would only take a quick minute for something to happen.

How could she have been so stupid. Roman was right, she was reckless.

Melody knew she needed to get back inside and soon. She had to remember to stay around people. Turning on her heel she made the first step to go back to work, but a voice off to the side stopped her. Her heart was in her throat as all sorts of devious scenarios played out in her mind. The moment her eyes lit on the person leaning against their car, he heart rate lowered and while she was surprised she was grateful to see a friendly face.

"Thank God, now I don't have to go looking for you."

Melody smiled at her acquaintance. Although she knew him, she was not overly close with him, and for some reason his tone seemed a bit off. It was as though his words had a different meaning. Melody shook her head, she was being ridiculous, the events of the night and her stalker were adding to her unease. "What brings you all the way down here?" She asked as looked back towards the door, she couldn't help it, the need to get back inside was building.

"Are you alright?" He asked.

Melody shook her head and plastered a smile on her face. "Sure, I am meant to be getting back to work that's all. I am sure my colleague will come looking for me soon."

Her acquaintance smiled and stood up from his seated position. "Well I guess I had better hurry up and tell you the reason for my coming here." Melody watched as he started to walk towards the back of his car.

"Professor Klein sent me down here to get some papers signed by you. Apparently she needs them pronto."

His voice dropped lower as he lifted the boot of his car and disappeared behind it.

"It will be easier for you to come and sign them back here as you can lean on my computer." He coaxed, leaning his head to the side of the boot so she could see him. Melody once more looked back towards the door of the bar. Roman's warning playing in her head.

"I can't leave until I have your signature." He added bringing her attention back to him.

The smile that was currently gracing his face put her at ease. She was letting her paranoia run wild, she had known this guy for over two years and if Professor Klein had needed any papers signed she *would* have sent him. It all made sense.

Pushing the bad feelings she had down, she stepped off of the pavement and made her way to the back of the car, she let out a sigh of relief when she saw a bunch of papers sitting on top of his computer. He offered her another smile as he handed her a pen.

"So this all seems pretty official." He commented as Melody leaned over the tailgate and went to sign the documents. It took her mind a moment to realise that the paperwork she was looking at appeared to be an assignment. Her eyebrows furrowed as she spoke, "I think you..." her words were cut off as a piece of cloth was placed over her mouth.

Melody panicked, she opened her mouth to scream but that just allowed him to shove some of the material into her mouth and manoeuvre it so it was also covering her nose. Melody struggled to remove the hand covering her mouth and nose, but his hold was too strong. The sweet smell and taste that coated the cloth now permeated her senses and was making her lightheaded and sleepy. She knew she had to do something drastic.

Melody kicked out with her heel and connected with his shin, it was enough to get her a momentary reprieve. The hand holding the cloth loosened enough to allow Melody the chance to move her head to the side and scream. The only problem was her voice was weak from having something shoved in her mouth and there was no-one within earshot that would have heard it.Melody knew her best hope was to make a run for it. Using her shoulder she shoved her assailant to the side and on wobbly legs she tried to make it to the door of the bar. Using her hand to steady herself against the car Melody pushed her way forward. She had only reached the passenger side window when a large weight hit her from behind. "You Bitch." He hissed as he rolled her over.

Melody whimpered and tried to punch him when she saw him bringing the cloth down to her mouth once more.

"Why are you doing this?" she rasped right before he placed the cloth over her nose and mouth again.

"You will find out soon my Dove. You are mine and not even your detective can save you now."

Melody continued to struggle for a few moments more, but as her lids grew heavier and her mind foggier, everything became clearer. Her stalker had finally shown himself, and there was no-one around who was going to be able to save her. As Melody faded off into the darkness that called her name, her final thoughts were of one person.

Roman.

* * *

Melody groaned as she placed a hand against her head. It felt like someone had taken a sledgehammer to it, it was pounding that hard. Melody tried to sit up and figure out what had happened. At first she thought she might have drunk too much with Gabby last night, but as she sat up her stomach lurched, it was then she realised she was lying on something hard in complete darkness. Melody reached her hand out to feel around her, only to realise she was touching something cold. Running her hand further around the area she was laying her memories flooded back. Tears started to fall down her cheek as she lay there trying to figure out what to do.

Her captor had locked her in the boot of his car. The only good thing Melody could make of the situation was that the car didn't appear to be moving. But that was the only thing. Melody had no way of telling how long or far they had driven, or even in which direction. For all she knew they could be in New Mexico.

This was bad. This was very bad.

Melody continued to feel around the back of the car hoping to find something she could use as a weapon against her attacker if and when he came back. She could not get over the fact that it had been 'him.' It all made sense now though, how he had gotten access to her personal records, how he always seemed to know where she was. Melody tried to think back over the last few months to determine when his fixation had started, but there was nothing. Nothing about their friendship had seemed off.

It dawned on her then. The 'Denver Dancer' Serial Killer. It all made sense as to how he was getting away with it. It had been under their noses the whole time. Melody's attention was brought back to the present when she heard footsteps coming towards the back of the car. At the same time her hand landed on something solid that moved. Not knowing what she held, but knowing it was better than nothing, Melody picked it up and brought it closer to her body. She knew she would need to surprise him so she did the only thing she could think of. She pretended to still be unconscious.

It took all of her might not to flinch as the lid opened and the cool air rushed forward. She felt some relief to know that he hadn't buried her alive. Melody waited for the right moment to attack, when his hands reached down for her she took her shot. Lifting her hand up she swung out with whatever she had picked up and felt a rush of elation as it connected with him and knocked him to the ground.

Melody didn't waste any time, groggily she sat up and climbed out of the car as quickly as she could. Neither her stomach nor her head liked the sudden movement, she wanted to throw up and pass out all at the same time. She stumbled, grabbed the edge of the car and stopped for a minute to get her bearings. As her mind cleared she came to realise that he had brought her to the motel that was just down the road from her own house.

They were still in Pagaso Springs.

With that in mind Melody started running, she ran as hard and as fast as she could to the safety of her home. When Melody heard him calling her name behind her she picked up the pace. She needed to get inside and ring 911. She would not alert her parents to what was going on as she did not want to see them hurt.

Melody was certain that this man would harm anything that stood in the way of what he wanted, and what he wanted was her. The minutes seemed to tick by as she ran home, what should have only taken four minutes seemed to take four hours, but soon her house came into view. Melody let out a small whimper of hope, her head was still hurting and with each step she took it became harder not to throw up.

As her foot hit the bottom step that lead to her apartment, Melody chanced a look behind her only to see him striding purposely across the lawn towards her. Gone was the good-natured man she had known and in his place was a monster. Melody reached into the pockets of her shorts and gave a sigh of relief that her keys were still there. She always kept them on her in case she had to get something from her car.

Without another thought Melody rushed up the stairs and tried to open her door, but as luck would have it, it was not as easy as it usually was. She was finding it hard to get the key in the hole and when she looked and saw that he was halfway to her stairs her panic started to take over. Melody was crying and swearing as she tried to open the door and keep an eye on where he was, finally the key slid in and she was able to open the door. Melody rushed in and slammed it shut behind her. She leaned against it and looked around for what to do next.

Melody knew she didn't have long before he reached her and when she heard his feet hit the bottom step followed by his singing she knew there was one hope left. There was only one person who knew what was going on.

With that in mind Melody reached for the phone that was sitting on the side table and dialled Roman's number.

"Pick up, pick up, pick up." She cried as she heard the footsteps getting closer.

"Are you ready for me?" She heard through the door just as Roman picked up.

"Hello." He answered.

Melody didn't bother about pleasantries she simply screamed into the phone, "Roman he's here. Help," at the same time the door crashed back against the frame.

"Honey I'm home," her captor remarked snidely. She could hear Roman shouting into he phone asking her all sorts of questions but the fear that was running through her body would not allow her to speak. All she could see was the evil look that entered his eyes as he reached up and ran a hand through the blood that was now trickling down over his left eye. That look made her fear that not even Roman would be able to save her.

She clutched the phone in her hand close to her ear as he looked from her to it. "That is going to cost you." He hissed as he came forward and grabbed her around the throat. Using all of his strength he lifted her off the floor.

Melody dropped the phone as she tried to pry his hands from around her throat, but this time she had no strength left. As the world around her darkened once more, her last sight was of her captors wicked smile and the sound of Roman screaming her name through the phone. Her final sight was her captor bring something shiny towards her head, before pain sent her reeling into total darkness.

It had all been for nothing.

25

Roman's tires squealed as he sped into the carpark of the bar, he had been on his way back to Pagosa Springs and was just outside of the town's limit when the phone call had come through. Looking down he noticed it was a private number. Thinking it was going to be Warren he picked it up and answered normally. The sound of Melody screaming through the phone had his blood running cold. Roman quickly pulled his car over on the side of the road and tried to make sense of what she was saying.

"Who is there?" Roman asked, knowing full well who she was taking about. What Roman was looking for was a name. If he could just get the name of the bastard he knew he could finally capture him, but Melody was too hysterical.

"Baby you have to talk to me." He tried to calm her but Melody had gone silent and that was when he heard the bastard. Roman listened astutely to what was happening on the other end of the phone, trying to get any indication of where they had gone, but all he could hear was a murmured voice and noises that sounded like someone struggling. When the phone finally went dead Roman hadn't wasted anytime getting back on the road and getting to the bar. He needed to find out what had happened from when he had last spoken to

Jax and the phone call.

As he drove along the highway as fast as he could without breaking too many laws, the sound of the perps voice kept playing over in his mind. It wasn't so much what he said that caught Roman's attention, it was more how he said it.

Roman could have sworn he'd heard his voice somewhere before.

Parking the car Roman didn't even bother locking it, he simply jumped out and started running to the bar. It was pure dumb luck that had him back here. He hadn't been planning on coming back until tomorrow, but the moment Jax had told him that Melody had agreed to work tonight he had a bad feeling. Giving his partner all the information he had gained from Jax's friend, he had hightailed it back to Pagosa Springs. He was not going to be happy until he had Melody in his sights again. He only wished now that he hadn't left.

What had she been thinking? Roman had warned her to stay around people. Pushing the door open he paused for a brief second to see if he could find Jax. It didn't take him long to spot Jax and Gabby having a heated discussion at the bar. He didn't have time to explain to them what was going on, he needed answers and there was only one way he was going to get them. Roman made a beeline to the back of the bar and the area that would take him to Warren's office.

"Roman, thank God you're here, we need…" Gabby's words trailed off as he kept on walking. He knew that Jax would follow. Roman didn't bother knocking when he reached his destination he simply threw open the door and blurted, "I need to see your security tapes."

"Well hello to you too Rome, please tell me you know who our blackmailer is?"

Roman's eyes furrowed as he tried to focus on Warren, "what? Oh yeah I do know but that is not what I need the tapes for. I need to check…."

"Roman, Melody is missing." Jax and Gabby said in unison as they burst through the door.

Warren stood up quickly and looked at Roman. Roman gave him a slight nod letting him know he already knew. "I think he already knows guys. Here." He pushed a few keys on his computer and the video of the bar was up and running.

"How do you rewind them?" Roman asked. Warren showed him how to work the system and soon Roman was rewinding back through the night. He went right back to the point when Melody started work that day, and as he watched her go about her duties and the thought of never seeing her smiling face again, the rage he was feeling increased.

He was going to kill this guy.

Nothing seemed out of the ordinary until she went into the staff quarters around eight-thirty. Roman knew when her breaks were, so he had expected her to reappear, but after five minutes and no Melody he started to wonder if this was when she'd disappeared.

"Here." He said stopping the tape. "Did you see her after this?" He turned and asked Gabby.

Both Jax and Gabby nodded. "Sure, that was when she had a headache. She was gone for about an hour and a half but was back in time for her next shift."

Roman groaned. Now a new kind of niggling feeling was playing in the back of his mind. Surely she wouldn't have been that stupid he thought to himself. As Roman continued to play the tape, he paid special attention to the dancer, and low and behold there was Melody on stage doing what she had promised she would never do again. He only hoped that the bastard who had her hadn't figured it out. Something like that was known to send men like him over the edge, all rationality left them. This made them twice as dangerous.

"FUCK!" Roman swore unable to control his rage any

longer.

"Did you find something?" Gabby asked tears forming in her eyes. Roman knew that they understood it was bad from his behaviour.

"No sorry, this is just frustrating. Did Melody ever tell you about her stalker?" Roman didn't want to frighten Gabby any more than he had to, but he needed to know if she knew anything that might help them.

Gabby's hand flew to her mouth at the same time the brothers said "what?"

Roman paid them no mind and continued to look at Gabby. She shook her head no as a tear feel down her cheek.

"Rome, what is going on?" Jax asked sitting down in one of the chairs opposite him.

"Look I don't have time to explain in depth, all you need to know is that Melody has had a stalker for a few months now and I am pretty sure he has her."

All three of his friends started shouting questions at him. Sticking his fingers in his mouth he let a whistle rip through the room. All three became quite.

"As I said, I will explain everything later. Right now we have to find Melody. Is there anything you can tell me about tonight when she came back on shift?"

Roman was trying to get as much information as he could without looking at the tapes. Just knowing it was her on stage was ripping his heart out. He was angry at her for not listening, but he was also angry that he may never get to tell her how he felt.

"No, nothing." Jax said in a flat tone. Roman could tell he was in shock.

"Hang on, yes. Right before she went missing she said she had to get something from her car. She never came back. I went outside to check for her, but her car was still here I just thought she was somewhere in the bar." Gabby answered through her tears.

"Oh God, that was when he got her wasn't it?" She added.

"I should have gone with her." Jax echoed, placing his head in his hands.

Roman agreed with him, but he knew he couldn't blame his friend for this. Roman had simply asked him to watch out for her. This was his fault. He never should have left Melody and maybe if he had told Jax what was going on none of this would be happening. There was no point assigning blame, all they could do was find the clue that would allow them to find her and fast.

"What time was this around?" Roman asked getting back to the task at hand. He knew he needed to put friend and lover aside. What Melody needed was Detective Fox.

"Um, it would have been around tenish." Jax answered as Gabby took the seat beside him.

"Alright now we have a time frame we just need an unsub." Roman stated going back to the footage.

It was time for him to start acting like the detective he was. He already had the guys voice, now he just needed a profile to go with it. Then he would be able to piece the puzzle together. Roman scanned the camera footage and found one of the cameras that was placed at the entrance of the Bar.

"Shouldn't you be looking inside. It is not like the guy will have taken her right at the door." Warren queried looking over Roman's shoulder.

"This will narrow the search down. It will give us an idea of who left the bar before she did."

"How do you even know they were in the bar? Maybe they were simply waiting outside." Gabby added in a small voice.

Roman knew his friends were only trying to help, but he had been chasing guys like this his entire career. What he had come to learn about these creations was that they loved to play with their prey. They would watch them and taunt them from afar, showing their victims who was in charge. They also loved to showcase how much smarter they were than the police. Roman was one hundred percent certain the creep had been here. He rewound the tape to just before Melody would have gone outside. The group of four watched on, Jax and Gabby having now joined Roman and Warren on the other side of the table. The only person they saw exit or enter the bar was Gabby and then a few men came in after her. They watched a few seconds more as Melody looked around and then walked off to her right out of sight of the cameras.

"What was she thinking?" Roman hissed under his breath.

"We need to extend the cameras to the end of the building." Jax offered to Warren as an afterthought.

Warren nodded his head in agreement. Roman stared at the computer screen trying to find any little bit of information that could lead him to his man. When Melody did not re-appear, Roman started to lose hope, especially when he saw himself bolting through the door. This was definitely the time she had been kidnapped.

"What do we do now?" Gabby asked.

Roman sat back in the chair that Warren had vacated to sooth Gabby. He knew without a doubt that the bastard would have been in here.

Perhaps he went out earlier.

Roman quickly started rewinding the tapes to as far back as half an hour before Melody went outside. He knew it was going to yield multiple perps, but too many was better than none.

The foursome watched, ruling out perspective suspects. Time and time again Roman paused and rewound the tapes. He could hear the frustration in Jax's voice when he asked. "How many times are you going to go over the same footage? Maybe he went out earlier."

Roman simply shook his head. This was what he did on a

daily bases. Sometime him and Shale would sit and go over the same footage for hours. Roman was sure the unsub was in there somewhere. Once more he rewound the tape and began to watch at a slower pace.

"Bingo." Roman shouted, pausing the video and pointing at the screen.

"Who?" Gabby asked, focusing on the screen trying to see what Roman saw.

"There is four of them. I am sure someone would have noticed four guys taking one girl." Jax commented, adding to Gabby's confusion.

Roman paused the tape before rewinding it so he could watch it again. He needed to make sure.

Oh yes this was his guy.

While everyone else saw a group of four drunken guys leaving the bar, Roman saw three drunk men and one killer.

"See how this guy seems to hang to the back of the group?" Everyone nodded and continued to stare at the screen.

"Well that tells me he is not part of the group. He also appears a lot more sober than the rest of them."

"Maybe he is their designated driver." Warren thought to add.

Roman shook his head. "No I am sure he is not with them, he simply followed them out, using them as part of his cover. This guy is smart he knows that we would be looking for one guy."

"Are you sure?" Jax asked. Roman could hear the tightness in his voice. He knew is friend was as worried about Melody as he was so he could forgive them their lack of confidence.

"Oh yeah I am sure, add that to the fact that he is wearing a cap at night and keeps on looking around him as though he has something to hide almost guarantees it."

As the others discussed what to do next Roman looked for more footage of the guy. He went back to the night that

Melody had first danced. He remembered she had gotten a message from her stalker that night, it suggested that the perp had been watching her. Roman smiled a wicked smile, now that he knew what his suspect looked like it wouldn't take him long to find the creep. All Roman needed was to get a good look at him and see if he could figure out who he was. Once Roman had a picture of the guy he knew he could link him with the voice. Finally, after a few minutes Roman found the footage he needed. It didn't take long for him to find the lone stranger walk in and wait for a table. Most of the time he kept his head down and barley spoke to anyone. The more Roman watched the man, the more he felt as though he knew him. Like the voice on the phone, his profile seemed vaguely familiar.

Roman wanted it to be Solomon, but something just wasn't adding up here.

"Hey, I know that guy. He was here about a week ago. He was really rude." Gabby intruded on Roman's thoughts. She was just in time to see herself walk up to his table and take his order.

Roman spun around in his chair to look at her. "Can you describe him?"

Gabby shook her head. "Not really, we were busy that night and as you can see on the video he kept his hat down over his eyes. I thought it was strange but we get strange people in here all of the time. I just served him and then left, if I was honest he creeped me the hell out. I should have paid more attention" Gabby burst into tears once more. Warren stepped forward and grabbed her into his embrace. "We all should have." He added.

"You need to start telling us about these guys." Jax added.

He was standing quietly off to the side, his face solemn as they all considered what could be happening to Melody. Roman faced the monitor and started to rewind it further back in the night, trying to find the time when he entered the bar. He was hoping he might be able to get a look at his face. What he found, was something else. It was not enough of his face to get a direct match, but it was enough of a front on to get the symbol on his jacket.

The bastard went to Denver University.

It all made sense now. The voice, the profile, Roman had met this guy, and not that long ago. Now he just had to jog his own memory of who it could be. Pausing the tapes on that frame Roman pulled out his cell and called his partner. "Do you know what time it is?" Shale asked as he picked up the phone.

"Don't even pretend you were sleeping. I know you're at the precinct. Listen I have a situation, I think our killer is here and he has a new victim."

Roman waited for that to sink in.

"How can you be certain it is him?" Shale asked.

"Same ammo. He has been stalking her for a few months and she is a dancer." Roman could feel all of his friends eyes on him.

"Damn. Sorry Rome." He heard through the phone. "What do you need from me?"

"We may have finally gotten the break we've been waiting for. I have video surveillance of the suspect we think may have taken her and on top of that I heard his voice tonight. I am sure it someone from the university."

"Is it Solomon?" Shale asked, his voice getting a little more excited.

Roman took a deep breath. They had been chasing Solomon for so long now, Roman was kind of hoping it was him, but he knew he needed to rule out all other possibilities fist. He couldn't let himself become single minded, Melody's life depended on it.

"I am not quite sure. What I am sure about is that the

unsub would have come into the station the day I left. I'd made too much of a ruckus on campus. He would have been dying to know what we had on him. His voice and profile seem familiar to me, what I need from you is a list of everyone who signed into the precinct that day."

"On it."

Roman waited patiently on the other end as Shale got the names. While he wanted the process to move faster, Roman knew that precision was key. If they rushed any part of this it could mean Melody's life.

"Got them, you ready?"

"Shoot."

Roman noted all the names of anyone form the university who had visited that day, then one name jumped out at him.

"Son of a bitch. It was under our noses the whole time."

He wrote the name on a post it note from Warren's desk and handed it to Jax. Go and ring every motel/hotel in town or just outside of town and find out if anyone by this name has checked in.

"We have him." Roman spoke excitedly into the phone. This had been the first break they'd had in the case in over a year.

"Rome, just so you know your friend might not have long. We got another call not long ago upping the deadline on the current missing girl. They have warned that if the parents don't pay up by morning their daughter will be returned piece by piece over the next year."

Roman slammed his fist down on the table.

"Hang on, how long ago did you say the call came in?"

There was a pause on the end of the phone.

"Just before ten." Shale answered.

Roman got Gabby to point out where the perp might have been sitting inside and once Roman found him, he fast forwarded until he left the bar. Not once did he pick up the phone.

"That's impossible." He mumbled into the phone.

"What?" Everyone, including Shale asked.

"He never touched his phone." Roman answered to the room and Shale as a whole.

"Did someone actually talk to him?" Roman asked confirming that it hadn't been a pre-set text.

Shale breathed deeply into the phone. "Yes. I took the call myself. Maybe he isn't our guy."

Roman was shaking his head, "no he is our guy, he has motive and opportunity. No, something else is going on here. I just have to figure out what. Shale I'm going to send you the name along with the screenshot from the bar. I want you to go through all of the evidence we have on these cases and see if anything pops up with this guy. He is connected somehow we just have to find it."

"Copy. Now you go and find your friend, hopefully this is one girl we can save."

Roman hung up the phone just as Jax came rushing back into the office.

"Got it, he is staying at the motel at the end of Main street." Roman didn't need to be told twice. He was out of his chair and out the door before anyone even had a chance to react.

* * *

Pulling up outside of the motel, Roman looked around while Jax ran inside to talk to the owner. It wasn't long before he was back with the room number. Running around the back they found the room they were looking for. But no-one was there.

Roman looked around the parking lot trying to figure out where they could have gone.

"Where is the bastard?" Jax asked beside him.

Roman shook his head indicating that he had no idea.

Roman needed to start thinking like a detective and stop letting his personal feelings get in the way.

This is just another case.

He kept the mantra going in his head trying to get into the right frame of mind. Looking back to the entrance he retraced his steps back to his car. He looked up and down the street before turning back to the car park of the motel. That was when he saw it. A few doors down from where Jax was currently standing a car was parked, everything about it looked normal, everything that was except the slightly ajar boot. It was a newer car and Roman would bet his money it was a rental. Running full speed towards the car he prayed that he was in time. He hoped that Melody was both in the boot, but also not. If she was in there without the unsub around it could only mean one thing. Roman placed his hand on the lid, took a deep breath and threw it open.

His breath left his body when he saw it was empty. There was no sign of Melody, but maybe there was a clue as to what happened to her. Turning the torch on his phone on, Roman shone it inside and looked around. Thankfully there was no blood, but that still didn't mean the bastard hadn't hurt her. Roman then moved his light over the bumper and around the outside of the car. He had no idea what he was looking for, he just needed something.

"What's that?" Jax asked leaning down and reaching under the car near the right-hand tire.

Leaning back on his heels he brought forward a pole from the car jack. Roman grabbed it from Jax and examined it carefully. "Good girl." He stated. There on the end of the pole was the tiniest bit of blood. Roman was not one to jump to conclusion, but with he knew instinctively that Melody would not go down without a fight. He had also taught the girls a long time ago that if they ever found themselves in trouble they were to use anything on hand to fight their way out. Roman hoped against hope that the blood on the bar was that of the unsubs and that his DNA was enough to connect this arsehole with the other murders.

He wasn't sure how the arsehole was connected with the 'Denver Dancer' Serial Killer, but Roman was positive he was.

"I need something I can bag this in for evidence." Roman stated to Jax.

"On it." He offered before he ran into the office of the motel.

With the bar in his hand Roman made his way back into the street and looked both ways. "Come on Mello, where are you?" He asked into the night. It only took him a minute more to figure it out. This motel was not far from her parents diner. He would have put it together sooner, but the private number threw him off. He was assuming that she was hiding somewhere else.

"This is all I could get." Jax offered he ran back to Roman holding an esky type lunchbox.

"That will work." Roman replied unzipping it and placing the bar inside. Thankfully it was deep enough to house it. Closing it he walked to his car and placed it under the front seat. He did not want to lose that.

"Now what?" Jax asked.

Roman opened the glove compartment. "Now we go and get Melody." Roman answered as he pulled out his own personal .44 and tucked it into the waistband of his trousers. He wished he had his badge with him but he knew that he would have to do this off the book. Make a citizen's arrest, as such. He let his jacket fall over it, locked the car and started to make his way towards her house. It didn't take long before Jax caught up to him. "I guess we have to take him in alive?" Jax asked.

"Depends on what shape Mello is in." Roman answered.

Jax gave him a look that spoke volumes. It was then Roman realised he had let his feelings for her seep into his answer. Roman looked his best friend in the eyes and let him see the depths of his feeling for her. He was through pretending. Melody meant the world to him and he didn't care who knew it. All he cared about now was getting to the bastard who had her.

"Got a problem with that?" Roman asked. The question was a double edge sword. It only took him a few minutes before Jax was shaking his head no. A small smile played at the corner of his lips. If the situation wasn't so dire, Roman was sure he would have a lot more to say.

"Good, let's go hunting."

With that a full blown smile spread across Jax's lips. "My three favourite words."

With that the two of them made their way silently up the road and into the forest that surrounded the diner and Melody's house. The bastard had picked the wrong girl to mess with. He thought himself a seasoned killer, he had nothing on the two men who were now hunting him.

Karma was about to coming knocking hard.

26

Melody groaned.

Why the hell did her head hurt so much?

Lifting her arm, she placed her hand against the side of her head to try and stop the pain, that was when she felt the huge lump.

Had she fallen?

Opening her eyes she groaned again as the light sent waves of pain shooting straight through her already pounding head. The pain was so intense Melody leaned to her side as nausea washed over her. With her head hanging off of the side of whatever it was she was laying on Melody remained still hoping that she would not lose whatever she had in her stomach. Finally the feeling passed and ever so cautiously she opened her eyes.

What the hell was going on?

Once her eyes were open Melody looked around trying to gauge where she was. With each piece of furniture that came into view the picture became clearer, she was in her own room.

How the hell had she gotten here? When had she come home?

Confusion was running rampant through her mind and Melody was about to sit up when a male voice on the veranda outside of her room caught her off guard. "Well deal with it for fuck sakes. I have my own problems here." There was silence for a moment before more talking reached her ears. "Remember our deal, it is your responsibility to get the families to pay and then to dispose of the bodies once I am finished with them." There was another moments silence as the person on the other end responded. "So get creative. Send her family a single piece of her body, that will show them that we are serious. If they haven't paid by tomorrow kill her anyway. It is time we moved on to the next one. Erica is proving to be too much of a problem." As the voice and conversation floated over her everything that had happened tonight came rushing back.

Melody was in the hands of the Serial Killer Roman had been chasing. She had to do something and fast. Remembering that she had a spare phone in her top draw she reached out and opened it. Melody cringed as the scrapping sound of wood on wood echoed in the room, it was only a tiny sound but in the silence that surrounded her it sounded like a gunshot. She held her breath and waited to see if the sound drew her captor's attention. Thankfully he went back to talking to his accomplice, although the sound become muffled as he walked further down the veranda away from her room. Melody breathed a sigh of relief when the draw finally opened far enough for her to stick her hand in. She wasn't going to waste time getting it open the whole way.

Sticking her hand inside Melody frantically felt around inside for the phone. As the minutes ticked by and the phone had yet to find its way into her hand Melody started panicking. She was not sure how much time she had before her captor came back. She knew that panic was not going to help the situation but she couldn't help the adrenaline surging through her body.

Tears started forming in her eyes and small sobs tried to

escape. Melody was giving up all hope when finally her hand landed on her prize.

"Thank God." She clutched her fist around the phone, holding on for dear life.

Please have charge.

She pulled the phone out and quickly hit the power button. For a few seconds her hope faded as nothing happened, but when the little white apple made an appearance a tear of happiness rolled down her face. The sound of footsteps clicking closer to the room had Melody laying back down on her back. Her hand rested by her side with the phone face down tucked just under her side. Her body blocked any sight of it from the door, just in case he was coming back to check on her. Melody held her breath in anticipation as she waited to see what his plan was. The footsteps finally stopped and her captor continued his conversation. He was closer to her room now, yet still hidden by the curtains on her door. She had to be quick.

Turning on her side she quickly and quietly brought the phone up to an angle she could see without drawing attention to it. It only had a few bars of power left, probably only enough for one message. She quickly opened her contacts and frantically went through them looking for Roman. This phone had been used last summer and while she kept it charged it only had the contacts in it from then.

"No, no, no." She whispered frantically. What was she going to do? Roman's number was not there. She tried to remember what it was, but her mind was foggy and she wasn't even sure she could remember her own phone, let alone his. Scrolling back up through her contacts she hoped that there was someone in it that would be able to get the message to Roman, asap. She was starting to give up hope until Jax's name crossed the screen.

Bingo.

She hit his name and then opened up a new message window. She knew she would not have time to write a whole essay so she opted for three quick words

My. House. Now.

Melody hit send then closed her eyes as the swooshing sound of a message being sent reverberated through the room. "You have your instructions Neil, now get the job done. Oh and make sure the Labs are left the same way you found them. We can't afford any more of your mistakes!" Melody flinched at how angry her captor sounded.

That was not a good sign for her. She pushed the off button on the phone and held it praying that it would hurry up and turn off, it always seemed to take forever when she was in a rush. The last thing she needed was for her captor to find it, that would send him over the edge and Melody was sure he would kill her.

"Should have bloody taken care of it myself." Melody began to panic as those grumbled words sounded closer outside. She gathered from the footsteps and the grumbling that her captor was finished talking to his partner.

Melody still could not believe there were two of them. It all made sense now.

How they had been able to evade the police for so long. How no consistent evidence showed up at any of the crime scenes, and finally how they had never been able to find the kill site.

They were smart, the pair committed their crimes where their fingerprints were expected to be, along with hundreds of other university students. They had been killing these girls under everyone's noses.

Hearing footsteps on the other side of the door she decided she would have to take her chance that the phone was off. As slowly as she could, Melody snuck her hand over the edge of her bed and tucked the phone in-between the mattress and the base of her bed. Luckily her bed frame was one solid piece and not slats so there was no chance of the phone falling through. Melody had just enough time to pull her hand back and rest it beside her before her captor walked in.

"I see you are awake." The chilling voice purred.

Melody's body crawled as his vileness washed over her. Somehow he had managed to make her feel dirty. Melody had hoped that if she continued to pretend to be asleep he would leave her alone. If he would just go out to the kitchen it would give her time to escape down the stairs from her balcony, but it was not meant to be. Of course he would not give her the chance to escape.

"Come on my pretty little dancer, the time for pretending is over." He whispered by her ear, right before he ran his tongue along her cheek. Melody was no longer able to keep her reactions to herself. Screaming she tried to roll away from him, but the movement reminded her that her head still hurt. She was now on her knees curled up in a little ball, her head resting in her palms as she tried to stop the pounding that was slicing through her brain, but it wasn't helping. Tears of pain and fear contained to rush down her face.

"You really should play nice." Her captor growled as he came around to her side of the bed.

Melody tried to get her body to work but the pain was too intense. She thought she might have suffered a concussion from ache in her head and from the way her stomach was lurching every time she moved.

This can't be good.

Melody wanted it all to stop. She had no way of knowing if Jax got her message he was her only hope now.

"Enough of this, it's time we got the real fun started."

Melody flinched when her captor's hand grabbed her upper arm like a vice and ripped her from the bed. She had no choice but to stand on wobbly legs or fall on her face. She didn't think her captor would be overly happy with that.

"Please let me go. I promise I won't tell anyone. I thought we were friends." She pleaded hoping to gain some sympathy by reminding her what they had shared. Her hopes dwindled further when her captor laughed and continued to drag her from her room into the lounge room.

"Now why would I do that. I have yet to have my fun with you. Besides you won't be alive long enough to tell anyone anyway."

Melody's worst fears were confirmed.

"Why me?"

Her captor laughed at that. "That's the beauty of this. Everyone always considers me their friend. That is what makes it so easy. All of you bitches are so trusting, you never consider the danger you put yourself in. Like you with your stripping."

Melody pulled up short. There was no way he could know about that. Only Roman knew and he would never have told anyone, let alone this maniac. "I.. haaave… no idea whaaat you are talking about." Melody stammered.

Her captor's grip tightened on her arm, the anger Melody saw in his eyes when he spun around and brought his face in line with hers made her tremble. "Don't lie to me. I know it was you up on that stage tonight. I have watched you dance for over a year now. I know every little movement you make, I know every inch of your body." He licked his lips as he raked an evil glare over her body.

Melody's body trembled again but for a whole new reason. The way he was looking at her made her feel as though she was standing naked before him. The idea that this creep had been watching her so closely, without her knowledge brought with it an intense invasion to her being. She felt as though someone had stolen something valuable from her, something she would never get back.

"How? Why?" Melody was stumbling over her words. She had so many questions she needed answers for and yet nothing could even come close to expressing how she felt.

Violated.

"Oh Melody; my sweet, sweet Melody, none of that matters now. All that matters is that I will be the last person that will ever see your body as unmarried as it is, and that is nothing but sweet justice." With that there was no more talking as he continued dragging her through her living room. Melody's eyes shoot to the door praying for it to burst open as Roman came to her rescue, but all she saw was the broken telephone and shattered glass from the bowl that he must have used to knock her out. She was so entranced in the mess that she didn't realise what was happening until it was too late. Her body was turned around so quickly her head spun, before she was roughly pushed up against her kitchen bench. She tried to fight her captor when he took both of her hands in his and raised them above her head.

Confusion began to set in, the grogginess from her head wound wasn't helping. Melody tried to pull her hands out of his grip but all of her strength was zapped. Her muscles felt foreign to her. It wasn't long before Melody felt something cold snap around her wrists, looking up in confusion she was surprised to see a set of handcuffs holding her in place. Something about this whole thing was starting to seem familiar but the fogginess was not letting her remember. Melody's attention was brought back to his face when he began talking again. "God you have a beautiful body." Her captor hissed as he reached out and ran a finger along her collar bone.

Melody couldn't help the shudder that ran though her. The anger that entered his eyes at the motion scared her. So much so she had to look away. Lowering her eyes she decided to look down at the floor. That was when she realised she was wearing nothing but the satin G-string and bra she had worn on stage.

This was beyond bad.

Everything Roman had tried to drum into her was starting to finally sink in. With thoughts of him came tears. *Where was he? He should have been here by now.* Tears began to flow down her face in earnest as the realisation that she might die tonight set in. She knew she could not blame Roman, he was in Denver and if she had listened to him she would not have found herself in this mess. Melody had to face facts. No-one was going to save her.

She was going to die. Alone.

Melody trembled violently when her captor placed his hand on her chin lifting her face to his once more. She knew it angered him when she did it, but she had no control over her body at this point. Once she was looking him in the eyes he leant in close and whispered, "by the end of this night you are going to learn to love my touch."

His breath on her skin made her stomach turn and the urge to lose the contents of her dinner became too overwhelming. Melody desperately tried to calm her nerves as she knew vomiting everywhere would be a bad idea. She was not prepared for the blow that came to her face however.

Her captor hit her hard enough to cause her teeth to cut the inside of her cheek. A small trickle of blood ran out the side of her mouth and the smile that crossed his face showed her just how evil this man was. Blood did not disgust him it only turned him on. The time for hope was over if she was going to survive this night then she had to do it herself. Melody gave one last ditch attempt to gain his sympathy, "Quinn please, you don't have to do this." She begged tears mixed with the blood on her lips. The moment his evil smile widened she knew begging was of no use. All Melody could do was pray. Pray that her parents weren't the ones to find her body. Pray that she held on long enough to see Roman one more time. Pray that when the time came for him to kill her, Quinn made it quick. With the threat of death in the air the only thought that crossed her mind was that everything she had done this summer had been for nothing.

Juilliard would forever remain a dream.

27

Roman and Jax had been standing in the trees behind Melodies house when Jax's phoned tinged. They were trying to figure out how to get inside without anyone seeing them. Roman ran his hands through his hair in exasperation at not being able to get to Melody. What use was it being a cop if he couldn't' save the ones he loved? He thought morosely.

NO! He would not allow it. Melody was not going to end up like the other girls.

Roman was pulled from his thoughts as Jax spoke. "You have to see this." He handed his phone to Roman, who at first was confused, this was not the time for his friend to be sharing messages with him. It was the name on the message that finally caught his eyes and everything made sense. It was from Melody.

"How?" he asked Jax in confusion.

"I don't know. I guess she had an old phone on her."

Roman looked back at the message. The three little words that were there were like a huge neon sign.

"Smart girl." He murmured as he started bolting towards the house.

Melody was telling them exactly where the arsehole had taken her. It didn't take Jax long to catch up to him. Once they were in the yard Roman signalled Jax to be quiet. "I am going to go up the stairs of the balcony. I will try and sneak in through the bedroom, hopefully they are in another part of the house. You head quietly up the front ones and wait for my signal."

"What if they're in the bedroom?" Jax questioned.

Reaching behind him Roman removed the gun he had placed in his waistband earlier. He checked if it was loaded before giving Jax the nod.

"Still wait for my signal. We can't chance this guy killing Melody." Jax nodded his understanding.

"Give me a few minutes to get into position before you head up." Roman ordered as he looked around the yard trying to gauge what other dangers there might be. Everything seemed normal, Roman hoped that Melody's parents were asleep, the last thing he needed was for them to get caught up in this mess. Roman jogged quickly and quietly to the steps of the balcony, once he neared them he slowed to a walk. With a few quick steps Roman found himself in position. Taking a deep breath and positioning his arms in front of him, readying his gun, Roman lifted his head to the heavens and sent up a quick prayer that the bedroom would be unoccupied. He started making his way up the worn wooden steps and when one creaked ominously giving away his intent, Roman paused and waited to see if he had been caught, when no-one showed he continued. Deciding that it was probably best to get the job over and done with, Roman quickened his steps. As his right foot hit the landing of the balcony Roman quickly rested his back against the wall of the house. Holding his gun against his chest he listened to see if he could gauge where Unser was keeping Melody. At first no sounds could be heard, so taking a chance Roman edged his way closer to the door of Melody's bedroom. Thankfully the curtains were still drawn so Roman had some protection. He was wondering how he would get around opening the door without being heard, when her red curtain flowed out of her room, the fabric being sucked out with the breeze.

Thank you God.

Roman edged closer to the open door, but before entering he took a moment to listen once more. That was when he heard her faint voice. It sounded as though it was coming from the living room.

"Please Quinn," The pain he heard ripped Roman's heart to shreds. Guilt racked his body and made it hard for him to breathe.

He should have been here protecting her.

"I so do love it when you beg me."

It took everything Roman had not to burst into the house and start shooting the bastard when his evil, sadistic voice floated out on the wind. Roman knew that Jax was probably feeling the same and he hoped that his friend didn't do anything stupid. He was running out of time, it was now or never. Tuning into his years of detective work to calm his nerves Roman prepared himself for his next move. Now was not the time to lose his mind. He knew from experience that when a detective let his emotions rule him things went south, quickly.

Putting all of his personal feelings for Melody aside Roman became the hard arse cop he had always been. He let the images of the previous murder victims run through his head as a reminder to who this guy was, this arsehole was done with torturing women. Stepping into the room, Roman did a quick surveillance to see if there was anything out of the ordinary happening in the room. One of the things Police Officers learnt while training on the job was to always prepare for the unexpected and with a maniac like Quinn, anything was possible.

Once satisfied that the coast was clear Roman crept around

the edge of the room until the living room was on the other side of the wall.

"Why are you doing this?" Roman cringed at how hollow and weak Melody's voice sounded.

"That's an easy one to answer. I love knowing that I am the smartest man in the room. You know I came up with the plan for my dancers while I was in my forensic class. The professor didn't even know that while he was teaching us how to look at crime scenes, he was also giving me the perfect opportunity to foil them. Oh it was perfect. The police are always looking for the evidence in the wrong places, they assume that the killer of the 'Denver Dancers' would be killing the girls somewhere remote. That's where they got it wrong."

"Why would they do it somewhere public?" Melody asked.

"That's my girl keep him talking." Roman whispered to himself. He knew Melody was trying to bide herself some time and it seemed to be working. It was also allowing him to gather some valuable information.

"Because that's the key sweet Melody. I worked out that it is easier to kill my prey in a place that is used for that type of thing all of the time. As an added bonus there are so many fingerprints there that the police are unable to pinpoint one suspect."

Roman was trying to take in what Quinn was saying. It was no wonder the police had been unable to figure this one out. It took all his willpower to keep from busting in and arresting this creep, especially when he referred to his victims as prey. The man was truly sick. His attention was brought back to the present when Melody's scream ripped through the apartment.

Unfortunately, Jax did not possesses the same training as Roman. "Let her go you bastard." Roman heard Jax yell as he kicked open the front door.

"Jax!" Melody screamed.

Roman couldn't see what was going on from his position. *Damnit, why hadn't Jax waited for the signal.* Roman had one of two options: he could make himself known now and possibly get everyone killed, or he could hope that Jax could take care of himself a little longer and wait for the perfect opportunity to make his move. The choice was taken from him.

"Well, well, well. Looks like we have more people to play with my dear." The evil son of a bitch crooned.

To Roman's ears it sounded as though his voice was getting further away from the bedroom. He could only assume that Quinn was making his way to Jax. "Try your worst you sick motherfucker." Jax spat.

"That's it keep him distracted." Roman whispered.

Roman crept closer to the entrance of the door and quickly shot his head to the side to try and gauge the situation. He didn't have much time, Quinn swung at Jax with the knife he was holding. Jax jumped back and was able to miss the first swipe of the blade, but the second one that came down in an arc met with the flesh of his arm. Jax didn't go down, he simply egged Quinn on further.

"Is that you best you got you little weasel. You had better make the next one a good one as it will be the last chance you get." After he made his statement Jax let out a quick whistle between his teeth.

It was their signal.

Jax was letting Roman know that he was going to position Quinn in a way that would allow Roman a good shot. Roman knew it was the best chance they had, Jax edged away from the front door and started walking in an arc like movement that would place Quinn's back to the bedroom. Thankfully he was smart enough to keep a safe distance from the outreach of Quinn's arm. Roman waited for the right moment and as soon as Quinn's back was to him and Roman was sure that his full attention was on Jax, he stepped into the living room and waited. He was waiting for some kind of sign to make his move. He didn't have to wait long.

"How is it that you ended up being here anyway? I knew that moron cop wouldn't be the one to come. I made sure that he was in Denver."

That statement gave Roman pause. How in the hell would Quinn have set him up to go to Denver? Things were not adding up again.

"Are you sure about that?" Jax coxed Quinn making sure to keep his attention on him.

Roman could hear Melody whimpering off to the side but he could not chance looking at her. He knew the minute he saw what this monster had done he would lose his cool. It was her whimpers of pain that were making it hard. He was thankful that she hadn't given away his presence. Roman quickly gave Jax a hand gesture that indicated him to keep Quinn talking.

"Oh I am completely sure. Do you have any idea how much joy I get watching those idiots run around with their hands on their cocks. They think they have everything figured out, but I'm going to let you in on a little secret. They know shit all about what's going on and no matter how close they think they are to catching me, what they don't know is I am always one step ahead of them."

Roman wished he'd been recording this conversation, but there wasn't time. He could tell by the way Quinn's body was twitching he was getting impatient. Roman quickly and quietly moved a little closer to the pair, he would have had no problem taking Quinn down from where he had been, but Roman was not willing to take the chance of something going wrong. One wrong move and the bullet he aimed at Quinn could easily hit Jax.

"Roman will catch you." Jax stated empathetically.

Quinn laughed at that. "How do you suppose he will do that when he is chasing his own tail?"

A small smile curved Jax's lips as he gave a slight nod to let Roman know to take the shot. Roman was only too happy to oblige. Placing his lips behind his teeth he let out a short, sharp whistle, it was enough to gain Quinn's attention and throw him off guard.

"Surprise arsehole." Roman spat at the same time he fired his gun.

The bullet shot out of Roman's gun with lighting speed and smashed into Quinn's kneecap. Quinn screamed in pain as he dropped the knife he was holding and crumpled to the floor where he withered around in pain. The shot in the small apartment sounded like a cannon going off, Jax covered his ears and the scream that came from Melody added to the cacophony of noise. Roman knew that the shot would have been heard by at least everyone on the block, and that the police force would be here in no time. That suited him just fine. He couldn't wait to have this psychopath dragged off to jail. Most of all though Roman couldn't wait to nail this guy to the wall and send him away for life. Quinn was still screaming when Roman walked up and placed his foot on Quinn's injured knee. Quinn clawed at Roman's leg trying to remove it.

"You are going to pay for this Pig, you and that little slut of yours." Quinn spat.

"Roman, Roman, ROMAN!"

Jax's voice drew Roman from his trance. He had been so focused on making this worm suffer as much as possible for the threat he'd just made towards Melody that he'd lost all reason. Looking up at Jax he saw him with his hand out. Roman's brows drew together in confusion.

"Give me the gun." Jax coxed as he walked closer.

It was then Roman noticed he had his gun pointed directly at Quinn's head. It would be so easy to pull the trigger and rid the world of one less perverted monster. He could easily claim self-defence.

"Not like this Rome." Jax pleaded as he placed his hand on Roman's.

Roman looked into his friend's eyes. "You know the world would be better off." He tried arguing.

Jax shook his head. "Maybe but think of those poor girls who wouldn't get justice for what he's done to them. Think of their families."

Roman looked back at Quinn who was laying on the floor, blood covered his hands and was starting to pool under his leg. Roman cocked the gun and took aim.

"Do it! You know you want to. You know as well as I do that I am going to get away with this and when I do your little whore will be the first one I come after."

While the words that were flowing from Quinn's mouth were strong and unbending, he could not mask the fear that was floating in his eyes. Jax was right, Quinn had to pay for the crimes he had committed and he knew that Roman had him dead to rights.

"DO IT YOU COWARD!" Quinn screamed sitting up as far as he could.

Roman gave him an evil smile, "no I think I will enjoy letting the inmates down at ADX have their way with you. A pretty little thing like you will get lots of attention." he threaten right before he cold-cocked him effectively knocking Quinn out.

"Damn Rome, you scared the shit out of me there for a minute bro. I seriously thought you were going to shoot him." Jax commented.

"I was." Roman answered truthfully.

The look that entered Jax's eyes told Roman he had not

been expecting that answer. "What now?"

"Now we find something to tie him up with." Roman turned his head, he could hear the police sirens off in the distance and he knew it wouldn't be long before they were here.

"I need you to restrain him as best you can, local law enforcement is on its way."

Jax nodded his head before he turned and made his way to the door, before he left he stopped and faced Roman. "How bad do you think it is?"

Roman didn't have to ask what Jax was talking about. The cries they'd heard from Melody earlier had faded away and Roman was afraid that when he turned around he would find out that he had been too late to save her.

Now that everything had settled down he had no choice but to look. "She is tough, it would take a lot more than this creep to take her down." He answered, hoping that his words held true. Jax nodded his head before he dashed down the stairs. Roman squared his shoulders, before placing his gun back into the waistband of his pants. Preparing himself for the worst Roman turned around to see Melody for the first time since he'd entered the apartment. The moment his eyes rested on her ravaged body he had to restrain himself from pulling his gun out once more and shooting Quinn.

Tears pooled in Romans eyes as he quickly rushed to her side. This was it. This was the moment of truth.

Please God let her be alive.

28

As Roman rushed over to where Quinn had handcuffed Melody to the bench, he pulled out his phone and dialled 911. "911 what's your emergency?" The young woman on the phone asked.

"Hello, my name is Detective Fox and I am requesting an ambulance for 678 Lakewood Drive, Pagosa Springs. I have a young woman who has been attacked in her home. Her condition is critical."

Roman listened as the woman confirmed that an ambulance was on its way. After thanking the operator, Roman tossed his phone on the bench behind Melody. He took a moment to categorise her injuries so he could inform the paramedics when they got here. Roman's blood boiled as he saw the various deep cuts and wounds on her body. She was dressed in only a bra and G-string, that were both equally soaked in her blood. Melody's head had fallen forward and her chin was resting on her chest. Blood ran from underneath her hair line in steady stream. Running his hands gently through her hair Roman felt two knots the size of golf balls and his fear for her welfare increased when she didn't make any movement to his touch.

He knew it was imperative to get her down from her

position and quickly. Looking up his hands followed the line of her arms until he saw that she had been attached to the top part of the bench with a pair of handcuffs. What fuelled his anger though was that they were of police grade. The little bastard must have stolen them from the station on one of his visits, Roman thought bitterly. He'd had it all planned out, right down to playing the police for the fool. Roman looked around and tried to figure out where the key might have been. With an unsub like Quinn there would have only been one place he would have kept it. On his person. He would have wanted to have it close on hand for that moment when he released her, the moment of her death.

Rushing back to Quinn's motionless body Roman didn't waste any time in searching his pockets. When he didn't find them in the front pockets Roman turned him over and searched the back.

Bingo.

A rush of gratitude for the lord flowed through him as his hands clasped the tiny silver key. Dumping Quinn's body unceremoniously back on the floor Roman ran back to Melody. Within seconds he had her arms released and she was falling forward into his arms. Roman gently sat down against the wall cradling her in his arms. Softly he patted her left cheek with the palm of his hand while he tried to coax her to open her eyes.

"Come on sleepy head it's time to wake up."

At first there was no reply. With each word that Roman spoke and no response forthcoming he was no longer able to keep his fear hidden.

"Melody Baby you have to open your eyes for me. Come on show me that you didn't let this bastard win."

He was now shaking her a little harder hoping that it would jar some pain through her body and it worked. The sound of her groan was like music to his ears. He hated hurting her but if it helped keep her conscious until the ambulance got here, he would do it.

"Tell me where it hurts." He asked in a shaky tone. Roman did not expect an answer of any kind he was simply trying to keep her connected to his voice.

"Is she alright?" Jax asked coming to stand beside them.

Roman looked up at his friend and saw his own rage reflected in Jax's eyes. "I don't know. I can't get her to open her eyes. She *is* breathing though. Is Quinn restrained?"

"Yeah, just wanted to check in with you before I took him downstairs."

Roman nodded his head, before he went back to talking to Melody, nothing matter now but her. He wasn't sure when Jax left, but the next time he looked up he was gone. Looking back down at Melody his heart started to break a little more, he couldn't lose her. Not when he'd only just found her. "I told you to be careful." He chastised her as he shook her once more. "When will you start listening?" The tears he was trying to hold back made his voice sound raspy.

"Sorry."

Roman's eyes flew to Melody's face as the barely audible whisper reached his ears. Looking down he was met with her pain filled ones, tears began to well up and fall down to the side of her face.

"Oh Baby, it's alright I promise. I just need you to hold on for a little while longer."

Roman was not sure if she understood him as her eyes filled with fear. Fear for her wellbeing deepened as she desperately tried to claw at his arms. Roman was worried that she was going into shock.

"Shhhh, it's oaky sweetheart you're safe. I've got you."

Melody didn't seem to be listening to him, she was shaking her head from side to side.

"Quiiiinnnn." She ground out. Her voice sounded scratchy

and dry to his ears, as though she had been holding back screams of pain.

"He is gone. Trust me Baby he can't hurt you anymore." Still she would not settle. She was still shaking her head, then it stopped and Melody's eyes were closed once more.

God please NO!

"Melody come on Sweetheart you have to keep your eyes open." Roman begged her. He was now shaking her whole body. Slowly her eyes opened, but the look that was there was no longer fear, instead it seemed as though she was fading away. Roman could hear that she was trying to say something, leaning down he put his head near her ear only to catch one word "Neil," before she lost consciousness once more. This time there was no waking her, Roman placed his finger on her neck to feel her pulse and he could feel it fading fast. Picking her up he cradled her body close to his. As he walked past the single chair in the living room he grabbed the blanket that rest over the arm and carried it with him out the door. Jax was waiting for him at the bottom of the stairs.

"We don't have time to wait we need to get her to the hospital now! Throw this over her." He ordered Jax.

"There are no cars here." Jax reminded Roman.

"FUCK!" Roman screamed into the night.

Jax took a step back from him. Roman was not sure what his friend had seen in his eyes but he knew it couldn't be good. Roman was searching the yard frantically when the sound of sirens reach his ears. The ambulance and police cars finally come speeding down the street, the ambulance in the front.

"I will ride with her to the hospital. You fill the cops in on what happened and meet me there." Roman ordered.

Jax didn't argue he simply nodded his head and waited. Within minutes the ambulance was stopping in front of Roman. The doors to the back swung open and one paramedic leapt out. She was soon joined by his partner as they brought the gurney out. Roman didn't give them time to bring it to him. He was placing Melody on the gurney before they could even finish unloading it. The paramedics didn't stop to question him, they took one look at Melody before both lifted the gurney with Melody back into the ambulance. One climbed in the back while the other prepared to shut the doors "are you riding with us?" the driver asked. Roman nodded his head before joining Melody in the back of the ambulance. Quicker than he could blink the doors were slammed shut and in time were speeding off to the local hospital, sirens blaring. Roman watched as the paramedic placed an oxygen mask on Melody's face. "Can you tell us what happened?" she asked Roman in a clam voice.

Roman knew that they were trained to be calm in situations like this, much like he had as a cop. Calling on his own training Roman proceeded to tell fill her in on what had happened. As Roman did so the paramedic was feeling all over Melody's body for broken bones. She didn't seem concerned until her hands were feeling Melody's head.

"How bad is it?" Roman asked.

"We won't know for sure until we can get a scan."

Roman knew that the paramedic was in no place to give him any real medical outcomes for Melody. All he could do was wait. Roman leaned forward and grasped her right hand between his, bending his head he placed his forehead against their intertwined hands and softly spoke to her. "Just hang in there Baby. Just a little longer, you are almost there." Before long the ambulance was coming to a stop. The driver got out and opened the back door. Roman climbed out first and moved off to the side so that the paramedics could get her out and into the emergency room. Roman followed after them.

As the doors slid open Roman was immediately hit with the smell of the hospital. Doctors and nurses came rushing as the ambulance driver filled them in on what had occurred. They immediately rushed Melody into one of the free bays and began examining her. Roman stood just inside the bay and listened as the doctors rushed around using medical jargon. Most of it he could not understand, but panic set in when he heard one of the doctors speak, "We are looking at a broken rib, possible punctured lung, minor head trauma and severe blood loss. The patient is in threat of going into cardiac arrest, we have to get her into radiology stat so we can determine if she needs surgery."

Roman stepped out of the way as the nurses began to wheel her bed out of the bay and down the hall. He quickly caught up with them.

"Can someone tell me what is happening?" He asked as they continued to wheel her down more halls.

One nurse looked at him and asked, "are you family?"

Roman shook his head. "Then I am sorry sir. We cannot give you any information on her condition."

"Her family is not here yet, isn't there something you can tell me so I can let them know what is going on?" Roman hoped that the nurse would cut him some slack, but it was not to be.

She simply shook her head and answered, "I'm really sorry sir, there is nothing I can do. You will have to wait until the doctor talks to her family."

Roman continued to follow Melody's bed right up until he hit the doors for radiology. "Sir this is as far as I can let you go. Please go to the waiting room."

Roman wanted nothing more than to argue with the nurse. He hated that he could not be with Melody. Roman felt that if he could just see her everything would be alright.

But it was not to be.

Roman didn't move, he continued to stand in the hallway and watch as the bed Melody lay on was wheeled through the double doors and beyond and he didn't move for a while after the doors stopped swinging. Roman wanted nothing more than to make this nightmare end, but for the second time in twenty-four hours he was made to wait. Turning on his heel Roman made his way back down the hall and found the waiting room, sitting down in one of the hospital-grade chairs he glanced at the clock. It was nearing midnight, he prayed the time went fast but as he watched the second-hand tick it's way around he had a feeling this was going to be a long night.

Leaning back and resting his head on the wall Roman closed his eyes and tried to focus on anything other than what was going on behind those doors. As images of Melody's crumbled body flashed behind his closed lids, the rushing of his blood mixed with the sound of the clock gave him an ominous feeling. Time was mocking him as he waited to find out what Melody's fate would be.

Tick, Tick, Tick.

29

Roman couldn't stand the sound any longer. With each tick of the clocks hands he was finding it harder not to scream. His body was filled with so much energy it was as though every nerve was being rubbed raw. Standing Roman began pacing the floor, he needed to focus on something else other than what was going on in the rooms beyond. He still had no idea if she was going to be alright, or even if they had taken her to surgery. Looking up at the clock he noted that it had been half an hour since she went behind those doors.

Where the hell was Jax?

He should have been here by now. Roman pulled out his phone and checked to see if anyone had rung. Seeing that he only had one bar of reception and no calls he sent Jax a quick message, to let him know where in the hospital he was. Once done Roman placed his phone back in his pocket and started pacing once more.

"Focus on anything else." Roman whispered to himself.

Roman's mind wandered to the whole situation back at the house, something was not right. He was damn sure Quinn was his man, and yet much of what Unser had revealed to Melody when he thought no-one was listening didn't add up. Then there was the information Shale had shared. The parents of the current missing girl had received a phone call at the same time Quinn had been at the bar. Yet Roman knew for sure that Quinn hadn't even touched his phone. Perhaps Quinn wasn't the 'Denver Dancer' killer and he was just an ordinary psychopath, but as quickly as the thought come Roman dismissed it. Quinn was involved in the disappearances of these girls he had all but admitted it to Melody. Besides he had the smarts and psychotic capacity to pull it off.

"What am I missing?" Roman growled. He knew he probably looked strange to any on lookers. Here he was pacing the floor like a mad man talking to himself.

Roman went over the whole night in his head again. From the moment he realised she had gone into work, until the moment he watched Melody go into surgery. Still nothing jumped out at him.

As the minutes ticked by so did the memory of the night. With each pace of the floor Roman rewound the night and paused on certain parts of his memory just as he had with the video in the bar. Then it hit him like a tone of bricks. Melody hadn't been scared that Quinn would hurt her at her house, she had been trying to tell him something before she had passed out.

What was it she had said?

"Neil, that was it." What had she meant.

Roman wondered if she had been trying to tell him there was another victim. He ran all the names of everyone they knew in town, but no Neil came to mind.

"Come on Baby, what were you trying to tell me?" Roman spoke out loud as though Melody could hear him. But as though by some miracle all the pieces of the puzzle fell into place, like cogs of a well-oiled machine.

"Fuck me." Roman swore. How could he have been so stupid? Without wasting another minute Roman rushed down the hallway of the hospital until he was almost back in the emergency room. He had just rounded a corner when he ran straight into Jax.

"Whoa, Rome, slowdown is everything okay, where is Melody?" Roman knew Jax had noticed how panicked he was. Roman nodded his head and then shook it. "I don't know what is going on they won't tell me anything. They took her into radiology to see if she would need surgery, but that is all I know. Look I have to make a phone call but I will be back. Let me know if anything happens."

"Can't it wait?"

Roman shook his head. "I have to get this information to Shale, a girl's life hangs in the balance."

Roman didn't need to say anything more, Jax moved out of his way and headed up to the waiting room. Roman didn't want to waste any more time, he also didn't want to be away from Melody for to long. As soon as he left the walls of the hospital Roman made his way off to the side of the emergency room so as not to block the path of those entering. Pulling his phone out of his pocket he dialled Shale's number. He knew his partner was waiting for his call.

"Talk to me, what happened?"

"Look I don't have a lot of time, we found her but she was in bad shape."

"Did you get Quinn?" Roman sighed at the interruption. He needed his partner to listen but he also knew how much Shale needed to catch this bastard as well.

"Yes, and before you ask, yes he is who we think he is?"

"Are you sure?" Roman could hear the excitement building in Shale's voice.

"The bastard all but practically admitted to it. I have no evidence though so you know he is going to lawyer up as soon as he can."

"Where is he?"

Roman was starting to get frustrated with the interruptions, but he held onto his patients a little longer, it wasn't Shale's fault. His partner had no idea how he felt about Melody. Taking a deep breath of the cool night air Roman started pacing the footpath. His eyes shot up when another ambulance pulled up and unloaded and elderly gentlemen.

"Fox, where is he?" Shale repeated.

Roman focused back on their conversation. "He is in county lock up. Don't worry the police have information on who he is. I needed you to call Detective Harsher down there and organise to have Quinn shipped up to Denver asap and Shale?" Roman could hear his partner writing down the name of the Detective but he needed Shale to be fully comprehensive for the next part.

"Yeah."

"I also need you to go and arrest Neil Solomon."

As Roman had expected radio silence greeted him. Right before "Are you crazy?" came through the phone.

"I know how it sounds, but Melody was trying to tell me something when she passed out. She said his name Shale and on top of that Quinn hinted that there was more than one killer when he was bragging about it. Think about it. It all makes sense, how we have never been able to catch Solomon on his own. How he always had an alibi for the days of the kidnappings and even his and Quinn's relationship. Just look into it please."

Roman listened as Shale groaned. "I am so going to get fired."

Roman laughed at that. "Trust me you won't, instead you will be known as one of the legends who solved the 'Denver Dancer' Serial Killer case. Now go, before Quinn finds a way to warn him."

Shale needed no more prompting than that. After saying a

quick goodbye and with a promise that he would call Roman when they had captured Neil he was gone. Roman took no time getting back to the waiting room, Jax was sitting in one of the chairs, his head hung in his hands while one foot shook from his impatience. Roman knew exactly how he felt, he had spent his first fifteen minutes in the same position. Taking a seat beside him Roman slapped him on the back.

"What's taking so long?"

Roman shook his head when Jax looked up at him, Roman had no answers to give him.

"Didn't they tell you anything before they took her in?"

Again Roman shook his head. "All I caught was that they suspected a punctured lung, some kind of head injury and excess blood lose. All I know is they took her to x-ray over an hour ago and haven't returned. They won't give us any more information as we are not family.

"Fuck." Jax swore.

An older lady who was now sitting across from them looked up with a frown. "Sorry Ma'am." Roman apologised for his friend. The lady didn't say anything she simply nodded her acceptance of his apology and went back to reading her magazine.

"Crap I had better ring Melody's parents." Roman spoke once again forgetting his language.

"Already done. They won't be here until morning though as they had gone away for the weekend and are five hours away." Roman ran his hands through his hair. Once again he felt terrible for leaving her.

"Gabby?"

Jax leaned back and placed his head against the wall. "I haven't rang her yet. I wanted to wait and see what the outcome was before I did."

"Jax she will be going crazy with worry. You need to let her know we found her."

"Alright, but if she ends up down here driving us crazy, that's on you."

Roman nodded his head and watched as Jax sent off the message. Instantly a ting came through followed by five more, Jax groaned. "She will be here as soon as she can." He ground out before placing the phone back in his pocket. Roman and Jax had nothing to do but wait, as another hour ticked by. Closing his eyes Roman sent up a prayer to keep Melody safe before once again focusing on his breathing and the clock.

Tick, tick, tick it went, counting its way down to his inevitable fate.

* * *

After three hours of waiting Roman couldn't sit still any longer, he was back to pacing the room. Melody's parents had called an hour ago to let Jax know they were about two hours away. Gabby was also here, she was currently curled up on one of the sofas asleep, Jax was haphazardly scrolling through his phone.

"Is the family of Miss Davenport here?" The doctor asked as he stepped into the waiting room, while removing his cap. Roman turned and took a deep breath.

"We are her friends, her parents are a few hours away. Is there anything you can tell us?"

Roman prayed that the doctor would be sympathetic to their plight. He let out the breath he had been holding when the doctor spoke.

"Look I can't give you all of the details but I can let you know that Miss Davenport sustained some serious injuries which required surgery. She is in a stable condition at the moment but the next forty-eight hours will be critical. If she pulls through she will have to remain in hospital for at least a week."

"Can we see her." Roman cut in. All he had needed was to hear that she was alive.

"She is pretty out of it from the anaesthetic, only one of you will be able to go in and only for a few minutes. Her room is down this hall and to the left. See the nurse at the station and she will let you know the number. There is a waiting room closer to that section for you if you'd like to move. "

"Thanks Doc," Jax replied from behind Roman as he shook the doctors hand.

"Please let her parents know that I will come and see them as soon as I they are here."

Roman nodded once more. Gabby was awake and tears were running down her face. Roman grabbed her and pulled her into his arms. "We almost lost her." She was sobbing. Roman was rubbing her back and Jax was once more sitting with his head in his hands. Roman needed to get control of the situation.

"I am going to go in and see Mello. Gabby can you go and ring her parents and let them know that she is okay, for now. Jax go and find us some coffee." Neither of his friend argued with him, they were too grateful to have something to do. Once his friends had gone on to do their perspective tasks Roman made his way down the hall. Turning left he made his way through two double doors that read intensive care and a little farther down was the nurses station.

"Hello, the doctor said that you would be able to tell me where to find Melody Davenport?" Roman asked.

The nurse typed the name up on the computer before offering him a smile, "she is in room 67, just down the hall."

Roman nodded his thanks before heading that way. Soon he was standing in the doorway of her room and his heart sank as he got a good look at her. Machines beeped and tubes ran from various bags into her arms. She was still covered in cuts and bruises, one of which was bright blue and purple on her cheek. Her head had a bandage wrapped around it and so did her left arm.

"I should have killed him." Roman mumbled to himself as he entered the room.

"Rome." Came a groggy voice from the bed. Roman quickly made his way over to the seat that was beside her and took her hand in his.

"Hey there Sweetheart, how are you feeling?" He knew it was a stupid question to ask but he wasn't sure how much she remembered.

"Where am I?" she asked looking around the room.

"In the hospital."

Melody's head shot back to the side, causing her to groan.

"Whoa ease up there Sparky, try to move slowly." He coaxed.

Melody's free hand lifted up to her head. Her eyes widened and tears began to fall as she felt the bandage there.

"What happened?" She asked once more, panic now filling her voice. Roman knew he had to calm her down. Leaning over he kissed her lips, a small smile played at the corner of his mouth when he felt her returning his action. Pulling away he saw that she was back to being calm.

"I promise I will explain everything when you are a little clear minded. For now know that you are safe and just concentrate on getting better." Melody closed her eyes and nodded slightly. As much as Roman wanted to ask her what she remembered, he knew it would have to wait. He did have one question for her though.

"Do you remember what you said to me earlier?"

Melody's eyes opened and slowly moved to his. They darted form side to side as she tried to remember.

"The last thing I remember was being at the bar. I had just finished…"

Melody stopped and closed her eyes. Roman knew what she was remembering. "Well needless to say that's the last thing I remember." Her voice was starting to fade and her eyes were dropping. Just then a nurse entered.

"I am afraid that's all the time I can give you. Miss Davenport needs to rest now." Roman nodded before standing, he leaned over and kissed her head one last time.

"I'm sorry Rome." Her voice sounded like that of a small child.

Roman squeezed her hand. "Don't be sorry Mello just get better. With that Melody faded off into a drug induced sleep. "How long will she be like this?" Roman asked. He wanted nothing more than to stay here with Melody, but he also wanted the satisfaction of nailing Quinn and Neil's arses to the wall.

"At least a few days."

Roman nodded and started to make his way out of the room. He stopped at the door and took one last look at Melody before he left. Now that he knew she was fine, it was time for him to finish this thing.

It was time for those monsters to pay.

30

Melody lay in her hospital bed listening to the beeping of the machine that was currently pushing antibiotics into her system. It had been five days since her surgery and, although she was still in a bit of pain, she was grateful to be alive. The first few days of her stay in hospital were still a blur. In fact, yesterday had been the first day she had been fully coherent and everything from the night of her attack came rushing back.

Melody could still feel the pain she felt when Quinn had sliced her open, or when he'd punched her repeatedly. She swore every time she breathed she still felt the pain from when her rib pierced her lung.

The last thing she remembered was him slamming the handle of his knife into the side of her head adding to the pain that was already there. Melody had never felt so sick in her life. Her head had felt as though it were splitting in two, she felt as though she wanted to vomit, pass out and scream from the pain all at once.

Thankfully, the darkness took her, the pain stopped and the next thing she remembered was waking up in this room, her parents sitting beside her, tears in their eyes knowing that she was going to be okay. Once she was able to take in the room Melody was able to see that everyone she loved was there.

Everyone except Roman.

Melody could have sworn that he had been here at some point, but as the days passed and there was no sign of him, she assumed that she had dreamed that he told her he loved her. She wanted to ask anyone who came in about him, but she was scared of what they would tell her. Either he was still working on the case or he was avoiding her. Either way, for Melody it was bad news.

"You awake Sleepy Head?"

Melody opened her eyes and turned her head to the knock that sounded on the door. A smile spread across her face, her best friend stood in the doorway with a sad smile on her face and her arms full of magazines.

"I am now." Melody answered, "what is all that?" She pushed the button on the bed to raise it so that she was in a sitting position. Melody couldn't help the twinge of pain that ran through her body as her lung stretched a little. One thing was for sure, a punctured lung was no laughing matter. It hurt like a son of a bitch. Not to mention the broken rib and other parts of her body that hurt every time she moved.

"Take it easy Dee." Gabby chastised as she rushed forward, put her bag on the chair, then placed the magazines and two yellow envelopes on the table. Melody gave her friend a sweet smile as she rearranged the pillows behind her head so that she was more comfortable.

"You don't have to do that you know? I am quite capable of taking care of myself." Melody quipped.

"As is evident by where you are." Gabby shot back with one raised eyebrow. Her friends expression reminded her of another, but before she could let her mind travel to unwanted thoughts Melody pushed her feelings down and focused on Gabby.

"Touché. Now are you going to tell me what all of this is?"

Gabby gave her a sly smile as she grabbed the two envelopes and placed them on the bed. She then spread the magazines out on the table.

"Well first the magazines here are for reading. Are you sure the doctors checked your head properly?" Gabby asked jokingly as she pretended to examine Melody's head a little closer.

"Very funny Gabs. What are the yellow envelopes for? Don't tell me they are full of pens for us to use on the quizzes in these books." With that Gabby rushed back to the chair and opened her bag, "thanks for reminding me." She laughed as she pulled out a roll of pens that were held together by a rubber band.

Melody laughed then winced as a pain shot through her rib. "Don't make me laugh." She groaned.

Gabby put her hands up in the air. "Sorry that wasn't my intention."

"I know. So are you going to tell me what's in the envelopes now."

Gabby shot her a sly smile as she placed the pens on the table beside the magazines. "I was actually thinking about taking the quiz, *'How annoying are you?'* What do you think?'"

Melody rolled her eyes, "I can answer that right now for you if you like. Just tell me what is in the envelopes."

Gabby made a tis-king sound. "You are extremely pushy today."

"Well being in pain and having to deal with annoying people will do that to a person."

"Alright keep your panties on." Gabby laughed.

Melody watched as she lent down and picked up the first envelope. She handed it to Melody and waited.

She didn't open it right away, instead she sat there holding it in her hands, looking at her friend. When nothing was forthcoming Melody groaned, "well?"

"Well nothing, open it." Gabby shot back as she sat down in the chair after placing her bag on the floor

Melody opened the envelope but almost dropped it when she saw all of the money that was in there.

Her eyes shot to Gabby's as she tried to find the words she needed, "how? When? Why? Please tell me you didn't sell your car." Gabby snorted.

"No I didn't sell my car. That there is money that was collected over the last few days from the bar. Once we had explained what had happened, everyone wanted to chip in and help you get the money you needed to go to Juilliard."

Tears formed in Melody's eyes and were soon falling when she counted that there was a thousand dollars in the envelop. Melody couldn't believe it. "You didn't have to do this." She cried.

Gabby shook her head, "no we didn't, but we wanted to and so did everyone else. With that in mind know that you will look like a huge bitch if you don't accept it."

Melody chuckled at her friends comment, then placed her hand to her side as pain once more sliced through her. She should really remember not to laugh so much.

"This is going to be such a bitch." She growled.

Gabby laughed at that, "maybe, but it is highly entertaining for us."

Gabby gave her a cheeky smile when Melody shot a glare her way. Even though she was in pain, she was glad that her friends and family could joke about the situation now. They needed too after the scare she had given them.

"So what is in the other envelope, more money?"

"Well funny you should say that." Gabby answered as she handed her the other one.

Melody opened it and sure enough there was more money inside. Only this one housed a lot more than the first.

Melody's eyes flew to Gabby's in question. "Don't look at me, that came from Honey. She said there is a note in there for you." Melody's heart raced. She wondered if Honey had filled Gabby in on why she would be giving her money, but she was too afraid to ask her friend. Instead she opened the envelope and noticed the small white piece of paper. Pulling it out and putting the money on the table, she unfolded it. Honey's neat scrawl stared back at her. A small smile played on the edge of her lips as Melody read the message:

I have been wanting to give this to you for days. You have more than earned it. I even added a little more of my own in there. Hope to see you back soon.

Melody re-folded the note and placed it back in the envelope. Once done she quickly looked at Gabby who was sitting with her hands resting on the bed in front of her face like a steeple.

"What did the note say?"

"Nothing much, she just wanted me to know they are all wishing me well and that her and a few of the other strippers chipped in a little extra." Melody hated lying to her friend, but she couldn't tell her the truth, not now.

"Why are you lying to me?" Gabby asked in a hurt voice.

Melody's heart sped up. "I'm not." She tried arguing.

"I read the note Dee." Gabby admitted softly.

Melody should have been mad at her friend for invading her privacy, but she wasn't. It was kind of a relief, now she had no other choice but to tell her.

"What did she mean by you more than earned it?" Gabby asked. Melody took a deep breath and prepared to tell Gabby everything.

"It was me on stage that night, not Honey."

Melody expected Gabby to chastise her in some way, but when no sound was forthcoming Melody looked up at Gabby to find her sitting in the chair in complete shock. It only lasted a second.

"You mean stripping?"

Melody nodded her head. That seemed to get Gabby moving. She sprung from her chair and started pacing the room.

"How? When? Why?" Gabby stumbled sounding like Melody had a few moments before.

"Gabby can you please stop pacing you are starting to make me feel dizzy again. Look I promise I will tell you everything if you will just sit and listen. You have to promise me that you won't say anything until the end though."

Gabby looked at Melody with surprise, "but."

Melody shook her head. "No buts. You either listen to the whole story with no interruptions or you don't hear it at all."

With that Gabby huffed and stomped her way over to the chair. She was like a small child who had just been told she could not have any ice-cream until she finished all of her dinner. Once she was in the chair she looked up at Melody. "Alright I am listening."

"Remember no interruptions." Melody reminded her.

Gabby closed her mouth and pretended to lock it and throw away the key. Melody smiled. "Don't be mad Gabs I promise you can ask all the questions you want when I am done. For now I need to get it all out or I won't be able too. Gabby nodded her head in understanding and some of the fire left her eyes. Melody took a deep breath and began to let her friend in on her deepest darkest secret. This time she was not going to leave anything out, she was going to tell Gabby all of it.

"Well it started with a Juilliard."

* * *

"And that is all of it." Melody ended. She had spent the

last twenty minutes filling Gabby in on the last few months of her life.

"This is unbelievable. I can't believe it was you up there stripping, or that you had a stalker and you never told me." Gabby hoped up from her chair and started pacing once more.

"I didn't want to worry you. Besides not telling you about the stripping was more for your benefit than mine."

Gabby stopped pacing and looked at Melody as though she had lost her mind. "Please explain."

"Deniable plausibility."

"Bullshit." Gabby spat as she started pacing again. "You just didn't want *anyone* to find out."

"Pft, fat lot of good that did me." Melody mumbled. She hadn't expected Gabby to hear her but when her friend stopped and placed her hands on the end of the bed, she knew she hadn't whispered it low enough.

"Explain." Gabby ground out.

"Rome found out." She could have lied or made up any excuse, but there was no point in that now. Melody had promised Gabby all of it, and that included Roman.

"WHAT?"

"Gabby please keep your voice down." Melody's eyes shot to the door hoping that nobody would come in.

"Are you serious? You tell me that Roman has known about all the times you stripped and you expect me to keep it down. How the hell did he react?" She was standing at the end of Melody's bed with her hands on the railing, waiting impatiently for Melody to explain.

"How do you think he reacted. He was not happy about it. He didn't know about the last time, just the first time. He made me promise never to do it again."

Gabby groaned. "You should have listened. I guarantee you he knows about the last time."

Melody looked up at her friend in confusion. "What do you mean?"

It was Gabby's turn to confess. "I am pretty sure he figured it out when he saw the security tape the night you were taken. Now it makes sense as to why he lost his shit when he saw the stripper."

Melody was shaking her head. "How could he have seen the tape that night? He was in Denver. I know I rang him when I got to the house, but he never showed." Gabby was shaking her head as she came around and sat on the bed just near her hip. She gently placed her hand on top of Melody's before she began talking.

"Melody, Rome was here. He and Jax are the ones who saved you that night, don't you remember?"

Tears filled Melody's eyes as she shook her head. She had prayed that Roman would be the one to save her. Now she knew that he was aware of what she'd done. It all made sense now. No wonder he hadn't come to see her. *What had she done?* Melody buried her head in her hands and let the tears fall, she had broken her promise to him, she couldn't blame him for not wanting anything to do with her. Gabby grabbed her and held her tight rubbing her back.

"I screwed up Gabs and now I have lost him for good."

"What do you mean?"

Melody sat up and wiped the tears away. "I mean I screwed up. Rome warned me what would happen if I stripped again, he also warned me about trusting people. I thought he meant strangers and I didn't listen. Look where it got me. I am in hospital and he is gone. He is gone and I will never get the opportunity to tell him."

The tears started once more. "The opportunity to tell him what Dee?"

Melody looked up into her friend's concerned eyes. She wanted to keep everything buried deep inside but she knew that over the coming months she would need her best friend's help. Her heart was breaking and Melody had no idea how to make it stop.

"To tell him I love him."

31

Roman walked through the department, past his old desk reminiscent of how he had a few months ago. Only this time he knew that he was not going to be getting into trouble. After leaving Melody at the hospital Roman had high tailed it back to Denver. Shale had informed him that after going to the chief and getting permission to find and arrest Solomon, a tip had come in about where the killers may have been doing their work.

Roman had gotten back to Denver just in time to tear the medical labs at the university apart. They searched a full day for any evidence and had almost given up when they found remnants of one of the victim's hair and clothes. Once they went to Solomon with what they'd found he rolled on Quinn like a baker on dough.

Neil told them about how it had all been Quinn's plan and what his role had been. He tried to gain a plea bargain for information, but instead settled for not getting the electric chair.   Both psychopaths were currently locked up in Englewood penitentiary awaiting trial. Unser and Solomon had both lawyered up and Solomon's folks were trying to push for the insanity plea. Roman and the department were adamant however that they were not going to let that happen. Both Neil and Quinn deserved to rot in jail for everything they'd done.

Roman knocked on the chiefs door. Turning in his chair he waved Roman in before he continued with his phone call. "Good, make sure you get as much evidence as you can. I do not want to see these shit for brains walking my streets ever again." With one final word the chief hung up the phone.

"Have a seat Fox."

"You wanted to see me Sir?"

"Yes I did, now while I am less than happy with the fact that you disobeyed me and continued to work on the case without my knowledge, I think we can let this one go. Especially since the outcome was in our favour."

"Thank you sir."

"But understand me when I say this is not an invitation for you a to ignore my commands in the future. Is that clear?"

"Perfectly Sir." Roman squirmed in his chair. Not because he was worried about getting into trouble, but because he wanted to get this meeting over with as soon as possible so he could get back to Pagosa Springs. It had already been three days and he was anxious to see how Melody was doing.

Roman knew she was getting better as he'd talked to Jax on more than one occasion, but he still had to see for himself. Roman could not believe how close he had come to losing Melody, his heart would not feel calm until he could hold her in his arms and tell her what she meant to him.

"Do you want me to tell her where you are and that you have called?" Jax had asked him during one such phone conversation. Roman had thought about it for a minute, but he didn't want to worry her. He wanted to know for sure that the monsters who had caused her so much pain were well and truly behind bars for good before he got her hopes up. So he decided to leave it to do in person.

"No, I don't want to worry her until I know for sure that

they will be going away. I want to be able to give her some good news. Telling her I am back here and what I am doing will only worry her. I need her to know that she is safe."

"Fox did you hear me?"

The chief's question brought Roman back to the present. Ever since he'd carried Melody into the hospital that night he'd been having a hard time keeping his mind off of her.

"Sorry Sir, I was just thinking about the case."

"I asked if you'd had a chance to talk to Quinn's victim about testifying yet."

Roman shook his head. "I have been thinking on that and I was wondering if is necessary to drag her through the court hearing. We have enough evidence to bag these guys. Not to mention the testimony of Erica."

The chief shook his head. "I know this his hard Son, but you have to know that your friend's testimony of what she heard that night, and what she endured will be the final nail in the coffin. It will aid in making sure the lid on this one is firmly shut."

Roman nodded, he did know that. It didn't mean he had to like it. "Alright I will ask."

"Good. Now when do you plan on coming back to work?"

Roman smiled at the gruffness of the chief's words. He would never say it out loud, but that was as close as the chief would get to admitting he was wrong. "If it is alright with you sir I would like to finish my holiday. I have a few things I need to finalise at home. I would be more than happy to start back next month.

The chief nodded. "Sure thing, you have more than earned it." Roman stood and shook the hand of his boss before he turned and exited the room.

"Be here bright and early on the first." Roman heard yelled from the office behind him.

A smile split his partner's face as Roman made his way

towards him and the chief's words rung out.

"See told you we would crack this case." Shale joked.

Roman snorted. "I think it was more like I told you."

"'Whatever Fox. So are you ready to get back to work?"

Roman shook his head. "Sorry, I am still on holidays," He picked up his bag and started making his way out of the building.

"Where are you going?" Shale yelled.

"Home." He called back and then to himself, "to claim the woman I love."

* * *

Melody smiled down at the cheque she was holding in her hand. She still couldn't believe it. Her parents had just given her the last of the money she needed for Juilliard. When she'd woken up this morning she had not seen her day going like this at all.

"What is this?" She asked them when they handed her the money.

"Why didn't you tell us about Juilliard?" Her mother asked. At first Melody had been shocked, then realisation set in.

"Gabby told you didn't she?"

Her father chuckled, which brought her eyes back to his. "Now don't you go blaming poor Gabs, she had nothing to do with it."

"No she didn't. Your professor rang us." Her mother added as confusion set in once more.

"Oh." Was all Melody could say.

"You should have come to us. Now I demand you tell us everything." Her mother chastised. The next half an hour was spent with Melody explaining the opportunity she had been given and how she was afraid that she wouldn't be able to dance like she used to. It had been a fear she'd had since waking up in so much pain. She wasn't sure how her body was going to heal and that scared her. She had the money to go to the camp, but would she have the strength and capabilities she needed to make an impression.

"Listen Sweetheart. You are tough. You have loved dancing since you were a little kid, and nothing as trivial as a few broken bones and battle wounds will be able to keep you down for long. You still have six months left before you have to be there, and I know that if you rest up and listen to what we are telling you, you will heal in no time and be back to your old self before you need to be. We will go home and ring your teacher to let her know that you *will* be going to Juilliard."

"Thanks Mom." Melody cried.

Then true to their word they left. Melody was so caught up in her own thoughts she didn't hear the soft knock at her door. "Mind if I come in?"

Melody's eyes flew to the door at the sound of a voice she'd missed these last couple of days. At first she thought her mind was playing tricks on her, but as her eyes landed on the form of the man she loved, her heart melted. He had never looked so good. He was wearing a pair of cargo shorts, coupled with a black polo shirt that stretched across his body. He was leaning against the door jam, arms crossed over his chest.

"Rome." She whispered his name like some sort of prayer.

"Were you expecting someone else Sweetheart?" He walked over to the side of the bed and kissed her.

Melody didn't know what to make of his appearance or his gesture. After Gabby had told her that Roman had left after talking to her that night in the hospital with no explanation, Melody hadn't expected to see him again. Now here he was smiling and kissing her as though nothing had happened.

"You came back?" Melody blurted out before she could stop herself.

Roman sat on the bed beside her, much as her mother had done earlier, and moved a strand of hair that had fallen over her forehead. Thankfully her head no longer hurt as much as it had that first day. It still killed like a son of a bitch when the bump was touched with any great force, but most of time she was pain free, in her head at least.

"Of course I came back. What made you think I wouldn't?" Roman asked, confusion marring his face.

Melody placed the cheque on the table before she looked down and started playing with the edge of the blanket. Tears started to form in her eyes as all the pain and fear she'd felt these last few days finally broke free. "Mello talk to me." Roman coaxed as he placed a finger under her chin and lifted her head. When she was looking at him he smiled and wiped away her tears.

"Baby?" he added as a question. Melody threw herself into his arms. "Oh Rome. I am so sorry for everything. I promise from now on I will listen to everything you say. I will be obedient and always tell you that you're right."

Roman laughed. "Now don't make promises you can't keep."

Melody leaned back and shot him a glare. Which only gained her more humour.

"Come on Mello, you and I both know that there is no way you will be able to remain meek and mild for long."

Melody sat back and wiped the tears from her cheek before crossing her arms. "You never know. I could do it if I wanted." She huffed.

Roman chuckled before leaning forward and kissing the pout from her face. "No you couldn't, and I wouldn't want you to. I love you just the way you are. Even if you are dangerous for a man's health."

Melody's eyes widened. "You. Love. Me?"

Roman shook his head. "Of course I love you. Do you really think I would put myself through this much torture if I didn't?"

"So you're not mad then?" He knew exactly what she was talking about. The change that came over him was the same as it had been the first night she'd stripped. Gone was his fun-loving side and in its place sat the hard detective.

"Oh I am mad alright. But we will discuss *that* issue at another date. Mark my words Melody, that will *never* happen again."

Melody nodded her head. "Cross my heart and hope to die." She said giving him a cheeky smile trying to break the tension. It didn't work. She probably shouldn't have reminded him how close she had come to dying.

Remembering that night brought back the fear she'd felt, she had to know. "Is…… is he in jail?" Melody asked unable to keep the fear out of her voice. Roman's hard features softened once more and he pulled her back into his arms. Melody assumed it was as much for his comfort as hers.

"Yes he is. You never have to fear him again Mello, that I can promise you." Melody should have felt relief at what he was telling her, but the knot in her stomach remained. Something was not right. There was something from that night she felt as though she was forgetting.

Then it hit her.

Melody sat up so quickly her head hit Roman's chin. They both groaned in unison at the pain, but Melody's didn't last long. Panic was quickly taking over. "Rome, you have to go back, you have to tell them. They don't know all of it. The evidence won't add up. He will get away with it." Melody could see the worry in Roman's eyes, but she was just not sure it was for the right reason.

"Whoa Mello calm down, you are speaking in riddles. Do

you feel okay? Should I call the doctor?"

Melody groaned in frustration. "Roman listen to me, it's not over. You have to find him."

Roman's eyes furrowed in confusion. "Find who Mello? Trust me it's over, Quinn is in jail and will never be able to get to you again."

This time Melody shook him. "Not Quinn Rome, Neil. You have to find Neil and save the other girl. There are two of them, don't you see. The 'Denver Dancer' Killer isn't' one man it's two."

Melody was on her knees begging Roman to understand. "Why are you smiling? This is not a time to smile. Look if you won't go at least ring your partner. I am not crazy Roman, I promise."

"It's alright Mello." Roman cooed.

"No it's not, and it won't be until you save the girl."

"Melody listen to me, we did save the girl. We found Neil and have all the evidence we need to lock them both away for a very long time." Melody froze her hands were gripping the tops of Roman's arms and she searched his eyes for the truth. She could see it in the very depths of his soul and she knew she was truly safe. Melody fell forward into his arms as relief that the nightmare she and others had faced was over. She had been one of the lucky ones. Melody sucked in a quick breath as the pain from her ribs spliced through her, but she didn't want to move.

"Mello?" Roman asked in concern.

"I'm alright I promise. You really found her?"

"Yes Baby we found her and it was all because of you."

Melody sat up again, this time more gingerly. "What did I have to do with it?"

"The night you were attacked, you were able to give me his name before you passed out."

"Oh." Was all Melody could say. Her eyes lowered to the

bed.

"I was so scared Rome."

"So was I." Roman confessed. His hand slid across the bed and captured hers. Lifting her eyes she met his.

"Can you tell me everything?"

"Are you sure you want to know?"

Melody thought about it for a moment, then nodded her head. "Alright. But first I need to get more comfortable, I need to feel you in my arms." With that Roman pushed the table away from the bed and stretched out beside her. Being careful so as not to rip out any of her tubes, Roman reclined on her bed and then opened his arms to allow her to lay in them, Melody was more than willing to oblige him. Laying down she placed her head on his chest and sighed with content as he wrapped his arms around her. Melody closed her eyes and listened to the strong beating of his heart, as he began to speak his voice washed over her like a long-lost song.

Her heart was full.

All of the fear and sorrow of the past week disappeared and she no longer worried about life. Deep in her heart Melody knew that as long as she was in his arms she was safe.

He was the end of her dangerous dance.

32

"Well Ladies and Gentlemen it has been a gruelling six weeks, but you have all done a magnificent job. I look forward to viewing your addition tapes next year when you apply to Juilliard. I expect there will be some stand out candidates."

Melody applauded along with everyone else in the group. The smile that spread across her face could not signify how amazing she felt.

She had done it.

Six intense weeks of learning dance moves she'd never known existed and using muscles she'd forgotten she had, but it had been worth every painful moment. Pushing herself up from the floor she shook the hands of some of her classmates.

"Promise us you will keep in touch." Caroline from Virginia demanded as she hugged Melody.

"You too." Melody returned.

"Don't forget to send us some photos of those hunky bartenders you always talk about." Nicole quipped.

The girls had become fast friends and they all prayed they

got in next year. Melody could see herself having a blast with them.

"I will. Make sure you send me your mother's famous Southern Fried Chicken recipe."

Nicole laughed and agreed to do just that. The girls hugged each other once more before finally saying their goodbyes. They were in a rush as their flights were leaving in an few hours. Melody's didn't leave town until tomorrow morning and she silently wondered what she would do in New York all by herself. There was plenty to see, but she was not sure she wanted to do it alone, understandably she still harboured deep fears about what could happen to her. Melody had booked a hotel close to the airport and that was where she was headed now, her car service would be arriving soon. Walking over to the far wall where she had placed her bag, Melody collected her stuff and prepared to leave. As she walked down the hallways of the school she hoped to attend, Melody committed every inch of this place to memory. Even though she planned to come her next year, she knew the competition was tough and doing a course like this was still no guarantee of entry.

After taking one more look at the grand staircase in the entrance Melody headed towards the double doors that would take her out to the streets of the Big Apple. It was bittersweet leaving, she knew this could be the last time she ever stepped foot into this magnificent school, yet Melody couldn't wait to get home and see her man.

The moment Melody had returned to Denver, Roman had moved her out of her depleted University accommodation and into his loft and life had been the sweetest it had ever been. The last six weeks without him, while amazing and everything she had dreamed, had also been torture. Melody missed having Roman's arms wrapped around her at night, not to mention his kisses and the way he greeted her in the morning, but Melody especially missed the way he made love to her whenever the mood took them.

Which was quite often.

"Only one more night." She told herself. Melody pulled her phone out of her back pocket and shot him a message. Her smile intensified when she got a message back within minutes.

Can't wait to hold you in my arms.

Melody was preparing to send another back when she heard her name being called. Turning around she saw that Mrs. Windrope the Head of Admissions was standing near the end of the staircase.

"Can I have a word?"

Melody's wondered why she would need to talk to her. The season had finished and the intake for next year was not due to happen for a few more months. "Sure." Melody answered as she made her way to where the imposing lady was standing. Although everyone here was nice enough, the teachers were true professionals. They all walked, talked and acted as though they were on a Broadway stage, and they expected nothing but perfection from all of their students. Melody followed Mrs. Windrope down the hall behind the stairs until they were in her office. The imposing woman stood by the door and ushered Melody inside.

"Please take a seat." She offered as she shut the door.

Melody nodded her head, placed her bag on the floor near the chair and then sat down. While her first instinct was to make up an excuse as to why she had to leave, Melody knew that impressing these people also played a part in her acceptance to the school. She had proven that she would do anything to get into the school, so sitting here and listening to Mrs. Windrope critique her was nothing compared to what she had endured in the past.

Melody placed her hands in her lap and proceeded to wring them. She was nervous as she was unsure as to why the Admissions lady would need to speak to her. All of her paperwork for the course had been filled in correctly and it had all been approved and paid for up front before she arrived. Surely there wasn't some outstanding money owing. With the idea that she may have to come up with some more money her worry increased.

"I know you are probably wondering why I wish to talk with you, and you probably have someone waiting to collect you so I will make this short. Every year we run this program for a particular reason. Do you know what that reason is Miss Davenport?"

Melody smiled. She had researched Juilliard for years and was certain she could answer any question thrown at her, she straightened her back before she answered. "Yes ma'am, so that students such as myself can come and learn techniques that will better help us apply to Juilliard."

Mrs Windrope nodded her head slightly before she continued. "Correct, but what most don't know is that we run this program so that we may find a candidate that is worthy of our Juilliard Scholarship. Every year we pick one extraordinary dancer from the program to be the recipient of a full ride to Juilliard the following year. This year that candidate was you Miss Davenport."

"Me?" Melody was in shock, she didn't know what else to say. She hadn't even thought about what she would do for money if she actually go into Juilliard. Mrs. Windrope simply nodded her head.

"Why me?" Melody asked.

She knew she shouldn't be questioning their decision but there had been so many talented students here this summer and she was not afraid to admit that there were many that were more deserving than herself.

"Well Miss Davenport, upon watching your audition video for the course and after your exemplary work over the last six weeks, we here at Juilliard have decided that we would benefit from having a student here with your drive to succeed. But if you would prefer us to give it to someone else…"

"Oh no Ma'am that will not be necessary. I would be more than honoured to accept." Melody cut in.

She knew it was rude to interrupt someone when they were talking, but she could not afford to lose this scholarship. This was everything she had been working her whole life towards. The reality of what had just happened finally hit her, this summer had been her audition into Juilliard. She had made it, she was going to be attending her dream school. It all made sense as to why her professor had pushed her as hard as she had. "I am glad to hear it. Now here are your papers, I will need you to fill these out and get them back to me by the end of the month, that way we can start processing everything so that you are ready and set up to start next year."

"Thank you so much. I will defiantly make sure these are back on time." Melody crooned as she reached over and took the A4 envelope that had been placed on the table in front of her. Melody clutched it to her chest like a lifeline.

"Well Miss Davenport. We look forward to seeing what great things you can achieve. Until next time I wish you a safe journey home." With that Mrs. Windrope stood, Melody followed suit and after shaking the woman's hand one last time she grabbed her bag and headed back towards the entrance. As she stepped out into the brightness of the afternoon sun Melody looked at the envelope once more.

She had done it. She had made her dreams come true.

Turning around she looked at the building and the

realisation that she would be attending this esteemed collage hit home. No longer was it out of her reach, her dream was now a reality. With that reality came the realisation that she would be moving away from Roman. Not that it was a surprise. They had discussed it over the last six months and Roman had promised that he would do everything he could to make it work if she got in, but now that she had the reality of what it would be like to live without him hit her. When she attended Juilliard she would not just be away from him for six weeks, but for months at a time. Melody was not sure she could do it and that was scared her to her core. Question after question plagued her mind.

Could their relationship last long distance? Would he find someone else and grow tired of her? Would he change his life for her? Would she have to change her life for him? On it went.

Melody was not sure she wanted to know the answer to any of the questions rushing around in her mind, because as much as she wanted to come here, she knew that she wanted Roman more.

"I thought you said you couldn't wait to see me?"

Melody spun around at the sound of his voice. "Rome." She screamed as she ran down the stairs and into his arms. Roman caught her mid leap and was laughing as she clung to him. Before he could say anything else Melody locked her lips with his and kissed him passionately. Soon they were both panting.

"Does that answer your question." She answered saucily.

Roman groaned. "Damn I've missed you." He put his head against hers.

She leant forward and kissed his lips tenderly this time. "Not as much as I've missed you."

Roman pulled out of her arms and leant against the car that was behind him. The look on his face bellied her last comment. "That's not the impression I got."

"What's that supposed to mean?"

"It means, tI was afraid by the way you were looking at this building you were regretting leaving here."

Melody laughed. "I was taking it all in one last time. What are you doing here?" she finally thought to ask.

Roman shrugged his shoulders. "I was in the neighbourhood and thought I would drop by and pick you up."

Melody crossed her arms over her chest which was quite difficult with the envelope still in her hands. "Just in the neighbourhood eh. What exactly were you doing in the neighbourhood might I ask?"

"You first. What's in the envelope?"

Melody narrowed her eyes. Roman was being evasive, something he only ever did when he was hiding something. Melody decided to play his game, she knew how stubborn he could be. Melody decided now was as good a time as any to tell him. At least they had a good six months to prepare for what came next.

"It's a scholarship. Apparently this camp is not only to hone the skills of some of the best dancers around the country, it also allows Juilliard the chance to award a scholarship to one of those dance. This year they chose me, I have been accepted into Juilliard with a full ride."

Melody had not been prepared for what happened next. Roman practically shouted in excitement before he picked her up and twirled her around. When her feet hit the ground once more he grabbed her face between his hands and kissed her deeply. People everywhere were watching them, but Melody didn't care. She only cared about the man in front of her.

"I am so proud of you Baby." He cooed.

"You know this is going to be hard on us, right?" Melody asked. She hadn't meant to spoil the moment but she couldn't help the worry that entered her voice. She had expected Roman to be a bit more disappointed that she was moving away, instead he acted like the last six weeks had not been hell.

"Oh I don't think we will have to worry about that." Roman replied cryptically.

Melody hit him in the stomach. "What aren't you telling me Rome?" she hissed.

Roman sucked in hair and let a little laugh, but when she went to hit him once more he put his hands up in surrender. "Alright, alright I will tell you. The reason I am not worried is because I will be living here with you."

Melody gave him a perplexed look. "How is that going to work, especially with your job?"

"Well considering that as of next year I will be working for the New York office I would say pretty good."

It was Melody's turn to squeal. "Are you serious?" She asked as she threw her arms around his neck.

Roman nodded before he kissed her neck and then placed her away from him. "They were so impressed with my work on the 'Denver Dancer' case they didn't think twice when I applied.

"How did you know I would get in?"

Melody's heart melted a little when he gave her his lopsided smile. "Because I know you Mello, and anyone in their right mind can see what an amazing dancer you are, I didn't doubt you for a minute."

Melody smiled a smile that was pure sunshine. She leant forward and kissed him, but was surprised when he pulled back and looked at her with a serious expression in his eyes. "I am warning you Mello, I had better not see you in any strip clubs."

Melody laughed. "The only person I strip for now is you Rome."

Roman growled. "Speaking of which, how about we put all talk of this away for later as I want nothing more than to take you back to our hotel room and have you show me what new dance moves you've learnt over the last six weeks."

"Are you sure you can handle it?" She replied sassily as she sashayed over to a waiting cab.

"I guess we will have to find out." Roman quipped as he opened the door and let her in.

"I guess we will." Melody leant over the door and kissed him before sliding in. Satisfaction washed through her as she watched Roman adjust himself before he slid in beside her. How had she gotten so lucky.

Melody still couldn't believe that this man was hers, all because she had the nerve to do a dangerous dance.

The End